About Requiem

'In 'Requiem', Berlie Doherty evokes a painful emotional and spiritual journey, as Cecilia faces the curse of her childhood and the sterility of her faith. Haunting and beautifully written, it powerfully conveys the mystery and anguish of Catholicism.'
Penguin Books

'The story of Cecilia's adolescence is exquisitely told in a style that is both economic and exuberant. There are moments of near-Joycean epiphany... the plot is tight and the narrative startling.'
Independent.

'I have great feelings of admiration for Requiem. Very good indeed.'
Beryl Bainbridge.

'This novel made me angry - for all the right reasons. Beautifully written in a style which combines poetic feeling with a scrupulous attention to the truth of things, it probes the tragic-comedy of Irish convent Catholicism with a rare power and sensitivity... 'Requiem' continued to disturb me long after I had finished it.'
Wendy Perriam.

'Doherty writes in and even beyond, the best tradition of Irish lyricism to explore the extremes of sacrifice and sin, love and rejection.'
Company.

'Requiem is an enchanting and lyrical portrait of childhood and growing up. Berlie Doherty is a real writer. Lovely prose.'
Barbara Trapido.

Copyrights;

Text:	© Berlie Doherty 1991, 2011 & 2014
Cover & Graphics:	© W. E. Allerton 2014
'Requiem' cover font	© Roland Huse (Rainy Wind)
Typeset & Layout:	© W. E. Allerton 2014
Font:	Garamond 12pt.

ISBN: 978-0-9548373-9-6

This revised edition published 2014 by;

Cybermouse MultiMedia Ltd.,
101 Cross Lane
Sheffield S10 1WN
www.cybermouse-multimedia.com

First published by Michael Joseph 1991

ybermouse MultiMedia Ltd.

Requiem

Berlie Doherty

Part One

Sacrament

It is quiet in the early fields. A bell begins to toll for Mass, and from all over the village dogs set up their baying. A priest in his long skirts stands on the steps of the church. People are coming, clutching their missals. The priest goes inside. He is old.

Latecomers shuffle in the porch. Men in their shirtsleeves stand leaning on the glass at the back of the church. Their shadows hunch about. The voices of the faithful rumble after the priest. A baby's hand taps on the glass.

Outside, the streets are empty. A rook on a post clucks to itself and squawks down, loud beaked, to its fellows.

Chapter One

How clearly I remember the day Mr Devlin nearly murdered Angelo Caravelli in class; Angelo who had the looks of a cherub on a holy Christmas card, and who had no sense at all about keeping still at his desk. I remember my particular terror because Angelo was my friend and because he sat in front of me, which meant that I saw the look in Mr Devlin's eyes just before he did. Like a cat he pounced as the boy turned round to talk to me, and all our chatter flew away up and into silence like birds scattering into treetops, and in shock we watched as the boy was lifted from his chair and flung onto his desk-top and pummelled many times; and all the while this was going on we could only stare, locked in terror, till Mr Heaney from the next classroom came through and spoke quietly and released us all.

Mr Heaney was the one who started the term by breaking his cane across his knee and throwing it into the waste basket; and because we didn't understand this we watched in the same fearing silence. And when Thomas Smiley, the grey-skinned boy from the top year was stripped of his trousers in the yard and tied to a chair by the headmistress, and left out to be taunted through playtime, and still left out when we lined back up to go to our lessons, wondering whether the crows would come down and peck at him, it was Mr Heaney who hurried out to him and untied him and found him something he could wear so he could run home without shame, though his disgrace was never to be forgotten while he lived in our village.

But for all that, the truth is that in my last year at that small school it was quiet Mr Heaney who committed a terrible act of violence against himself. He killed himself. Some said he did it by slitting his wrists in his bath, till the water was cold and crimson with his own blood; so it wasn't he who gave me the news but Mr Devlin. He made me stand up in class while he told me that I had passed the scholarship to go to the convent school.

'Well, it's an honour, that's what it is,' said my Uncle Rory, who had hair like a lion's, red and silky and loose to his shoulders. 'You'll be off with the toffs now, Cecilia. Mixing with the young ladies from the convent school.'

'Did you thank the Lord for this gift?' my Aunt Bridget asked, removing her teeth to search out a strip of apple skin that was bothering her. My little brother Terence watched for her to slide them back in again, and screamed as she dropped the top set back down again and lowered her head at him like a grinning skull. 'Where's that child? Let me eat up his bones!' she cackled.

'Don't give her ideas yet about going, Rory,' my mother said. 'We've no money for this. Why can't she go to Geraldine's old school, and be satisfied?'

'Because Geraldine is only a soft lump, and you know it,' said Aunt Bridget. My big sister, laundry girl at the local hospital, getting on and still in white socks, smiled at my aunt and folded her red hands on the table to show that her meal was finished. 'Whereas Cecilia has brains, and many of them. She shouldn't waste those brains. They're God's gift.'

'Brains are one thing. They're handed out quite free of charge. But I'd like to see God handing out school uniforms.'

'I should be careful what you're saying there, Nancy,' Aunt Bridget warned her. 'There might just be a touch of blasphemy in that. Don't you think, Rory?'

'To hell with blasphemy,' said my mother, reckless.

My aunt pushed back her chair and scraped the meal's leftovers onto one plate for the hens. 'You have no real faith, Nancy,' she suggested. 'You must trust that God will provide. Remember the child's first communion day?'

'I do,' said my mother. 'It was a humiliation, Bridget.'

'Which is good for the soul,' Aunt Bridget reminded her. 'But the child would have gone to the altar in her street clothes if I hadn't thought about the curtains and made a white frock for her out of them in the nick of time. The child should never have fussed in the way that she did.'

'You left a pin in the armhole. No wonder she cried. There was blood on her! Blood on her first holy communion frock, Bridget!'

The women were grim in their clearing up. Uncle Rory leaned back in his chair and grinned. My sister Geraldine laughed across at him, her face rosy from the fire. Little Terence ran out with the plate for the hens.

'Can't I go, then?' I asked at last.

'We'll see,' my mother sighed. 'Wait till your father comes in.'

But Uncle Rory rolled a bright coin across the cloth to me and winked. 'That's for being so clever!' he whispered, and put his finger to his wet red lips.

When my father came in with dry soil still powdery on his hands he kissed my hair and sent me skipping off to see Father Carolyn, and because it was like a holiday in our house that day Geraldine and Terence were sent with me too. On the way we met our big brother Michael coming home from the milking and we shouted out our news to him as we ran down the lane towards him. He whipped me up in the air and swung me round till my hair tangled in the hawthorn bush and I screamed out for mercy. When he set me down again Geraldine grabbed my hand in hers and pulled me over to the stile that would take us down and across the fields to the church and the presbytery. And there was the sea, the great long gleam of it pink with the evening, and the red sun dipping down into it, and as we raced down into the valley the colour deepened and spread till at last the sun gave itself up to drowning.

Father Carolyn and his housekeeper were in their garden. She bent over, stiff legged, to pluck out dandelions, and I pulled Terence behind me so he wouldn't see how her skirt rose wantonly over the backs of her knees. Father was clipping lilac for the altar. The air was sweet with the scent of it as he plunged his fists into the tree to find the finest heads.

'What's this?' he said, seeing us. 'Not sickness in your house?'

Geraldine pushed me forward, her fat fist in the small of my back.

'My daddy said I was to tell you I've passed the scholarship to the convent school.'

He held his hand out to me, soil stained as it was from the gardening, rough-skinned like a farmer's, and as I slipped the tips of my fingers onto his palm he squeezed them till I could feel the nails going in. 'That is good!' he whispered, and I could smell his breath, sweet and sharp. 'That is going home for you, Cecilia Deardon. Come with me now, and give thanks.'

He led us into the church, holding still to my fingertips and clutching his spray of lilac in his other hand like a bride, and he took us up the choir stairs to the organ. He nodded to Terence and Geraldine to tread the pedals for the wind to come, and he dabbed his fingers over the keys till he found the chord he was after.

'Sing for me, Cecilia, and give thanks!' he said, and my tiny voice came like a small bird in the church, and he joined in, deep as dogs and rumbling, and down in the aisle the housekeeper stood with her white face turned up to us and put her wandering harmony in, and I wanted my voice to soar then, the way the skylark takes herself up and spills her singing over the fields.

'Was there any other message for me?' Father Carolyn said, as the last notes died and Geraldine wiped her armpit sweat on her skirts.

'Yes,' I whispered, timid after that glory. 'My mam said I was to tell you we can't afford the uniform.'

When we got home to the house there was a row going on. We could hear my mother's voice raised, rough and railing in temper, and my father laughing, mocking her, riling her on with his calmness. It wasn't dark, though the sun had long gone down; the sky was heavy and sultry, and against the side of the white house the poppies were hectic in their blowsiness, blown out too big for themselves. We waited by the porch for the rowing to finish.

'How many brains have you got?' Terence whispered to me, and I said I had about three, but I wasn't sure: one each side and one in the middle, maybe, and then the shouting stopped and we went in, with Geraldine hanging behind us as though this was a house she was a guest in.

My mother's cheeks were flushed and her hair was loose about her face the way my father loves to see it, and she was leaning down laughing to him as he lounged on the sofa, his hands up around her waist and pulling her down to him.

'Get on up to bed!' he shouted to us without taking his eyes off her, and we scampered past them to the stairs.

'Cecilia, what did the Father say?' my mother called up sharply.

I hung back, not looking down at them. 'He said I'd be going home,' I said. 'What did he mean, Mam?'

'How should I know? It would be a bit of piety, coming from him. What about the uniform?'

'He said there'd be no trouble about that, none at all.'

'Oh, Nancy my girl, my love,' my father crooned, his voice soft and thick and growly. 'Oh, my Nancy.'

'Off you go, then, Cecilia. Off to bed.' But her voice was as soft as his, and I didn't need to be told.

In my bed I waited for Geraldine to finish her prayers. That afternoon I had left school early, sent home to give my news, and the children had been in the yard playing rounders. Their voices were lusty in the ecstasy of their game, and I was on the other side of the railings, walking away from them. I began to run, turning my head sideways to watch their playing, and the pictures I saw through each slat of railing were like new movements in the choreography of a familiar dance. My stomach had fidgeted then with thrill at the news I was carrying, and with a kind of helpless sorrowing that I could not understand.

And I remember the day I started at the convent school. My father was to take me that first morning after the milk round in case I fell off my bicycle in my nervousness and spoilt my uniform - after the first day I was to go on my own, and be careful, and my Uncle Rory's scholarship present for me was a handlebar basket to put my school books in. Geraldine made a lining for it so that the books wouldn't be scratched.

It was raining that first morning. I jogged about on the back of the milk-cart looking at the house and the lane as they disappeared away from me, and the hedges and the walls and all the farm buildings we passed as though I was seeing them for the first time, though it was a route that we used to take every Sunday to my grandmother's cottage after Mass when I was a little girl.

My father pulled up at the gates just long enough for me to jump down, and shouted to me to be good, and I watched the lane he went down until the sound of the cart-wheels was only a remembered one, and then I walked slowly up the drive to the convent school. I was far too early. There was no one in sight, and the grey house with its high narrow windows was frightening. I hid among bushes of mauve hydrangeas with water bouncing off their leaves and onto the brim of my velour hat, waiting for the girls to come down the lane. They came at last in laughing bunches of twos and threes, and when I counted fifty of them past and was sure no one was watching me I scrambled out of my hiding-place and shook the damp leaves off my coat. I followed them up the drive, my heart lurching in my chest with pride and fright.

The school smelt of the spice of carnations, and it had corridors that rang with the smart striding of the girls, and its stairs and panels gleamed with polish. The girls all seemed to know each other, and their laughter shrieked like sudden peals of bells till the nuns hushed them. 'Pssshh!' like pistol cracks ricocheting off the tiles. 'Psssssh!' and all the bells stopped pealing.

The day started with Mass in the convent chapel. It was quite tiny compared with our parish church, and had white walls and a carved wooden ceiling, and pictures of lambs and flowers and young child saints in its stained glass windows. It was Father Carolyn who came to celebrate the Mass. I wanted to smile at him as he came out from the vestry with the serving nuns. Instead, timid, I bowed my head. I had never been in any other church but my own before, and it was comforting to recognise the statues on the shelves, because they had the same faces as the ones in our parish church and the ones in every room of our house at home. There were flowers everywhere; we could smell them as soon as we went in, and beneath them the waxy smell of candles and polish. And I knew the perfumes of the incense. I stopped trembling for the first time, feeling at last that I was in a place as familiar as my home, and when the nuns and the choir started to sing the responses I closed my eyes and smiled to myself. Gently I pitched my voice into theirs, knowing how it shone.

In class nobody spoke after the Hail Mary. A nun who was more beautiful than any painting I'd seen of the Blessed Virgin wrote 'Algebra' on the board for us to copy, and said the word signified the reunion of broken parts, and promised us we would understand it some time, and would consider it an excellent ordering of mathematical notions, and I slid my eyes from her and saw how the other girls watched her with admiration and awe. She had a low, calm voice and grey eyes, and she said her name was Mother Philomena, which was the poetic name for a nightingale. I wondered whether she knew the story my Uncle Rory had told me, where Philomel had had her tongue cut out before she was changed into a nightingale, but I daren't ask her. I kept my head down and listened to her low voice telling me about things I'd never heard of before, and the magical transformation of numbers into letters.

The room we were in was panelled to the ceiling with dark brown wood. High up at the top was a narrow slit of a window tickled with the scuttle of leaves. There was one bare light bulb, and the only colour came from the sky-blue robes of the Virgin's statue in the corner, where we addressed our prayers at the beginning and end of every lesson and at the twelve o'clock Angelus.

Next to our classroom was the kitchen, and the reek of boiling cabbage rose like the salt of the incoming tide halfway through the morning, and lingered throughout the day.

When my brother brought the cart for me at four o'clock I could hardly keep back my grief, and I sat behind him with my throat aching for tears all the way home, and sat silent at the table while my mother and Aunt Bridget coaxed me with scones to talk about my day. Little Terence squatted at my feet, anxious. It wasn't till Geraldine came home spattered with mud from running up the wet lane from the hospital and came straight to me to hold my face in her fat hands that I could let out my weeping.

'Dear God, what's up with you child?' Aunt Bridget said. 'Did they beat you?'

'Nobody talked to me,' I blurted out, though that wasn't it.

'Well, that's a fine thing to grieve about!' My mother, impatient and relieved, went back to her cooking.

'Everybody knew each other and nobody talked to me. At playtime they all walked around the gardens, and nobody walked with me. And at dinner we had hard potatoes and wet cabbage and a nun read to us about the life of Juliana.'

'Not a nice story to be eating your dinner with,' Aunt Bridget agreed. 'She was the one whose body was broken on a wheel till the very marrow spurted out, if I remember my martyrs and virgins right. Yet she would not give up her chastity, no she would not. Actually I like her story, Cecilia.'

I sat back, exhausted. Geraldine dropped her hands from my face and sat down on a stool opposite me, still searching my eyes. But I couldn't look at her. How could I paint for her the picture of the dark corridors, the classrooms with wooden walls and high, tiny windows, the black line of nuns parading round the hall at assembly, the pistol-crack of their voices, the smell of carnations and cabbage, the long and dreadful walk down the drive in the rain, the climbing onto the milk-cart with Michael grinning at the staring girls?

For that is what I remember of my first day, and that is what came to me the day I left, when I stood alone in the holy of holies, the nun's burial ground, that forbidden place. The blank row of little flat stones was well-ordered, protected by the trees and shrubs that crowded in on all sides. Beneath my feet the soil was rich, moist, newly turned and tossed on the bed of Mother Mary Rose.

Take away the black robes, Mother, and the bowing at the altar. Take away the hushed prayer and the magic telling of the beads. And take away your mystery.

Chapter Two

We had our first choir practice on my second or third day at school. At last here I could look forward to something wonderful, because like my lion-haired Uncle Rory I loved to sing. One of my favourite places to sing was down the yard in the old lavatory with the door shut tight and the hens scratching at the broken planks to get underneath it, and dust tumbling with the sunlight through the cracks. I reasoned that because no one could see me there then no one would hear me, and I could sing popular songs without my Aunt Bridget scolding me for their coarseness, or Christmas carols at any time of the year. Sometimes I could sing the sweet sad songs you heard the fiddlers playing in between the hooligan jigs at the ceilidhs. And there was a hollow in the hills up behind our barns, with boulders clutching the sides of it like seats in a theatre, and every time I sang there it would be different...

'Oh, the days of the Kerry dancing... Oh, the ring of the piper's tune...'

If the sun was heavy and full the tune would skip through it, but a sea wind would snatch it up away from me and fling it back again. The best time to sing was just before rain, when the air felt thin as silk; that was when everything echoed for me. And in church, listening to my mother and father each side of me, and Uncle Rory rich as peat, and all the voices rising up, rising up like waves, and my own sound there, bright inside them all.

When we went in to choir practice that first time it was in the gym, and Mother Mary Rose, teacher of music, was playing a hymn on the piano. It made us march, and it made us laugh. I caught the eye of one of the girls, Veronica, and we smiled at each other. I was excited. We filed into the row of chairs that had been set out for us and the playing stopped.

'Which of you girls is Cecilia Deardon?'

'Me, Mother.' I said.

'Who? Who? Who spoke?'

I put up my hand. I was in the middle of a row, somewhere near the back of the class. The nun made no effort to see me, but shouted, her old woman's voice ringing in the lofty gym.

'Who? Stand up. Stand up. Don't be such a goose, child. Stand up.'

I stood up, blushing fiercely as heads turned to look at me.

'Come out here to the front. I want to look at you. So.'

I stumbled over sandaled feet and out to the front. I knew my skirt was too long and that I wasn't wearing the uniform cardigan. It was nearly the same colour, but cheaper. My Aunt Bridget had knitted it for me. I knew that.

'So you're Cecilia.'

'Yes, Mother.'

The old nun stared at me, and I stared at her half-gloved fingers as they fidgeted like moths on the yellow keys.

'And do you know, child, who it is you're called after?'

'I think it was my granny, Mother.'

There was a titter round the girls.

'Your granny, is it? Is that what you think?'

'Yes, Mother.'

'You don't know much, do you?'

'No, Mother.' I whispered.

'She was a far greater lady than your granny is, or was, or will ever be, girl. Remember that. You can tell your granny that Mother Mary Rose said that to you.'

'Yes, Mother.'

She slapped down the piano lid and sprang up from her chair. Her fingers grasped my arm as she turned me round to face the rest of the class.

'Well, who was she then? Who can tell me? November 22nd. Look in your missals, girls. Look in your missals. November 22nd is..?'

There was a fluttering of pages as girls rustled through their missals. I was holding mine but was too much of a fool to open it.

She had made me stupid. There was no redemption.

'Please, Mother!'

'Yes?' Mother Rose pointed at one of the raised hands.

'Please, Mother. Saint Cecilia's day, Mother.'

'Good girl. What's your name, dear?'

'Veronica Murphy, Mother.'

'I believe I taught your dear mother. And who was Saint Cecilia, if she wasn't this girl's granny?'

The class tittered again. The missals had been closed and were reopened, pages shuffled in the fever of the race.

'Please, Mother!'

'Yes, Veronica.'

'Please, Mother. Martyr and Virgin, Mother.'

'...and?'

'Please Mother! Patron saint of music, Mother.'

'Yes, Veronica.'

The sigh was like the wind hushing through trees, as the girls sank back into their chairs. Mother Rose let go my arm. 'Saint Cecilia, Martyr and Virgin, patron saint of music. Did you hear that, child?'

'Yes, Mother.'

'And are you worthy to be named after her?'

My head swam. 'I don't know, Mother.'

I could see the fine hairs on her pale cheeks, the fluff of spittle on her lips. 'It's yes or no, child. Yes or no. Do you love music? Yes or no?'

Do I love music? With my soul.

That night after Terence had gone up to bed I sat with my mother and Aunt Bridget round the kitchen table. I had homework to do for the first time ever, but first I had something to ask my mother. She was reading the paper, her face puckered with the effort, even though she was wearing the reading-glasses that she would never put on when my father was in the house.

Geraldine was in the yard at the back, chopping logs. We could hear the gasp of breath that came just before the chuck of the axe, then the splintering of the wood and the thud of it as it was tossed into pile. When we moved the pile after the summer into the porch with the drying wood and turves we would find toads there, squat and loose-limbed, blinking.

My question was a bluebottle, buzzing in my head.

'Mam,' I said, when at last she folded up the paper and shoved it across the table to Aunt Bridget along with the reading-glasses. 'Mam, what's a virgin?'

Hadn't I known that it was not a question to be asked? Aunt Bridget tapped the edge of the table sharply with her fingers flat out. I saw mischief glimmer in my mother's eyes and out again as quick, and the sides of her neck glow pink.

'Oh shush!' she said.

'It's not a bad word,' I insisted. 'There's the Virgin Mary.'

'Then you know what it means,' said Aunt Bridget.

'No,' I said. 'I don't.'

My mother fiddled with her hair, which was curling down loose from its pins. Aunt Bridget pushed back her chair abruptly, screeching it, making the sleeping cats sheer up. Geraldine's gasping had come to a rhythm. Oosh chuck oosh chuck oosh chuck.

'Mam?'

'Well now,' she said. 'It's a woman who doesn't have a husband.'

'And that's all she needs to know, Nancy, a child of her age, a child of eleven.'

'Twelve,' I reminded her. 'On Sunday.'

'That's all there is to know,' my mother agreed.

But the bluebottle was still buzzing. 'Mary had a husband,' I pointed out. 'Joseph. Mary and Joseph.'

'She was different.' My mother glanced across at my aunt who refused to look but kept up her tapping on the table. 'Different. She was the mother of God, but the holy child was placed inside her by a miracle. Usually a vir... Usually it means someone who does not have a baby. A woman without a husband.'

'Like Geraldine?' She had just come in, red-faced and damp-haired, clutching splintered sticks to burn when the men came home.

'Exactly,' my aunt said, dry, ending all prospects of pursuing the interesting subject. 'Exactly. You have it exactly, Cecilia. Like Geraldine.'

And Geraldine, standing in the kitchen in Michael's wellingtons, laughed with pleasure at hearing herself discussed and made a mock curtsey, as though she was in the centre of a stage.

I was in my bed by the time the men came home. I could hear them coming in, their voices loud and echoing along the lane, and the stamp of their feet in the porch as they worked mud off their boots. Uncle Rory was whistling. My Aunt Bridget's voice rose up to scold, and my father's laugh came back, light and easy. As soon as they came into the kitchen Geraldine came up to bed. She stood by the window for a long time, just gazing out into the night on the hills. It was September, the month of daddy-long-legs. I could hear them prancing on the plaster, and in the dark I could imagine their stalky legs running across my face. Thomas Smiley used to eat them whole, and that's the truth. He said they were delicious.

That night I wanted to be comforted from them, and gave a little squeak of dismay when I was sure one had danced down onto the pillow. Geraldine came over and knelt down next to the bed. She stroked my hair with the back of her hand and put her head down on the pillow next to mine. I stretched out my fingers to touch her cheek. It was wet.

'Geraldine,' I said. 'What's the matter?'

She took off her clothes and climbed into the creaking bed, and rocked me close against her warm, soft body.

Chapter Three

We had singing lessons twice a week with Mother Mary Rose. I would sit, anonymous and obedient, watching the twisted arthritic fingers, bandaged and black-gloved to the knuckles, find the notes on the piano. Her eyes darted irritably from face to face, searching for mouths that did not open and close in time, for the inadequate mimers. Her routine was unfailing, and on the day that I had been waiting for, the day when she was to choose junior members for the choir, Mother Mary Rose picked on me.

'*Visibilium et invisibilium.* Say it girls. Say it. Say it.'

The chair was suddenly scraped back, twisted fingers clutched the edge of the keyboard as she levered herself up, darted forward, bird-like, chin out; hovered and stopped, trembling, in front of me.

'You say it.'

'Me, Mother?'

'You. Say it.'

'Velum. Velum et invelum, Mother.'

Someone spluttered behind me. In my terror I smiled.

'I'm not laughing girl. I'm not laughing. Veronica. Where is she? You say it.'

'*Visibilium et invisibilium*, Mother.'

Perfect.

'Now you say it, child.'

I was without hope, wishing only to be taken up immediately into eternity. 'Vibilum et inviblum.'

'You're a giddy goat, child. Sing it out. Sing it out.'

Her spittle sprayed my cheek. I closed my eyes that were burning, willed the white face to go away, the flashing darting spectacles to crack and shatter and stream blood and tears.

'Sing it, Miss Giddy Goat!'

I swayed away from her. Giggles spurted round me.

'Vimbilum et... Please, Mother.'

'Sing it!'

'Vib...vib...'

'Sing it!'

'Mother...' Traitor sobs. Traitor traitor laughter. 'I can't.'

'So. Girls. We have a baby in our midst. Girls, will you just look at the big baby we have here in our class.'

Out of my tears I saw her fold her arms like wings around herself, thrust her beaked face into mine, heard her croak a harsh quavering note.

'Give me lah to that doh, child.'

My shame cocooned me in deep quiet throughout that day. In the evening it was my Uncle Rory who tried to rouse me from it.

'How's my little singing bird today?'

'Uncle Rory, I'm not a singing bird. I can't sing.'

'What's this,' he smiled. 'Can't sing?'

'The singing teacher told me I can't sing. I'm a non-singer and not fit to be in her choir.' I said it slowly, head bent into the swing of my hair so they wouldn't see my face. I had rehearsed the words very carefully on my bicycle ride home to make sure they made no mistake about it.

'What idiot talk is this? Cecilia Deardon, not fit!'

My uncle laughed, dismissing my nonsense, but after the meal that night he brought out his set of tin whistles and started to play on one for me, leaning forward with the lilting of it, glancing over to me to make me start, because this was a song we often sang together; after my verse my mother would take one up and then my father and then Michael and so on round the family till the sound swelled and swelled, but mine was always the starting verse. But though I tried the white scorning face came back at me again, spittle frothing at the corners of her mouth, the pale moth-fingers fluttering.

'Sing!' my Aunt Bridget said, prodding my back with her knitting needle, and I curled away from her, ashamed. So she sang for me, in her loud flat voice, concentrating at the same time on counting her stitches. I hugged my knees and stared into the firelight watching the flames that danced in the wake of the whistling pipe, waiting out for the voices to follow one another. When it came to my father's turn he knelt down next to me and turned my hot face up to his.

'Sing, Cessy. Sing!' he whispered, and I shook my head, not understanding myself.

The piping stopped.

'Leave her alone, Francis,' my uncle said.

'I will not,' said my father. 'I'll not have her playing sulks with me like this. She'll sing if I tell her to.'

'I said leave her.' My uncle's voice was quiet. I could feel my father's hand tensing against my cheek. My aunt tutted behind me. Uncle Rory never took his eyes off my father but slowly lifted the whistle to his lips again and started playing, and this time nobody sang. In her chair by the window Geraldine hugged herself and laughed.

And so at school I was declared a non-singer, and was obliged to sit at the back of the singing-class and suffer the hopeless meanderings of the tone-deaf. I was given no further audition for the chapel choir, and when we filed into chapel for daily Mass and Thursday afternoon Benediction I had to separate myself from the chosen ones and sit downstairs. Like the sweet spice of the incense swung in the thurible the incantation of the plainchant wafted round me, balm to my adolescent yearnings:

Tantum ergo, sacramentum
Veneremur cernui;
Et antiquum documentum
Novo cedat ritui...

Above and around me, music centuries old.

During my first year the soloist in the choir was a girl called Patricia Keenan. She had a thin, sweet boy's voice which people said was beautiful, though I did not find it so. When I listened to her singing I found I was stretching my own throat and arching up the back of my tongue, as if by doing that I would be able to urge her to a fullness that went beyond her natural and easy head notes. I felt she sang without passion, though I could not have explained that at the time. She was a sixth-former, and when she walked round school I found that I could not help watching her, and that my awareness of her made me nervous and warm; and that, too, was something I could not understand. I would watch her in the gardens, where she walked with the other girls of her year. The shrubberies there were dark with rich foliage, and the paths wound through them, dank under the canopies of the trees. This was where the nuns would walk alone, heads bowed in private meditation. When the sixth-formers were given leave to go there they walked casually, arms folded or linked with each others', chatting and laughing softly. Patricia Keenan was one of them. She was olive-skinned and light like a dancer, brown-eyed. She always smiled at me as I hung on the perimeter of my permitted ground, and one day she walked over to me with her friends and touched my hair.

'What a glory this little one's hair is! Sunset!' She bent down towards me. I was hot and fierce with the closeness of her; my blood banged in my head. 'Do you know your Latin?'

'Yes,' I whispered.

'*Pulchra*,' she murmured.

Pulchra. Beautiful. *Amo amas amat*. I love, you love, he she it loves.

She walked away from me, forgetting. She had been standing in front of the rockery grotto of Our Lady, the Blessed Virgin, and as she moved away I found the statue's cool eyes fixed on mine. The Virgin wore a cream dress and a long blue cloak which went over her loose brown hair. Her lips were thin. Her statues were everywhere, in the gardens, in all the classrooms, in the long passages that threaded the basement of the school, and in the chapel, shadowy in the light of the candles. We had them in all the rooms of our house. She was very young, I always thought, to be the mother of Jesus, who was bearded and kind-eyed, who wore red, and whose bulging heart was visible.

When I turned to go away from the shrine I found the tall girl, Veronica, watching me.

'My mother says I can ask a someone home for tea.' she said.

'Oh.'

'Would you like to come?'

'Would it be tonight?' I was too shy to thank her in the proper way. I had never been asked to anyone's house to tea before.

'Oh no. We only have people to tea on Sundays. But I can show you how to get there tonight.'

After school she stood waiting for me when I went to collect my bike from the shed. We walked up the lane a little and she helped me to hump the bike over a padlocked gate. We had a meadow full of poppies to cross.

'Wait and I'll leave the bike in the hedge, Veronica. I can pick it up on the way back.'

'No, bring the bike. You can go home on the lanes. This is just the quick way for now. And you can call me Noni, only not in front of my dad.'

I did not like pushing the bike through the choking grass. Once I laid it down and she yanked it up again. 'Push it,' she ordered. 'It's not far.' It was very hot. I could feel my school blouse clinging to me, and my heavy skirt damp around my thighs. The grass was above our knees.

'Do you always come this way?' I asked her.

'No. I thought you'd like it. Don't you like it?'

'I do. It's nice.'

Just below us we could see the wooden spars and supports of a house that was being built.

'We're near the lane now,' she promised. 'That place is for the new doctor. It's an eyesore.'

She pushed ahead of me and then stopped. She put out her hand behind her to shush me as I tugged my wheels through a new tangle.

'What is it?' I asked, and she shushed me again. I joined her and stood with her, stared down with her at a place where the grass was squashed flat and a long pinkish shape lay there on the downward slope towards the eyesore. It was a naked man that we could see, his arms folded underneath his face, and he was still, quite still, and all we could hear was the cracking of the black gorse pods. We stood together and stared at the creased lines around his neck and at the dark fuzz of hair that tufted under his armpits, and at the bulge of wet flesh where his waist was, and at the pale flat buttocks, the arch of his crossed feet, at the slight fanning of his yellow hair.

'Jesus Mary and Joseph,' Noni whispered. 'It's a dead corpse, so it is.'

'Jesus Mary and Joseph.' My fingers were clenched round my handlebars. I tried to ease them up, one by one, and they were like twigs with their stiffness. My knees were tight as nuts. The man's flesh was pinky white, and his shoulder blades were sharp red angles. The flat strange buttocks had a grinning dark line.

'Let's go back,' I whispered.

'We will not,' Noni whispered back. 'We'll tiptoe round it. Are you ready?'

I nodded.

She moved forward and as I tried to follow her my bike wheels locked in the grass.

'Help!' I hissed.

She glanced back and lifted up the bike at the saddle and I heaved it up with the handlebars across my chest. We skirted the corpse step by step, facing each other with our mouths stretched over our teeth with the effort of the lifting and the silence.

And then the corpse stood up. Shocked, he stared at us. We stared back, motionless. Then Noni dropped her end of the bike and ran with her arms stretched out in front of her, stumbling down towards the lane; and the corpse grabbed out for his pants in the long grass and fumbled wildly on one leg to put them on and I heaved my rattling bike down the lane behind me. I caught up with Noni and we ran, heads down, our feet thudding up dust and the pedals of the bike clanging against our calves, and we didn't stop till we came to the big house where a man with a straw hat was mowing a long green lawn.

'This is it,' Noni panted. 'Will you come on Sunday?'

'All right.' My breath came in huge gasps. I straddled my bike and put my foot on the pedal. My legs started to shake. 'I'll go now.'

Then Noni's mouth went sideways as if she was going to cry. She folded her arms across her chest and bent right over. I slid forward till my head was on the handlebars and let my hands slide right down. I could hear myself howling. Noni whooped and toppled backwards onto the verge and lay with her legs kicked up in front of her. She tugged out handfuls of grass and stuffed them in her mouth and spat them out in bursts. We howled with our mouths right open and no way of stopping the tears that streamed and streamed.

'Will you tell anyone?' I gasped out at last. I felt as if my jawbones had been stretched.

'I will not!' She whooped again.

'Did you see his bottom!' I howled. 'He looked like a pig!'

Noni couldn't speak. She flung herself over and banged her head on the grass. 'Yum yum pig's bum!' she yelled.

The man with the straw hat peered over the hedge at us and I rode away slowly, my bike swaying from side to side, my face aching. 'Yum yum.'

Yet I longed to tell Geraldine about it. I stole sideways glances at her in our bed and thought about telling her. Over and over in my head I thought of the shock of the sight of him, and wished I'd had a better look while I'd had the chance. It would be a wicked thing to talk about, I knew. I did my best to think about holy things instead.

Chapter Four

Wherever I went about the school and the grounds there was music. If it wasn't the organ in chapel or the sound of the choir at practice it would be the nuns at their private service, or it would be an instrument, a piano or a violin, flutes. The music rooms were below our classroom, lined up along the tiled passage that led to chapel. Piano notes trickled from them hour after hour; they would echo round the school like the sound of water on pebbles. I could not listen to the lessons for their sweet distraction. And one day when I was waiting for Veronica to come down from class for her lunch and I saw Mother Mary Rose coming from the music rooms, a sudden impulse made me speak to her. Didn't she, of all people, know how much I wanted to be worthy of my name? Perhaps she would teach me piano if she wouldn't let me sing. The notion was so good and obvious that it drove away my fear of her. I hovered on the edge of the chapel passage for her. Here we could speak. One step further, and speech was sin.

St. Cecilia, help me.

'Mother..'

'Pssssh!'

'Please, Mother…'

She stopped next to me. 'Well, what is it, girl, what is it? I'm in a hurry. Speak quickly now.'

'Yes, Mother. I wanted to ask you something.'

She darted a sideways look at me.

'I don't know you, do I?'

'Yes, Mother. I'm Cecilia Deardon.'

'Do you love music, Cecilia Deardon?'

'Yes, Mother.'

She peered at me again. 'But you're not in my chapel choir, are you? I've never seen you at the practice, is that not so?'

'No, Mother. You said I couldn't be in the choir.'

'So what do you want with me?'

'Please, Mother. Can I have piano lessons? May I have piano lessons?'

'Of course you may, if you can pay. Well, don't look at me like that, girl. Four guineas a term, that's what it costs.'

'I don't think we can afford that, Mother.'

'Of course you don't think!' she snapped. Her fingers were groping in the folds of her skirts for her dangling rosary beads. 'You think music is free, don't you? You're all the same, you scholarship girls. I know you. I know you. Something for nothing all the time. I can tell you scholarship girls all right - by the cut of your uniform dear, and your knitted cardigans. That's how I can tell. By the way you speak, child. And by your fingernails.'

She made away from me, and in despair I blurted out, 'Please Mother. I'd really like to be in the chapel choir. If I could.'

Her rapid steps were halted by the sound of the midday bell.

'Psssh! The Angelus.'

'Please, Mother.'

She crossed herself. 'The Angel of the Lord declared unto Mary, say it with me, girl, say it with me...'

'And she conceived of the Holy Ghost...'

'Hail Mary, full of Grace...'

'What were you doing with Rosie?' Noni asked me later, when she was eating boiled fish and red cabbage and I was eating my cheese sandwiches from home. We had learnt the skill of speaking between courses under the clatter of the serving bowls, before Mother Joseph again took up her daily reading from the lives of the saints.

'I was asking her for piano lessons.'

'Are you going to have some?'

'Of course not. They cost four guineas a term, Noni. You never told me that.'

'How was I to know that?' She ducked her head down, a string of cabbage dangling between her mouth and the plate. She sucked it in, spattering red vinegar on the backs of her hands. 'I don't pay the bills. Is it too much?'

'Of course it is. I wouldn't even ask them. It doesn't matter.'

The reading had begun. Cutlery chinked on plates.

'I'll teach you if you want,' Noni mouthed, head down.

'What?'

'I'll teach you.'

'Noni, will you? D'you mean it, really?'

'Who's that speaking?'

The clinking stopped. Noni's plate of fish and my box of sandwiches were removed and we were made to stand, heads bowed, while the reading continued.

'After I've had my lessons,' she said, as we left the refectory at the end of the meal. 'You come to the music room straight after my lesson and I'll teach you what she's just taught me. It'll serve the old crow right.'

I cycled home in great joy that evening to tell them that I was to have music lessons, though I decided not to tell them that it was Veronica who would be teaching me. In my heart I knew that Mother Mary Rose would hear me playing and would be so moved by the beauty of it that she would teach me herself, free, and would put me in her choir.

But nobody heard my news. There was unhappiness in our house at the time, though I didn't know the cause of it. I knew the crops on our smallholding had been poor, and that there was precious little for eating, let alone for selling. That night at the meal my brother Michael told us that he was leaving home to find work.

'I might even go over to Liverpool,' he told us.

My mother pushed her plate away from her. 'Dear God,' she whispered, her hand to her mouth.

'He's twenty-one,' my father said. 'A man, Nancy. Old enough to look after himself.'

'Did you put him up to this?' my mother asked. 'Michael, was this your daddy's doing?'

Michael nodded. 'We talked about it. But it's something I want to do, Mam.'

'Well, it's not something I want you to do, for God's sake.'

Aunt Bridget slid my mother's plate back to her. 'Eat, Nancy, while we still have food to eat.'

'I can't eat. How can I eat when there's this sort of talk going on at the table?' my mother demanded.

I put my knife and fork together on my plate, a whole potato still untouched.

'He's old enough to leave home,' my father told her gently. 'He's not a child any more. You must face that, Nancy.'

'A child leaves home when there's another home to go to, and not before. If you'd found a wife, Michael, and were wanting to set up together, young as you are, it would be different. But to go off on your own! No, it's not right. You're not ready to leave home yet.'

I glanced at Geraldine and wondered if she would be allowed to leave home, ever. And would it ever come to me that I would have another home to go to? I would be a priest's housekeeper, perhaps. I would move into Father Carolyn's presbytery and cook his meals for him.

'We can't all live here, Mam. I need to find work. And I'll be sending money home to you.' Michael put out his hand to stroke my mother's arm, and she clung on to it.

'Digging roads, you'll be!' she said. 'Labouring. And with no one to cook your meals for you.'

'Something will turn up,' my Aunt Bridget said. 'You have no faith in the power of prayer.'

'And a fat lot of good prayer did for you!' my mother said, bitter with everyone in the room for the thing that was taking her son away from her. 'Night after night I sat up with you, Bridget, till your forty-eighth birthday, praying to Saint Elizabeth to help you out before it was too late.'

'Hush,' said my Uncle Rory. 'Hush now.'

'An empty womb.' My Aunt Bridget's sigh had a tremor in it. 'Never used, Rory, and that's the truth. Shrivelled up now, long since, like a walnut.' She drained back her mug of stout and wiped the froth from her lips with the back of her hand,

and held her hand there, pressed to her mouth as if she was kissing it, or biting it, her eyes shut tight.

'Nancy,' my father said. 'That was not a thing to be spoken of with the children still around.'

'Better to have no children at all, Bridget, than to lose them,' my mother said, and her voice was soft as though Terence and I in our shocked stillness were quite forgotten, and she was alone with her sister in some quiet dark place.

'Better to have none at all, I'd say, than to have dead things in you.'

And I remembered then what had happened a year or so before Terence had been born, when I was three or four. I could remember it clearly. My father coming down from the bedroom and saying that the baby had come and going out into the rain to stand in his shirt sleeves by the wall. And Geraldine and I going tiptoed up the stairs. I can smell the dust on the wood. Twilight, and rain seething against the window, and my mother sleeping in her bed with her eyes opened, she was so still, watching us as we crept to the door. My Aunt Bridget, midwifing her, rolling up a red sheet. Geraldine running forward, and a white bundle on the floor. 'Baby!' Laughing, and holding it as if it were her own, rocking it. And Aunt Bridget turning in the half-light to snap at her to put it down. 'It's dead,' she had said. 'Mustn't touch. Dead.'

And I will never forget the sound my mother had made then, like the sound animals make, even though she was lying there quite still and sleeping with her eyes open; a kind of bellow.

Chapter Five

'When are you thinking of leaving, Michael?' my Uncle Rory asked. 'Not too soon?'

Michael touched my mother's arm again. 'Saturday,' he said quickly. She said nothing.

'Just for the winter it would be, Nancy,' said my father. 'He can send us money from over the water, and feed himself too, and be back for the planting.'

'Geraldine can do the planting,' Uncle Rory laughed. 'She's got fine muscles. She's as good as any man when it comes to muscles, that one.'

Geraldine nodded round to us, proud of her muscles and of the attention they were getting. I squeezed the top of my arm. Not much there, I was thinking, and all of a sudden my mother clattered the tea things together, pulling Rory's half-finished plate of food from underneath his knife and fork.

'If everyone worked as hard as Michael does, there'd be more than enough food for all of us,' she said. She spoke it firmly and levelly, as though it was something she had been saving up in her head to say for weeks and months, and she didn't look at anyone, just walked on past us all out to the yard and stood leaning against the doorway with her arms folded and her hair being tugged down by the wind.

'I hadn't finished yet,' said Uncle Rory.

'Have hers,' Aunt Bridget suggested. 'She's hardly touched it. There's no point in letting two dinners go to waste.'

Still my mother leaned there, staring out into the yard and letting her hair frisk down around her neck.

'I want to go, Mam,' Michael called out to her, his voice tight.

'You hear that, Nancy. The boy wants to go. Let him.'

'When people go to Liverpool, they never come back,' Aunt Bridget warned my father.

Uncle Rory shook his head at her.

'I'll be back at Christmas,' Michael promised.

'Oh, they all say that, and they mean it too. They come home at Christmas, and at Easter, and maybe for a week in the summer if they have the money, and the next year they leave out the Easter bit, and after a couple of years you'll be lucky if they're sitting down to Christmas dinner with you. I've seen it,' she insisted. 'Time and time again.'

'Time and time again,' repeated Terence, liking the sound of it.

Michael took his jacket off the hook by the door and pushed past my mother.

'Where d'you think you're going?' she asked him.

'Out,' he said. 'O.U.T.'

'Oh you teapot,' said Terence.

My mother followed Michael. She tried to touch him but he ducked away from her and edged back, his jacket slung over his shoulder and its tape looped around his finger hook, while she talked to him. Their eyes had the same ash-green. It was not possible for us to hear what they were saying, though we all sat in a listening silence till Aunt Bridget said, 'Mothers always love their sons best.'

I looked anxiously at Geraldine.

'And daddies love their daughters.'

'And how would you know that?' Uncle Rory asked her.

'It's a well known fact. I've known that all my life. And sisters are closer than brothers.'

'There's no law about that, either.'

'Oh, it's true!' she insisted. 'And the youngest stay babies for a long, long time.' She rolled a plum across the table to Terence. 'Too many plums are bad for the tums.'

'Too much jelly is bad for the -'

'Terence!'

My mother came back in alone and stood in front of the fire, tidying her hair in the mirror that was propped on the high mantelpiece. 'Will you look how flabby my arms are getting at the top,' she said. 'You'll not be wanting to take me dancing soon, Francis.'

My father glanced at Rory and winked. 'Now you see, as soon as she's got that big lad off her hands she's wanting to act the girl again. What's this Nancy, flirting with your husband like a sweetheart!'

He jumped up and kissed the back of her neck, and turned her round with his hands still on her waist. I could see that her eyes still had hurt in them. He slipped his hand into hers so they could dance.

'Softly, softly, come to me
Touch my lips so tenderly

Softly, softly, turn the key
And open
Up my
Heart.'

'Great idiot!' my mother held her laughing face up to his.

'Will you just look at the pair of them now!' Aunt Bridget shoved chairs out of the way and stood them upended on the table so my father could plough his route, eyes shut, around the ballroom of the kitchen. 'You're never romantic like this with me.'

'I have a sore back, Bridget,' Rory reminded her.

My mother spoke up from the snug of my father's shoulder. 'It was on account of that sore back, Rory Brunton, that you came here in the first place.'

'Shush!' my father whispered. 'One two three, one two three…'

'You came for one week, I remember.'

Uncle Rory laughed. 'It's been a long week.'

'It was before Cecilia was born, even.'

'Is that so?' he mused. 'Indeed, Nancy. Is that so?'

Michael left home that Saturday, and I went down with my father to see him off. Michael had a tune in his head that he would not stop whistling. It was carried on from the ceilidh we had held in the house the night before for him, as though all that dancing and music and laughter, all those smiles and handshakes had been distilled down into his solitary whistling; an echo of yesterday, but such a sad thin one at that. There were three fiddles in the house that night, and tin whistles and banjos. They must have heard the noise across the water. My Aunt Bridget told us ghost stories in between the dancing, and had her shawl over her head and her top set of teeth dropping every now and again to frighten the little ones. My mother's other sister had come over with all her family, and most of the people down the lane had called in at some time or another to admire Michael and to wish him well.

'I remember the time,' Mrs O'Leary told my mother, 'When my brother left home to go to England. There were fourteen of us in the house and all my mother could say was 'Ah, but it will be so quiet at home now without the boy!' And do you know Mrs Deardon, it was. Like death,' she said.

When the house was too full and noisy to breathe in I had gone out for the calm air. I wandered up the hill, sleepy and happy, having had a bit to drink myself, not too sad about Michael, but knowing inside myself that nothing would make me want to leave home like this, when so much was expected of him, so much hope going with him. It would be easier to stay at home forever maybe. How wide the sea must be, I thought.

And the next morning the house was quiet as the church. My mother had said she would come with us to see him off and then at the last minute she changed her mind. She laughed and joked at the door with him with her eyes dancing about as though she couldn't look at him straight, even when she reached up to stroke his hair and laughed as he shook it forward again. As I watched her I wondered, is it true, does she love him more than she loves me? When my father looked at his watch and said, 'Come on, we'll be late,' and my mother hugged Michael quickly and went inside the house, I wanted to stay with her.

And Michael whistled all the way to the station. It was a tune that had no end, and he repeated it over and over again as if he was trying to learn it so he could hold it in his head for ever. I didn't know what to say to him and it seemed as if my father didn't either, to tell the truth, so we walked along behind him in silence with Terence running from one to the other of us with high prattle that nobody wanted to hear.

'What would you like me to buy you for Christmas?' Michael asked us when we were standing on the platform. 'Something to eat, or something to wear?'

'Can I have something to read?' I asked him shyly.

'Beano,' said Terence.

'A proper book,' I said.

'Oh, a proper book,' said Michael. 'Like a missal, you mean? That smells of leather, maybe?'

He stood on the very edge of the platform with his back to the lines, the tips of his heels just over the sill. He laughed down at me because I begged him to move in. When at last we heard the train coming up the valley he stepped forward and lifted me up high as if I was as young as Terence, and rubbed his stubbly chin on my cheek.

'Don't you ever cut off that hair of yours, Cessy,' he told me. 'Ever.'

'I won't.'

He set me down and swung Terence round and threatened to throw him on the lines if he didn't look after Mam now, and Terence screamed with laughing as the train hurtled towards us. And he hugged my father with both arms, his face buried in his shoulder. As soon as the train arrived he picked up his case and climbed on. Terence and I ran along the platform with the moving train, trying to keep his waving hand in sight, laughing with excitement as we tried to beat his carriage to the bridge, and when I turned Terence was panting behind me and Daddy had gone. He was waiting for us by the road. 'Come on,' he shouted, holding out his hand to me. 'Run.'

Terence danced ahead of us and ran on home, but I was out of breath by now. My father's hand hurt me. He tugged me behind him and I was bent nearly double, pulling myself away from him, hating this roughness. When we reached the top of the hill he leaned against the wall, his breath coming in sharp rasps.

'Look. Away down there. Michael's train.'

The voice of the train was a rumble through the hills, steadfast and purposeful.

'He'll come back again, won't he?'

'Oh, he'll come back. But he's left home now Cessy, that's the thing, you see. He's left home.'

'Do you want Uncle Rory and Aunt Bridget to leave home?'

He shielded his eyes with his elbow propped against the wall, watching the train that he could no longer see. 'What's that?'

'Do you want...?'

'No. Why should I? Do you?'

'No,' I said. 'I don't. I'd hate to see them go.'

'Then why d'you ask, eh?'

'Because Mam wants them to go.'

'Mam?'

'She does. I know she does.'

He swung away from the wall and we walked down home together. He seemed to have picked up the tune that Michael had been whistling, and he kept his head down and his hands in his pockets, not sad I would have thought, not the way he was whistling it, but a long way from me.

Father Carolyn's housekeeper came up the hill with a hen under each arm. When she saw us she called out that she had a brother in Liverpool who would look out for Michael, she had his address somewhere safe, she was sure of that, though she hadn't written to him for twenty years.

'There'll be keening in your house tonight then,' she said into my father's whistling, and I answered for him that there would not.

'They're going ballroom dancing at the hall. The lot of them. Even my Uncle Rory with his sore back.'

She planted herself then for a good long gossip, shifting the hens as they fluttered for freedom. She told us that her sister used to be an exhibition dancer in Dublin with five hundred sequins on her frock, and that her career in glamour had been cut short when she married a man with two left feet, and though this information interested me a lot it seemed that my father didn't even hear her but kept on walking and whistling. I caught up with him, disappointed all right, and then, just as we came in front of the house, I remembered my news.

'Daddy,' I said, planning to cheer him up with it, 'I'm going to have piano lessons at school.'

'Are you?' he asked, not stopping. 'What for?'

'To learn music,' I said, surprised, and then I added, 'For nothing.'

'We don't have a piano.' He frowned down at me. 'Tell them thank you, but you don't need them.'

'But Daddy...'

'I've told you, Cessy. No.'

I ran ahead of him into the house, past my mother and Geraldine who were working in the kitchen, and up the stairs to my room. Terence was in the room next door; Michael's room. His now. Already he was thumping round in it, heaving Michael's bedding off the mattress, bringing his own in from the big old cot he had always slept in next to my mother and father's bed.

'Will you help me?' he shouted through the doorway.

'No,' I said. That brought my mother shouting up the stairs after me and I followed Terence through, wanting only to be on my own, lifting up the debris he'd scattered on the landing. The room smelt of Michael. His sweat, I supposed, and the stuff he put on his hair when he went dancing, and the polish he used for his best shoes. Christ on his crucifix suffered over the bed, his eyes young and pained and looking straight into mine, making me guilty always. For him I cleared up the used sheets and straightened out some for Terence on the mattress and opened up the window to let in the air of the sea. 'Look after Michael,' I whispered to him, and his young eyes sorrowed.

When my mother and Aunt Bridget came upstairs to wash themselves for the dance I went back down. My father was round the back scraping the shoes, and I found myself alone in the kitchen with Geraldine and Uncle Rory. He had his tin whistles laid out like the pipes of an organ in front of him, and I picked out one and tried to peep out Michael's tune on it, it was so strong and persistent in my head. Uncle Rory watched me and picked up another pipe and played out the tune with all the fanciful extra bits he always slips in.

'Here,' he said. 'You'll find that kind of jigging tune simpler on a D whistle.'

'Will you teach me to play, Uncle Rory?' I asked him. 'Instead of the piano?'

'Instead of the piano?' he laughed. 'Well, it's a lot handier than the piano, I'll give you that. You can't slip a piano into your top pocket and take it down to the dancing with you.'

'So will you?'

'The piano is the queen of the instruments,' he said. 'Don't you know that, Cessy? It opens up like rivers and oceans, like all manner of rolling things, and it's as deep as the dark of caves. I would love to play a piano. If I had a piano I would not be playing tin whistles, except when I was out in the fields and the piano was too heavy to hump over the wall with me. Or maybe when I was standing by the window, just standing there you know, and looking out at the night coming, and playing just what came into my head, like I do.'

'My daddy won't let me play one.'

He looked at me over his whistle, resting his fingers on the holes as he drew it out of his mouth. 'Do your friends at the convent school play the piano?'

I nodded.

'Well, you mustn't be asking for things like that. We don't have their sort of money. That's what he'd be thinking.'

'I could have the lessons for nothing.'

'And still your daddy said no?'

'He wasn't really listening.'

'Oh, he was. I should say he was. But not to you. To himself. He's a proud man.'

'Yes.'

'And you know, your instrument is your voice. You know that, don't you?'

'Mother Mary Rose says I'm a non-singer. I can't be in her choir.'

He sighed. 'Sing for me. Come on, come on. Sing for me.'

I shook my head, bewildered. At the sink Geraldine shouted the tune she'd heard my uncle play, the way a child in the schoolyard shouts a skipping chant.

Uncle Rory leaned forward to hide his whisper inside her shouting. 'Well now, this is our secret. I'll let you have the lessons.'

'But daddy said…'

'Ssh! Your daddy doesn't understand. He can't do. Let me see your fingers.'

I put my hand down flat on the table beside his.

'Give me one word for your fingers now.'

I giggled. 'Skinny.'

'All right. Now give me one word for mine.'

'Bony?'

His hands were long and brown and thin, his nails round and smooth as eggshells.

'Some people have farmer's fingers, and some people have fingers that are good for making shoes, or baskets, or for doing fine lacework, or for butchering meat. And some people have musical fingers. Like mine. Like yours. But don't tell your daddy, because he has farmer's fingers, and he wouldn't understand.'

'Are you ready, Rory?'

The women had come down smelling of soap, their hair newly curled. Uncle Rory squeezed my hand and stooped through the door after them to bellow at my father for taking his time so, and all night till they came home I sat up playing made-up tunes on the D whistle with my musical fingers, and worrying a great deal about the sin of disobedience.

Even so, a few days later there I was waiting at the stairs of our classroom for the sound of Mother Mary Rose walking away from the music rooms after Noni's lesson. Noni put her head round the door and hissed at me.

'Cecilia! Are you there?'

'Yes,' I whispered, scared.

'Then come on quick. She thinks I've stayed behind to practise. It's all right.'

The music room was gloomy, having a small high window that let in a yellowish light. I sat on the frayed piano stool, still warm, and stroked the stained keys, enjoying the feel of them under my fingers and the musty smell that rose up when I pressed them.

'This piano's got bad breath,' I giggled, nervous.

'There'll be dead mice and all sorts in it, I shouldn't wonder.'

Noni closed the door and came to stand behind me, leaning over me. She put her hand over mine and guided my fingers onto separate keys.

'This is what Rosie does, Cessy. She puts her hand right over mine, like this, and it's all dry and scratchy and cold. Honest to God, it's like paper. She gives me the creeps. It's like dead moths landing on you.'

I pressed down my fingers. 'What do I do? Where do I start?'

Noni guided my thumb out towards the middle note.

'That's middle C. Everything to the right of there is usually played by the right hand. And everything to the left is usually played by the left hand. Understand?'

I grinned.

'Well, we'll only be concentrating on the right hand for the first lesson. So, you have to move up the scale a note at a time. Press down the C.'

I did so.

'Now press down the next note with the next finger. Good. Now three. Now thumb under. No, thumb under, idiot, and on the next key. God, you're a simpleton! Now, one, good, two three four five. Good!'

'I did it!'

'You did.'

'Easy as anything. It's easy!'

'Of course. That was the scale of the key of C. Major.'

'Now what?'

'Now you come back.'

'I can't.'

'Idiot, you can.'

'I'm stuck.'

'Follow me, giddy goat. Follow me.'

We must have been making a fine old noise, with Noni imitating Mother Rose's croaked commands, and me in a great shriek of excitement. Anyway, neither of us heard the door open.

'What wickedness is this?'

I pushed myself up from the stool so abruptly that I cracked my head against Noni's chin.

'Well?'

'Nothing, Mother,' I said. Noni nursed her chin in both hands, her eyes smarting.

'What sin is this?'

'Mother,' said Noni, 'I told Cecilia I would...'

'No,' I cut in. 'I asked her. I asked Veronica if she would teach me.'

'What sin is this?'

We both looked away from her fury. Noni was shaking away an eruption of nervous giggles.

'Well? Well? You're sinning against the holy commandments. Don't you know that?'

'No, Mother,' I said.

'Yes, Mother. I do know that,' said Noni, taking control of herself.

'And..?'

'And I'm truly sorry, Mother.'

'So am I,' I said.

'Which commandment are you sinning against? You child, with the terrible hair, you're the one I'm asking. You tell me.'

'Thou shalt not... Thou shalt not...'

'Pschaw! Veronica?'

'Steal, Mother?'

Mother Rose turned away from her and placed a hand on each of my shoulders, shaking me till my head loosened like a doll's and my hair tousled down over my face. 'Thou shalt not steal! Thou shalt not steal! Stealing music lessons for which you in your poverty cannot pay! For which you in your slyness had no intention of paying.'

She released me and I sank back down onto the piano stool. She pulled me up again and turned her back on me.

'And you, Veronica Murphy. I'm surprised at you.'

'Yes, Mother.'

'This is my piano! My piano! My music room.'

'Yes, Mother. I'm sorry, Mother.'

'Sorry!' The nun's bright glasses winked round at her. 'Sorry? Sorry is not enough. What kind of a word is sorry? I want you down on your knees child, and I want to hear your Act of Contrition. And you...' she turned back to me. 'Get to chapel. Father Carolyn is in there now to hear confessions. Go to him this minute and tell him of your wickedness, child, and beg him to find a way in his heart of absolving you from your sin.'

The chapel was dim and quiet, with a few whispering nuns and some older girls waiting for confession. I slid along a bench and waited for my turn. I could hear the whisper of the penitents in the confessional and the low rumble of Father Carolyn's questions. He would know my voice when I went in. I thought of trying to disguise it but knew that God would know my voice too. It was a sin even to think of doing that. I would have to confess that, too. I daren't even begin to think about the complexities of stealing music lessons, because my thoughts skated dangerously near to doubts, sure as I was that Mother Mary Rose was mistaken and that there was no such sin. Yet it must be a sin to doubt the word of a nun. I was trapped. It was a sin to think.

At last it was my turn. I went into the dark, stuffy cubicle and closed the door. There was just room for me to kneel up against the grille that separated me from Father. I could hear him shifting himself for comfort. I could tell that he was leaning forward, his head pressed right against the side of the grille, inches away from me. He had a really bad cold. I pressed my knuckles together on the ledge and put my mouth close to where his ear must be. My voice was tiny. I told my story and he did not reject it. So Mother Mary Rose was right. I had sinned. Of course.

His thickened whisper warmed my ear. 'How many times have you committed this sin, child?'

'Once only, Father.'

'But you had it in your heart to commit it many times, is that not so?'

I nodded. He waited.

'Yes,' I whispered.

'And are you truly sorry now for what you've done?'

'Yes, Father.'

There was a smell of polish as he moved again, a creaking of his chair. He would be feeling for his handkerchief, perhaps.

'And do you promise me that you will never, never do it again?'

'Yes, Father. No, Father.'

There was a long pause while he blew his nose.

'I won't do it again, Father.'

'Now for your penance I want you to say for me five decades of the rosary.'

'Thank you, Father.'

'Say for me now the Act of Contrition, and I will absolve you from your sins.' The air fluttered as he moved his hand to cross himself. *'In nomine patris, et filii, et spiritus sancti...'*

I squeezed shut my eyes. 'Oh my God, I am sorry, and beg pardon for all my sins. I detest them above all things, because they deserve thy dreadful punishment...'

The chapel seemed filled with light after the black womb of the confessional. I sat a few rows from the front to say my punishment of Hail Marys from the rosary, and then lingered to watch the big girls, the sixth formers, who had come in to change the altar flowers. They worked in silence, taking the water jugs from the nuns who were allowed to approach the altar. Only the head girl and her prefects were permitted to help with the flowers. I loved the quick and quiet bustle they made, the light step of their feet as they came in from the rose garden and to the vestry and back again with empty jars and full, scattering loose pale petals on the polished floor. I was watching out for Patricia Keenan. She bobbed like a dancer as she crossed in front of the tabernacle, her genuflection free and in rhythm with her walk, not interrupting it. She caught my stare and smiled, and I closed my eyes against her as she tiptoed down the aisle towards me.

'Cecilia. Is that your name?'

I began my rosary again, not opening my eyes to her.

'Cecilia, I have something for you. Take it.'

I felt her lean down towards me. She touched my hand with something, then took hold of my fingers and opened them out. She pressed a fisted rose into my palm.

'For you. Go on. Take it.'

'Please don't. I can't.'

'You don't want it? Take it, little one. Put it into your missal for me. For me. Put it into the page for Saint Valentine's Day. Keep it there forever, *puella pulchra.*'

I kept my head bowed right down till her footsteps had died away. My stomach fluttered black and cold and faint. When I lifted up my hot face and opened my eyes the statues of the sacred heart of Jesus and of the Virgin Mary were both watching me.

'Jesus, mercy,' I whispered. 'Mary, help.'

Chapter Six

Yellow leaves flirted in a rush where the lane from school met the lane from home. Out of a cave of darkness they came in a tumble, catching lights from the dance of branches with a vivid autumn sun glancing through. Wind snatched at my breath as I pedalled, so my chest hurt and the calves of my legs ached with the effort I had to make. I would be glad to be home. But as I rounded the next bend and came out into the calm again I saw Uncle Rory swaying dangerously on Michael's bike, his big white jacket flapping open and the wide hem of his trouser legs flouncing. He raised his hand to greet me and clamped it down again quickly onto the handlebars as his bike swerved round.

'I thought maybe I'd just catch you,' he called. 'I'm wanting you to come with me. Turn round.' He swayed on past me.

'Where to?'

'To my mother's. Bridget's out, so I want you to come instead.'

'But what for?' I stood with my bike half-turned and my legs straddled each side of it. I was disappointed and annoyed. 'What about my tea? And my homework too?'

'We'll see about things like that,' he called over his shoulder, swerving towards the hedge. 'But you have to come. She's been taken ill.'

'What's the matter with her?'

'I don't know. It was the postman who told me. Your mother's gone queer, he said. Queer, now that was the word he used, not ill. The Lord knows what that means. I don't Cecilia, do you?'

The wind came at us again, veering Uncle Rory's bike into mine.

'I don't like bicycles,' he shouted. 'They hurtle you about without any motivation. They have no sense of direction.'

'Your bike has no brakes,' I warned him. 'That's why Michael always wore his boot soles out so fast.'

'It's a bleak and lonesome thing, to be told your mother's gone queer.'

The thought of visiting my uncle's grim old mother worried me. To my mind she had been queer a long time. She lived on her own in a house with bare stone floors that smelt of mushrooms. Since her husband died she wandered round people's smallholdings helping herself to what she wanted when she needed it, more or less. She would follow a hen round till it dropped its eggs and she'd stuff a couple into the pocket of her apron, or she'd pull up a potato root or break off a cabbage head with her hands. It was said that nobody minded at all, and that she was pitied round about. But she was a clean woman for all her wanton ways, with a stern stare that frightened me. She wore a white lace cap such as her grandmother might have worn, and the hair that strayed down from it was the colour of sand, but streaked with amber as though it had the stains of tobacco in it. Her eyes were red-rimmed from the peat fire in her room. People said she'd been a fine-looking woman once, with a sweet, strong voice, but I was afraid of the silence in her red-eyed stare.

We leaned our bikes against the house door, which was locked, and waited for Uncle Rory's knock to be answered. 'I was born here,' he told me. 'I had a den round the back, under the pear trees. I hid things there.'

'What kind of things?'

He glanced down at me, surprised at the question. He looked tense and remote from me. The skin around his mouth was pinched. 'I don't remember.' He rapped on the door. 'Mother! Will you come! Mother!'

'Shall we try round the back?' I suggested. He lingered by the front door, standing with his back to it and his hands in his pockets while I made my way round the back, pulling myself through brambles that tugged at my school skirt. It was half-dark already, yet there was no light on in the house. I glanced through the window and found the shock of the stare of the old woman, grey-faced and quite still, hunched as she was in a chair that was pulled up close to the glass; a cold blank stare locking mine.

'Uncle Rory!' I shouted, afraid.

He ran round the back of the house and shoved past me to open the back door. An appalling smell rushed out to meet us. I backed away.

'Come in, child,' the woman called. 'I'll make you a little drink of tea in a minute.'

Uncle Rory went down on his knees next to his mother. Her legs were caked. I knew what it was and daren't look again. I wanted to retch with the stench of it.

'Open up the window,' Uncle Rory told me. His voice caught in the back of his throat. 'Prop the door back now, or it'll slam.'

I edged past the staring old woman and moved the unwashed dishes at the sink to try to get at the window catch, which seemed to be stuck. 'I can't do it,' I said. 'It won't budge.'

'You have to stand on the stool,' the old woman said. 'It sticks at the top. Give it a good old thump.'

I did as I was told without looking at her.

'I'm just watching out for my son,' she went on. 'He should be here any minute.'

'Glory be, Mother, I'm here.'

'He's a fine boy. Now what about a drink?'

'I'll make some tea for us all, Mother. You be still. I'll make some.'

'That's it. He'll not be long now.'

Uncle Rory came and stood beside me. He filled the kettle and emptied it again and filled it again, not looking once at his mother.

'I'll need to light the fire to boil this. For God's sake, how long is it since the fire's been lit?' He was talking to me. We stood side by side with our backs to his mother looking out into the gloom of the tangled garden where he once used to have a den.

'Would you like some tea, Cecilia?'

'She needs to be washed, Uncle Rory.'

'I know that.'

He was a helpless thing. He put down the black kettle and searched for matches, for cups and for matching saucers.

'There's no milk.'

'You mustn't ask me to wash her,' I told him. 'I can't do it.'

'I can't do it.' His face was creased and old, yellowing round the eyes. His throat had a hollow in it under the Adam's apple.

'She must be washed.'

'I know that.'

'Is there hot water?'

'Yes, there's a geyser. I'd quite forgotten that. I had it put in for her. Yes, it's coming hot.'

'Then I'll lift down the bath and I'll fill it up. But you mustn't ask me to wash her.'

Uncle Rory turned round to her at last, bending down to look in her eyes as if she was really hiding behind them somewhere.

'Mother. Can you wash yourself?'

Like a small child she unbuttoned her cardigan and slipped it off onto the floor, and pulled down her grey vest. Uncle Rory supported her while she struggled to her feet and peeled off the rest of her clothes, wincing where they were stuck to her and pulling at her skin. She didn't look at him once, or at me, but stared out of the window. Her flesh pimpled up with the cold, and Uncle Rory leaned back without leaving go of her and kicked away the chair that was propping open the door.

'Rory will come,' she told him.

'The bath's ready now.'

I hung in the doorway to the room, shocked at the sight of the old woman's dry hanging flesh, and my uncle picked up his mother like a baby and carried her through and lowered her into the water I'd prepared for her in the tin tub. 'That's nice for you,' he whispered to her. 'Nice and warm for you.'

'He's a fine boy,' she said.

I found some old paper and wrapped her clothes in them and carried them outside to the rubbish. Someone could burn them, maybe. I gasped as the wind slammed into me. I wanted to gulp down its cold, clean gusts. Stars were coming out, glinting through black racing clouds. I went back in and pulled the stinking sheets off her bed, saying my rosary fast under my breath. I wrapped them up and took them round to my bike. There would be just room for them in my saddlebag if I shoved my homework books down into my blazer pockets. I searched in the tall cupboards and found sheets that were clean and sweet-smelling, and a nightdress too.

My uncle towelled his mother down. She held up her arms for him. Her sandy hair was damp on her shoulders. She ran her fingers through it and tossed it back like a girl, her eyes closed. She allowed him to slip her nightdress over her head and then followed him through to her clean bed. He tucked the sheets in round her, binding her tightly, and she lay watching me as I slipped past to empty the bath tub with a tin jug. Uncle Rory took the kitchen chair out into the back garden and threw off the covers and scrubbed it down with a kind of venom. I went out to him. It was quite dark now.

'Will it happen again?' I asked him.

'Yes.'

'Will you stay here?'

'Yes. You get off away home. Tell Bridget to come over in the morning.'

I went round to the front of the house. I was too tired to cycle, so I walked home, struggling to keep the bike upright in the wind, one hand on the handlebars and the other on the saddle, and my thoughts solemn and still with the secrets of my new maturity. 'I am grown now. Nothing is more dreadful than that thing I saw tonight. It has made a grown woman of me, capable of anything.'

Trees rushed with the wind. The moon was a brazen copper ball tossed in their heaving branches. At last I saw the blaze and glimmer of my own house lights, and ran down to them.

'Geraldine,' I said that night. 'Do you love anyone?'

There was no light in the room, and no sounds except for that deep voice the wind makes round walls. In the bed beside me my sister drew up her knees to her chin and giggled, hugging herself in a luxurious mystery. And underneath my pillow was my missal, and it seemed to me that I could still smell the fisted rose that had been given to me that morning, and that had come too late to open out. I tried to float a picture of Patricia Keenan into my mind, but couldn't. The only one that came to me was of the white-fleshed old woman being carried like a baby in her own son's arms.

Berlie Doherty

Chapter Seven

Mother Mary Rose bustled into the classroom the next morning when we were waiting for our history lesson.

'Girls, girls, I have a surprise for you. A lovely surprise now. We have a visiting priest called to the convent and he's offered to give you midday Mass! Put your books away quickly now. Quick, quick, quick. Stand up straight. Fasten your cardigans, that's right, fasten them up. Put on your mantillas. Be quick now. Choir girls line up on the right. Quick, quick, quick. And all have your missals out and ready where I can see them.'

There was no need for me to rummage in my desk as the other girls were doing. I knew very well where my missal was - underneath my pillow. And it was necessary for us to have our missals with us always, because we never knew when we might be called to Mass, or to take part in any of the services, you just never knew. You must always be prepared. I knew that.

And yet, idle sloth that I was, I had left my missal lounging and guilty under my pillow.

'Noni,' I whispered, as she passed me to join the choir line. 'What shall I do? I haven't got it!'

'What?'

'My missal! I've left it at home.'

She whistled softly. 'You've had it. She'll murder you.'

'It's not my fault. How was I to know there was going to be a Mass today? Father Carolyn's supposed to be away all week.'

'Who's talking?'

Noni bent over to me. 'Why don't you take in a dictionary?'

'I daren't!'

Mother Rose began her inspection of missals. 'Look at this, girls!'

She held up the one belonging to Mary O'Donahue.

'Stuffed full of holy picture cards. It's a wonder you don't spill the lot every time you open your missal, child.' She frilled open the pages so the holy cards fluttered down to the floor. 'Leave them, leave them,' she snapped as Mary bent down to scoop them up. 'I would like Mother Joseph to see how you waste your time.' She stamped her heel on Mary's spread fingers, then walked on.

'Help me, Noni,' I begged.

'Ask Biddy to lend you her new missal case.'

Noni turned round to Bridget and dug her fingers into each side of the girl's waist.

'No,' said Bridget. 'I only just got it.'

'Please, Biddy,' I said. 'I'll pray for you.'

'Go on, you mean cat.' Noni's fingers dug deeper.

Biddy slid the box-cover off her leather-bound missal and passed it to me.

'Now shove in your dictionary,' Noni ordered.

I did as I was told, fingers shaking, but the dictionary looked pathetically slim inside the grand case. We crouched over my desk while Mother's back was turned, rummaging through the contents. We slid in my Latin vocabulary notebook, then Noni's holy cards. Still the contents bumped about.

'Geometry cards!' suggested Biddy.

'Your hankie, quick. That'll muffle them all up.' Noni was starting to giggle. 'Your sandwiches, Cessy! Shove 'em in! Shove 'em in!'

'Shush! Oh shush!'

We were in a hunch of helpless giggles by the time Mother Mary Rose reached us. Noni and Biddy stepped smartly sideways into the choir line. Stony, Mother Rose put out her hand for Biddy's missal.

'Now, Bridget Maloney, with her lovely new birthday missal. Isn't this a lovely new missal, girls? Hold it up for everyone to see. And Veronica, good girl Veronica, with the missal your dear mother used to use. I don't mind. I don't mind at all. Now.' She turned aside from the line to where I was still standing, stupid, at my desk. 'Who's this?'

'Cecilia Deardon, Mother.'

'Will you tie back your terrible hair, Cecilia Deardon. You are a disgrace to your namesake, child, don't you know that? But you've a lovely missal case.'

'Thank you, Mother.'

'Isn't this a lovely new missal case, girls?'

'Yes, Mother,' said Noni.

'I'd like to see a little more. Yes I would. Will you show us all your lovely missal?'

'Please, Mother...'

'Let me have it, dear.'

For a second the nun's watery eyes met mine as she bent her hooked white face towards me. Her fingers that were as dry as moths closed over my own. 'I know you. I know you,' she hissed. I released my grasp and Mother Rose tilted the case slowly, without even looking at it, so the contents slid down her habit and out in a circle round her booted feet.

'*Corpus Dominum nostrum Jesu Christi custodiat animam tuam in vitam aeternam amen.. Corpus dominum nostrum Jesu Christi custodiat animam tuam in vitam aeternam amen...*'

Girls shuffled in and out of the benches to join the communion queue at the altar. The visiting priest mumbled his prayer as he bent towards each communicant and slipped the white disc that was the body and blood of Christ onto their proffered tongues. The organ notes fluttered and surged as first the soloist, Patricia Keenan, and then the choir took up the motet... *Panis angelicus, fit panis hominum...* and the music swelled over our bowed heads. I moved out when my turn came and was aware of a commotion up in the choir stalls.

The music was going astray. I glanced up to see the back of Mother Rose's head bobbing as she tried to focus on the aisle from her mirror over the organ. The choir voices faltered.

'Patricia Keenan. Are you going down to receive communion?'

'I am, Mother.'

Their whispers flickered over the sound of our shuffling feet and the priest's murmur.

'Will you look over the choir rails a moment. Do you see that girl at the end of the queue of communicants down there?'

'I think it's little Cecilia Deardon, Mother. She's a second year.'

I ducked my face, cold with sweat. The whisperings were drowned in loud thumped organ chords and the choir's new start. I made my way slowly forward behind the other non-singers, and as the first of the choir girls crept their way downstairs I approached the altar, repeating to myself the pattern of words that were like the stitches in an embroidered cloth... 'I am not worthy that thou should'st enter under my roof, say but the word and my soul will be healed... Lord, I am not worthy that thou should'st enter...'

'Cecilia Deardon.' The stitches were snipped. I looked up at Patricia Keenan, startled. I was almost at the altar rails as she bent down to speak to me.

'Mother Rose says you must not receive Holy Communion today because you are in sin.'

In sin, Cecilia Deardon. In sin.

Aren't you always in sin?

Please God, make me good.

Please Saint Cecilia, martyr and virgin, make me worthy.

I was alone in chapel one day waiting for Father Carolyn to come for the confessions when I heard a rustling and hushing behind me. Mother Mary Rose was calling me up to the choir balcony for the very first time.

'Pst! Girl! You, girl. Come up here! Pst!'

Her whisper was a whiplash, flailing the candle-shadows, stinging my flesh cold. I turned, afraid, and saw her leaning over the choir rails. Her spectacles glinted candles. Her black-robed arms waved in an urgent upward gesture.

'You, girl! Come straight up here.'

I scrambled from my pew and ran to the back of the chapel and up the polished choir stairs that were narrow and worn with years of footsteps. Mother Mary Rose was waiting at the top for me. She clutched at my arm and pulled me over towards the organ.

'Look, girl. There's a bird. See it?'

'A bird, Mother?' I was panting. Her fingers hurt my arm.

'On the organ. Get it down.'

'Me, Mother?'

She pushed me forward. 'Yes, quick, get it down. Before it gets stuck in the pipes. Get it down.'

I couldn't see a bird. I climbed onto the organ stool, trembling, and it flung itself down at me, into my face nearly, into my hair, a black and beating thing that rushed cold air with it. I fended it off, shouting, covering my face with my hands.

'What have you done now? You've driven it back up, you giddy goose! Get it down! Get it out of here!'

I stumbled down from the organ stool and ran to fetch the long window pole that was kept at the back of the chapel. I carried it up the choir steps like a knight bearing a lance, and all the time I could hear the tap of Mother's shoes as she ran backwards and forwards along the balcony floor, squawking and fluttering herself, a hen in a barn.

'Knock it off!' she told me as I tried to hand her the window pole. 'Clout it.'

'I don't want to hurt the little thing,' I said.

She gripped my elbow so the pole swung and clanged against the organ pipes and as she let go of me I released my grip and it clattered down onto the floor. The bird tumbled down from its perch and launched itself into the dark spaces of the chapel, and back to the pipes, and into air again.

And that trapped bird was a terrifying thing. It lost its grace and control of movement, it fumbled wildly. It flung itself against shut windows, testing its fragile weight, its splinter bones and wings. It stole into dark corners, eyes bright, beak open and pitiful, small body bursting. So it was, stuttering and stumbling in crazy sightless flight, and Mother Mary Rose with cold triumph in her eyes was darting from one end of the organ to the other, and over to the choir rails and back again, shooing and hissing and flapping her bent, gaunt arms, her long black robes beating; and I was running uselessly balancing my pole again, cheering it down, and there was sheet music floating like feathers in a farmyard and settling on the polished benches below.

And Father Carolyn caught us at it.

'What in the name of God is this?'

Out of the depths his voice thundered. We waited, silent, conspirators.

'Is this not the House of God you are in?'

His voice shouted up from all the corners of the chapel. Mother Mary Rose sat down, heaving for breath, crossing herself.

'Answer me, girl.'

I walked with my lance upright to the front of the balcony. 'Father... Father... it's a bird.'

And there it was, brilliant blue-black sheened, perched shyly on the foot of the Virgin Mary, head cocked to one side, eyes watchful, silent, waiting. Father Carolyn scooped it up in his big labourer's hands. Its bright eyes watched him. He smiled up at us, an actor, superb.

'A starling, Mother Mary Rose, is the greatest sham amongst your singing birds. He chatters and scolds in the gutters as if he has no song in his heart at all, and all of a sudden he hears a blackbird sing, and he copies it, the little devil, till you wouldn't know the one from the other.'

He held the bird up above his head, like a host to be venerated, and left.

And it was that very afternoon that we were to hold a dance at school as a treat to celebrate the anniversary of our patron saint. We were allowed to bring coloured jumpers or blouses to change into after school, though we still had to wear our uniform gym slips. Noni put on nylon stockings underneath her school socks. She said that no one would notice because her skirt came below the tops of her garters.

'What's the point then?' I asked, not believing that she had them on at all.

'What's the point?' She was astonished. 'They make my legs feel like film stars'. Look...' And she hoisted up the corner of her skirt to show her shining smooth legs, and the white tip of the suspender strap with its little button snug in the stocking top.

'You'll have to get some, Cecilia,' she told me, and I promised her that I would.

The nuns didn't dance, but sat round the sides of the gym watching us and smiling. Reverend Mother sat with Father Carolyn and they whispered together like old chums. Mother Philomena put the dance records on the gramophone. For the most part of the afternoon we stood in a bunch watching the big girls dancing until they were told by Mother Philomena that they should choose a partner from among us, and then we became hot and shy, nervous in case we were chosen. I was picked by Miss Maher, who came in twice a week to help out with the Games. I was too embarrassed to look at her. I danced with my head to one side, wondering if she had noticed that she was holding me so tightly that her large breasts squashed out soft and spreading across my chest. I had not been hugged so closely since I was a little girl in my mother's arms, with my head snuggled into her softnesses. I thought the Games teacher was being a bit indecent, and wished she wouldn't hum so happily and loudly. I noticed that

Noni was dancing with one of her arms held stiffly at her side and with her skirt puckered in her fingers against her thigh. She told me afterwards that her suspender had snapped and that she had been in mortal fear of her nylon stockings drifting down like the wrinkled skins of snakes to droop over the tops of her garters and give the game away.

On the way home down the drive we were met by a small contingent from the boys' school who had heard about the dance from their sisters and who, or so they told us, had been spying at us through the windows of the gym.

'You have not,' said Noni, clutching at her thigh again.

'We have,' said Biddy's brother, who was going to be a priest. 'And you dance like a gazelle, Veronica Murphy.'

We were all high spirited, with the music still in our ears and our cheeks hot with the efforts, and the cold air spanking us to brightness; and it was that time of dusk when the light is hardly there any more, and movements are a shifting of shapes to be heard and felt rather than seen. It would be Noni and Brendan who started the dancing, and then we all began to grope round for partners, no one talking, but laughing softly as we touched hands. The Italian boy came to me, and he put his arms round me trembling with shyness and then pressed himself against me as Miss Maher had done, but this time I didn't think it was indecent, and could feel my own softness pressing against him. We danced without music on the lawn between the trees, and our feet stirred the leaves and rustled them like whispers. Angelo bent down so his nose bumped against mine and I held up my face to him. He placed his mouth neatly on mine then drew away and breathed out, then in again, and came down on me again, lips to lips, wet, and stayed there a dizzy time.

The lights in the nuns' house were switched on and flooded the lawn and we scattered with shrieks like startled sparrows, all running in different directions. With my heart thumping I ran straight down the drive, holding down my hat. I heard footsteps behind me and ran faster towards the gates.

'Cecilia! Is that you?'

I stopped. 'It is, Father.'

Father Carolyn caught up with me and took my hand in his, leading me up the lane as if I was a little child.

'Did you enjoy the dancing?' he asked.

'I did, Father.'

'You dance well, like your mother.'

I couldn't free my hand.

'Cecilia, don't you ever do anything to make your parents ashamed of you.' His grip tightened. 'You won't now, will you?'

I shook my head. I couldn't trust myself to speak.

'I have to tell you that dancing can be an occasion of sin. Did you know that?'

I shook my head. My eyes hurt.

'You're not too young to know that. And I'm only telling you that because you dance so well, do you understand?'

'I think so,' I whispered.

He let go of my hand so he could fish out his handkerchief for a good blow.

'Have you heard from Michael this month?' he asked.

'No, Father. He said he would be coming home for Easter but he didn't make it.'

'And he didn't make it at Christmas, either. Your mother must be broken-hearted, watching out for news of her son.'

'She is, Father.'

'And praying for him every day and night. That's what children do to their mothers. You must be a comfort to her now. Don't ever hurt her, Cecilia.'

He took my hand again and we walked on, and I knew then that I was as much to blame as Michael was for my mother's unhappiness, even though she had not seen me dancing in the darkness of the lawns or known how my body had grown soft and faint with my first kiss.

Chapter Eight

We were in preparation for our first open day, to be held in the summer term of my third year. When the exams were over we were sent out into the gardens to make them fit for our visitors to see. The day came at last, a Saturday of glorious sunshine. The nuns had seen to that the evening before by bringing out all the statues and placing them round the gardens with umbrellas over their heads. The roses were in full bloom, yellow against the white convent house; deep pinks and mauves in the rosary walks. The air was sweet with their scent. The drive up to the school was lined with the last rhododendrons and the hydrangeas that had hidden me in my fear on the first September morning there. The flower-heads now were huge and overgrown, and their petals scattered the dusty drive. Inside the chapel, where we began the day with our hymns to Mary, the rich spiced smell of white carnations mingled with the smoke of candles. We processed out into the light with the last boom of the organ in our ears and with flowers in our hands, and then Mother Mary Rose scuttered down the choir stairs with her skirts bunched up in her fists, and ran from group to group of us desperate to keep us in even rhythm but spoiling our singing with her own harsh voice. I hummed the melody in my head, and that was enough for me. I knew that for me to sing out loud would be a sin of disobedience and pride.

My mother and Geraldine were among the first visitors to arrive. I watched them coming up the drive together, arms linked, and my throat hurt with pride at the sight of them. Geraldine had on a straw boater that she'd kept from her own schooldays, and she had tucked rhododendron petals into its cream band. I wanted to run to them but we had to keep in our lines till the courtyard in front of the convent house was filled with visitors and they swelled out our singing of hymns. The walls trapped our voices and the perfumes of the flowers; held and distilled them. Light breezes played with the veils about our faces and with the soft summer frocks of the women and girls.

Geraldine came straight to me when the singing was finished. She gripped my hands in both of hers, entranced, and I led her in to see my favourite place, the chapel. My mother followed behind us, chattering and laughing with Father Carolyn's housekeeper, who had a niece in the school.

The chapel was crowded already. The visitors came in and crossed themselves with holy water and genuflected to the altar, but instead of slipping quietly into one of the benches for private prayer they walked round in groups humming hymns to themselves, lifting down the frilled carnation heads to breathe in their scent, lighting yet more candles that had been set specially for them in a trough of sand in front of the altar; and they all talked softly to one another and moved round the place as if it was the room of a fine house and they were guests at a party. Geraldine went right up the altar rails, still holding my hand. The altar cloth was white brocaded satin, like a bridal gown, and it took on the pale gleam of the candle flames. I thought I would never move her from it; she seemed to want to take in every white petal of carnation and wisp of gypsophila. She responded at last to the pressure of my fingers on her own and turned with me, dreamy-eyed, to come face to face with Mother Mary Rose. The nun must have been behind us for some time, watching us.

'Who's this?' she asked me sharply.

'Mother, it's Geraldine,' I whispered, aware of the chapel.

Mother Rose took off her spectacles and rubbed them on her arm, on the hem of her looped skirt. The skin round her eyes was as white and moist as the flesh of a fish.

'I know you!' she snapped at last.

My sister will touch people when she can. She took her fingers out of my clasp and tried to stroke the paper skin of Mother Rose's hand. The nun shook her away as she put up her arms to replace her spectacles. People moved between us, and my mother came to link her arm in Geraldine's and to lead her out of the chapel.

'Come and see all the lovely flowers in the gardens now,' she told her. 'We don't want to be in a dark old house on a day like this, do we?' She took her arm to lead her out, but my sister twisted round, her eyes intent on Mother Rose's face till the old nun snapped away from her.

I had to join my class on the lawns, where stalls had been set up with spinning roulette wheels for bottle prizes, and cakes with currants to be counted. I took my place with Noni and Biddy behind the homemade marmalades.

'Is your mother here?' I asked them. Noni pointed out an elegant, toothy woman in smiling conversation with Mother Rose.

'Is yours?' she asked.

I nodded towards my mother, shy of the stir of pride I felt at the sight of her, bare-armed now she was out of chapel, in the blue cotton dress my father loved her to wear for the dances, her grey-sand hair looping free on her shoulders.

'There's the simple girl I told you about,' said Biddy, just as I was pointing her out.

'Hush!' Noni said to her.

'The girl in the straw boater and white socks. Is it a girl or a woman?'

'Hush!' Noni said again. 'She's with Cecilia's mother.'

'Is she?' said Biddy. 'Do you know her, Cessy?'

'She's my sister,' I told her, surprised. Biddy pulled Noni round till they both had their backs to me. 'You didn't tell me you had a simple sister.' I could hear their giggles splurting from behind their cupped hands.

My sister, stocky, her red legs plump above her white socks, her cotton dress stained with grass, her eyes blinking through her long fringe, her round face freckled, smiled across at Mother Mary Rose, waiting for her to catch her gaze and smile back.

'Don't worry,' Noni had turned round and seen the look on my face. 'We won't tell anyone.'

But they had told me, and like a stranger I watched her trotting behind my mother round the stalls, slapping her feet down to watch how the grass blades sank down and sprang up again. I had to stay with my class through lunchtime, helping to serve out sandwiches and cakes in the refectory, and though Geraldine kept turning round to wave at me I pretended to be too busy to go to her. Later in the afternoon

Uncle Rory came to help Father Carolyn on the whiskey roulette stall, and made him open up a bottle to prove it wasn't cold tea. You'd think it was all a party held in his honour, the way he shouted greetings to everyone, the way he stood on the wooden classroom chair that balanced precariously on the lawn and challenged everyone to take their luck in the game, the way they came to him, laughing and arguing as if he was an old, good friend. My mother came over to me, her face flushed with laughter at his antics. She bought jam from my stall and told me that my father would be waiting for her with the cart now Rory had come.

'Do you want to come back with us now?' she asked me. 'You'll be tired, Cessy.'

I told her I had to stay till the end, but as soon as they'd gone I wanted to be with them. I told one of the nuns that my mother had asked me to go home with her and, surprised, she gave me permission to follow them. I ran down the long drive after them, flurrying up the brown petals that had been trodden down to powder now. I could hear Geraldine singing in her high and tuneless shout that distorted the hymns she'd heard that morning:

'Oh Mary we crown thee with blossoms today,' she bellowed. 'Quee nov the angel sand quee nov the May...'

She had taken off the straw hat and had the elastic strap bound tight round her wrist. Her hair was thin and damp with sweat, lank around her ears. Her calves rubbed against each other as she walked. Her socks were dirty with the dust of the paths, and one of them had slipped down under her heel. Her sandals were worn down. Her feet turned in slightly. 'With blossoms today...'

I had never noticed her before.

She and my mother turned round when they heard me running, and Geraldine laughed and held out her fat hand for me to take. I could smell her familiar sweet-sharp smell, and hear the rasping wheeze of her breath, and I ran on past them, on up to the tall wrought-iron gates where my father sat whistling while he waited with the milk-cart to take us home; past him, and when the cart swayed up to me with leaves dancing round its wheels I walked on with my head down all along the quiet lanes till Uncle Rory caught up with me on Michael's bike and with whiskey on his breath and shouted out to me to perch on the saddle while he stood up and pedalled, and we teetered hysterically off to our house.

'When are you coming back home, Uncle Rory?' I asked him, breathless with laughter, as we scraped to a stop by our wall.

'Home? I've my own home now Cessy, now Mother's in the Old Folk's Place. You know that well enough.'

'Can I live in your house, then?'

He caught in his breath, as astonished as I was at my blurted request. He rubbed his stubbly chin against my cheek and rode off without saying a word.

And when I went into the house there was a surprise waiting for me. My brother Michael had come home unexpectedly. We hadn't heard from him for over a year now, and it was two years nearly since we had last seen him. My mother prayed for him every night of the week. He had arrived while my father and Terence were out bringing my mother and Geraldine back from the open day at school, and by the time I turned up he was used to being in the house again and was lying where he always used to lie after a day of hard work, legs stretched out on the sofa, hands folded behind his head. It was as if he had never been away, and I was shy of him, and embarrassed myself by blushing. His neck and shoulders had thickened out; I could see where he shaved now.

'Look who's here,' my mother said to me, her eyes dancing. 'What d'you think of this young man?'

He held out his hands to me and I went over and knelt by him to kiss him.

'You're fatter,' I said.

'Now then,' he laughed. 'And I was just about to tell you how pretty you've grown, Cessy. A woman, now.'

I dodged away from his hands, not knowing how to answer this.

'Shush,' my mother told him. 'Don't spoil her. She's only fourteen.'

'Let's look at you,' he said.

I stood still to be looked at, pouting out my breasts, hanging my head so my hair would hide them.

'Head up!'

I risked a glance at him and, catching my father's fond smile, stood straight.

'My!' Michael whistled slowly, and then I caught him glancing sidelong at my father and risking a wink. I flung myself at him, pummelling my fists into him while he laughed at me. He held back my fists with his hand and I butted my head into his chest.

'I've missed this little wild cat!' he told my mother. 'Can she still scratch? Yes, she can too!'

'Stop it now. Stop it, the both of you! I'll be kicking you out in the yard like a pair of dogs.' My mother flapped the tea towel over our faces and, hot and breathless, I drew my head out of his arms and pulled myself away from him.

'Have you come home for good?' I asked him, panting.

He laughed and stood up, stretching, too big now for the room, ducking his head as he went over to where my mother was standing in the extension by the sink. 'Come home?' He tucked my mother's hair back into its grips, leaning back to admire his work. 'You should see where I'm living now, Cessy.'

'Why? What's it like?'

My mother turned away from him, her hand in her hair. 'He's in the middle of a city,' she said. 'He can go to the films every night of the week, if he wants to.'

'Which I don't,' added Michael, with pride. 'Because I've even better things to do.'

'Well now,' my mother smiled.

'What sort of things?' asked Terence, who had been sitting on the window seat next to Geraldine, staring at Michael, half-afraid both of them of this stranger.

'Like dancing maybe, or going to the bars,' my father suggested.

Michael laughed again; not his old, easy laugh. 'What time will we eat?' he asked my mother.

'When it's ready. Half an hour, maybe.'

'I'll go out, then. Up the hill and back.'

Terence jumped off his seat and ran to go with him.

'You stay here,' said Michael sharply.

Terence, shocked, turned to my mother for comfort. 'He'll want to be on his own,' she told him.

'Cecilia. You come with me,' Michael said and surprised, shy again, I followed him.

He strode up the hill ahead of me. I was tired from my long day and my walk home. I loitered after him till he was way ahead of me. 'Come on!' he called.

I hung back, cross with him. 'Why did you say that?' I shouted after him. 'About our house?'

'I said nothing about our house.'

'You hurt Mam. And why didn't you write to her?'

'Too busy. Too busy.'

'You could have been ill, or dead, for all we knew.'

'Oh, you'd soon have heard if I was dead.' He turned round at last, waiting for me, taunting me with his smile. 'What's it to you if I was?'

'You should have seen them both watching out for the post every day. They still do, every day. I don't know how you could do it to them. You can't just go away and come back when you feel like it.'

'The Prodigal Son did. It's the only way. I don't like writing. How can I write a letter every day?'

'Not every day. Once a week would do. Once a month.' I had caught up with him but was still shouting, excited at seeing him again.

'I'm no good at writing letters. I don't know where to start.'

'Dear Mam. A postcard would have done.'

'A postcard! They're for holidays. Dear Mam, wish you were here on the building site...'

'We didn't know what had happened to you.'

'And now I am here all anybody can do is shout at me. They've all been on at me. I wish I hadn't come home.'

'Well,' I said. 'And how is it on the building site?'

'Oh,' he shrugged. 'All right.'

'You like it, though?'

'I said. It's good enough.'

We walked on together in silence. He's different, I thought. I don't really like him any more.

'I want to tell you something, Cecilia.' He was frilling off the flower heads of sweet cicely as he picked it on the laneside, sharpening the air with their early aniseed smell.

'What, then?'

'I've stopped going to Mass.'

This was a burden to be given. I didn't know how to take it, except in grief and disbelief. I needed to think about it alone, but he persisted as if I were his confessor, absolving him from his guilt by hearing him tell of it.

'Listen, Cessy. I mean for ever, you know. I've thrown it off.'

'Thrown it off! Like a skin, or a sickness!'

'Like a tyranny.' He looked down at me, at my sharp hurt gasp. 'It's an awful sham, all this church business. I had to get away from home to find that out for sure. And once I'd found it out I didn't see how I could come back. We're so bound up in it here. I feel as if I come from another country now. And when I sat in that kitchen just now, with the crucifix over the fire and the rosaries hanging on their nails for the evening prayers...'

'You felt ashamed of yourself.'

'No, I didn't. I wanted to laugh at you all.'

I turned away from him and he caught me and cupped my face in his rough hands. 'Don't be hurt. It's not you I'm laughing at, no it's not. I was caught in that trap too.'

I closed my eyes against him, my face tight, my fists gripped at my sides so the nails hurt my palms. I wanted to be in another place, in another time, not hearing these nightmare words.

'Talk to me, Cessy. You'll understand, one day you will.' He shook my face to try to make me open my eyes. 'You'll look at the statues, and you'll see they're all painted plaster. And you'll realise that's all there is to it. They're dolls. And we're children saying our nursery rhymes to the dolls, over and over and over again in case we get spanked...'

'Stop it! Stop it!'

'And we like to be told we'll be spanked, isn't that so, because it's nice for us to be little children still. It's easier than being grown-up and having to decide what's right and what's wrong all for ourselves.'

'You used to be an altar-boy!'

He threw back his head and laughed, so startled birds flung themselves away from the branches above our heads. When he looked down at me I saw that there was no sign of laughter in his eyes.

'What do I do tomorrow, Cessy?'

I bit my lip. 'You must come to Mass with us all, for all that. What else can you do?'

'And pretend? Do you want me to go into your church and pretend?'

'You've hurt Mam enough,' I reminded him. 'I think you should go to Mass.'

'And what about when you all go up to receive communion? I can't pretend then.'

No. That was unthinkable. He was not fit to receive the body and blood of Christ.

'I can't go through all that wizardry.'

I shuddered. He clutched at my shoulders, keeping my thoughts to practical matters.

'Then tell them you thought you'd be home in time to go to confession, and you missed Father Carolyn,' I suggested. 'He wasn't at the church today, anyway. He was at the open day at school. There would be another priest hearing confessions. Say you wanted him.' Oh, my deviousness, my deviance. Father, forgive me. It's only to spare my mother's grief.

'Right then.' Michael let go of me at last. He bent down to pluck another spray of sweet cicely, and spiked it into my hair. 'And when I've gone, I want you to tell them for me.'

'It would kill my mother. Don't make me...'

'And I've some other news, though I'll tell them this myself. I'm getting married.'

'It's ready!' My mother's voice sang out from the house, faint below us.

'Let me tell you everything, Cecilia. You're the only one in this house I can talk to.'

'So your girl's not a Catholic,' I sighed. I felt older than my years now.

'Tch, no. That's no problem. I've told you.'

'Then what?'

His face twitched into a smile. 'I'm going to be a daddy soon.'

I knew nothing about sex. I had no idea how babies were born or conceived. But I knew it was something to do with nakedness and passionate kissing, that adult thing, and with the first sin of man. I knew it was to do with virginity and that there was a wild word lust connected with it if it happened outside the sacrament of marriage, and that to commit this thing was a mortal sin that would make my brother burn in hell for all eternity. These thoughts, and especially the white thoughts of Michael's nakedness, swam like scared fishes in my mind's whirlpool. I pressed my hands over my face.

'It's not a bad thing, Cessy. I love her.'

'Don't tell me that,' I said through my hands, hotter still at the sound of the strange word that I could not understand. 'You can't love her if you did that thing to her. And you don't love us...'

'Mam says it's ready.' Terence came running up the hill to us.

'Cessy...'

'You've no right to come home and tell me all this and make me feel the guilt of it all for you, and you feeling no shame at all.'

'Will you come in now?' Awkward, Terence edged across to Michael and tried to pull him back down towards the house.

'I wish you'd never come back! You don't belong any more.' Michael wouldn't have heard me say that, because it was in a whisper, and he laughing down the hill in front of me with Terence swung up on his shoulders. My hair was damp across my face, and I was heavy then with the deep strange knowledge that it wasn't Michael who had lost his place in the family that day; for when the time came they would hear the news and in sadness they would pray for things to be right for him. But the child that I was had slipped away from her kneeling place on the hearth forever.

Berlie Doherty

Chapter Nine

By the time I was halfway through school it began to appal me like a sickness; the tedium of the classes, the furtive incessant whisperings of girls who knew more than I did and who would not tell. My only focus was the chapel, and I escaped there whenever I could. I loved the heavy smell of polish and incense and flowers, the rich patterns thrown by sunlight through stained-glass windows. I loved to watch the candles flickering and fussing palely as the quiet nuns fluttered to their benches. I liked to close my eyes and listen to the whispered susurrations of their prayers, sibilant and rhythmic, breath snatched at each Hail Mary's end, as fingers moved along the warm worn rosary beads that chinked and kissed like dried peas in a jar.

One morning in the late June of my fourth year we were waiting for the Latin lesson when Mother Mary Rose hustled into the classroom.

'Come along girls,' she said. 'Hurry in now. Mother Joseph is waiting to give you your Fourth Year talk. Be quick now, quick. Fasten your cardigans. Put on your mantillas.'

I joined Noni and Biddy in the whispering queue in the chapel corridor.

'Fourth Year talk, did she say?' I asked them. 'What's that about?'

'Boys!' whispered Bridget. 'What else?'

Noni laughed. 'Boys! What does she know about them?'

I followed them into chapel, wondering the same thing myself. Mother Joseph, the headmistress of the school, had a wide red-cheeked face that would never lose the glow of the years she'd spent working in her father's fields. She had never learnt the quiet glide of the other nuns, but clomped with brisk, manly strides round the school on her daily tour. From time to time her healthy face would appear behind the glass of classroom doors. It would have been easy to have been fooled into smiling at her and welcoming her presence, but for the ice-cold glitter in her eyes, which let us remember that she was searching for the sin in us at all times. She seemed like a kindly aunty seeing that all was well for us; instead she was a prison warder.

Now as we filed into chapel she stood in front of the altar rails with her arms folded under her robes and her legs apart; a matriarch defending the tabernacle. Yet she spoke to us as if she loved us.

'Children,' she said when our coughs had died down and our shuffling feet had come together at the kneelers. 'Dear children, you are approaching a very special age now. You have the bodies of women.'

She said this last bit abruptly, and stared at us in our discomfort.

'You know what I mean when I say this to you? Girls, is there anyone here who does not know what I mean when I say you have the bodies of women?'

Our silence danced with questions. Deep inside ourselves we sought the answers. The nuns parading the aisles turned to us, interested.

'Good. Now in a short time some of you will be leaving the convent walls to go out into the world. Children, it is a wicked world. I must tell you that men have only one thought in their heads. I must tell you that everything a woman does is destined to arouse that thought.'

In our new, deep silence we could no longer look at her. Naked Christ on his crucifix stared down on us. The nuns and the statues watched us all.

'Girls, is there anybody here who does not know what that thought might be? Good.'

She had a last confidence to share with us, and had no need to lower her voice for the telling of it, yet she did. As if she didn't want the watching nuns, or the virgin statues, or the humiliated Christ to hear, she whispered it.

'I have been told, girls, that not even a priest in prayer would be able to resist the temptations of an unclothed woman. Now, you are responsible. Dear girls, I pray that you will remember that always.'

Her voice rose as she clasped her hands together, beseeching us.

'Keep your body sacred. You are the bride of Christ. Your body is the temple of the Holy Spirit...'

At Mass the next Sunday I followed my mother up the aisle and stood waiting to receive communion. Father Carolyn and the two farm lads who were his altar servers were not watching me. With a glow of deep warm shame I unbuttoned my school coat, which I always wore on Sundays. I let it drape onto the polished floor. One by one my fingers slid open the buttons of my new cardigan. I languidly peeled it back across my shoulders, allowing my hands to brush against my breasts. My fingers ruffled the fabric of my skirt, kinking it up towards my thighs.

'*Domine, non sum dignus…*' Father Carolyn murmured to my young flesh. 'Lord, I am not worthy that thou should'st enter under my roof…'

A few days later I faced him in the confessional. I had no other priest to go to. We were in a dark wooden cupboard with a grille between us, and though I couldn't see him I could see the looming deeper darkness of his shape, and when I pressed my head against the grille to whisper my sins I could feel the warmth of his breath.

'Father, forgive me, for I have sinned.'

He waited.

'I have had dirty thoughts, Father.'

'How many times, child?' His voice was kind, as it had always been. I remembered my first confession, and how he had cajoled sin out of me then, eager as I had been to please. I had had nothing to confess; I could not think of one single sin. Yet how could I have received my first holy communion, and gone up to the altar dressed as a child bride, if I hadn't made my first confession and had my soul wiped clean? I would disgrace my family if I did not confess.

'Can you not think of something you shouldn't have done, and yet you did?' he had coaxed. 'I have bitten my nails,' I had lied. And then, grateful for his sigh, 'I have told lies.'

'How many times?'

'I don't know, Father,' I whispered.

How many times since Sunday had I draped and undraped the bath towel round myself in front of the long mirror, faint with the sin and the joy of it? 'Quite a lot of times.'

He blew softly into his hands. I could hear him wiping his face with them. He must know me. He must have read my eyes when he offered me the Host last Sunday. He must have seen the young urgent ashamed body beneath the buttoned cardigan and the heavy school coat.

'And are you truly sorry?'

'Yes, Father.'

'You must avoid the occasions of sin, child. You must avoid the places and people that arouse these impure thoughts in you. Do you promise me that?'

You don't understand, Father. I would never come to church again. Never see you, or Christ pinned to his crucifix.

'I don't know why the impure thoughts come though, Father. They just come, and then they go. And then they seem to come back again, Father. I don't know what to do.'

'Pray to the Blessed Virgin.'

'Yes, Father. Thank you, Father.'

As I knelt in the church saying my penance he lumbered out of his confessional box. I pressed my hands over my face. His skirt swished against my bench as he passed. I was the only girl in the church. I tried to rush through my penance prayers but in a few minutes he was back. He'd changed into his gardening trousers. His shoes squeaked as he walked out of the vestry. He tried to tiptoe as he approached my bench, and he stood by me, breathing deeply, until at last I roused myself to look up at him.

'Cecilia child, I didn't want to interrupt your prayers, but I have a message for your mother.'

'Oh, Father.'

'Will you tell her I've more lupins than I need, and she's welcome to some. Tell her to bring her wheelbarrow down any time for them. She'll love the scent of them at night, she will, in that little back garden of hers.'

On Monday I lurked in the corridors for Mother Joseph. When I saw her cheery face I almost wanted to blurt out the wicked thoughts I'd had on the way to Holy Communion. She must understand, knowing as she did about the real thoughts of all the men in the world. But when her blue eyes caught mine and she hovered, impatient, her fingers on her rosary, I knew there was no prospect of sharing that shame.

'Yes, dear?'

'Mother, I don't understand.'

'What, child?' Already as she talked to me her eyes darted to detect sounds in the corridor. 'What is it you don't understand?'

'The Virgin birth.' My face and my ears were scarlet as I spoke. 'How did she..?'

Her eyes glittered. 'She had no husband, dear. That she conceived was a miracle.'

I had heard that phrase mentioned in connection with Father Carolyn's housekeeper's cousin Bernadette, who was having her first child at the age of forty-eight.

'She was married to Joseph, Mother,' I tried.

She swung her rosary beads on her belt so they clicked past her thumb. I watched them, mesmerised, too embarrassed to look at her.

'Don't be misled into thinking that Joseph was that sort of husband, dear. Mary knew no man.'

She was ready to move on her way. Classes would start soon. I was a nuisance.

'But how did it happen, Mother?' Miserable, I clung on, as a drowning woman clings to bending reeds. I was an evil-minded child, I could see that in her eyes. She would pluck out the reeds and fling them far away.

'The Angel of the Lord declared unto Mary...'

'Yes, Mother. Angel Gabriel.'

'And she conceived of the Holy Ghost.'

'But how?'

She sucked air through her clenched teeth. 'Don't worry if you don't understand,' she said kindly. 'Do you believe?'

'I think so, Mother.'

'Think so?'

'I do believe, Mother.'

'Good!' She threw open her arms as though she would embrace me, her eyes now on the clock. 'Well, that's all that matters. Smile for me, dear, I don't like to see a young face so puckered up with bewilderment. As long as you believe, that's all that matters.'

'Thank you, Mother.'

I watched her brisk stride down the corridor, her black skirt swishing.

Let me believe.

That evening when I was cycling home I caught up with Aunt Bridget, who had just climbed down from the bus with her shopping. I balanced her bag in my saddle-basket and walked down home with her.

'There's the rooks, going home to roost,' she said.

There was such comfort in that word she used, roost.

'Your Uncle Rory should be giving me a hand with this. Do you know Cecilia, sometimes I wish I'd never married the man.'

'Do you, Aunt Bridget?' I asked, surprised.

'Oh, you girls think he's the sun and the moon, but I tell you, he's the laziest piece of work you can imagine.'

'He's good fun though, isn't he?' I suggested.

She tutted, as though fun never came into it. 'My advice to you is never to think of getting married, and that's a fact. It's nothing but hard work.'

'Did you love him when you met him though?' I asked, shy of my question, but deeply interested.

'Oh, love, that's another matter altogether. Yes, if you must know then, I did. Don't you let yourself be teased by that thing, Cecilia. He was a fine looking man, but that doesn't make a husband. Now you, you see, a handsome girl like you, you'll have all the fellers after you and that'll bring you problems. Whereas Geraldine, poor simple pudding that she is, is quite safe.'

And that was the turmoil where my aunt set me, peering into my own future, that vast and unknown landscape, as if I was on the peak of our hill that climbs up from the valley, looking out on the fields and shores of my own childhood, its tides; looking beyond them to a whispering horizon. And there, lumbering up behind me, holding out her hands for me to haul her up too, would be Geraldine.

Chapter Ten

But that was before Geraldine met the bad boy. He was the strange man who lived down the valley from us. My mother called him the bad boy but I believe he'd been a man for many years by the time I noticed him. But I knew he was bad because he never went to Mass, not even at Christmas or Easter. For all that, I liked him. He had a gypsy face and black hair that curled like a child's, and his beard was always just about to grow. His voice was husky with too much smoking and drinking, and when he talked to you one of his eyes would turn slowly, casually towards the other. I don't know how he did it, but it used to fascinate me. He was pretty slow. His father used to go out fishing, and sometimes he went out with him and sometimes he just sat on the rocks by the slipway waiting to haul the boats back in. And sometimes you saw him following the tide out when he was in the mood for cockling with the gangs.

My mother was the first to notice that he was interested in Geraldine.

The first sign was when he cycled home with her one night from the hospital. I saw them coming up the lane together and thought nothing of it, because when Geraldine swerved in at our gate he cycled straight on past with neither of them looking at the other; but my mother stood up from her gardening and thought everything. She watched while Geraldine pulled off her bicycle clips. She liked to wear a pair of Michael's old corduroys to cycle in during the winter; she would tuck down her skirt inside them, not noticing how it made them bulge.

My mother followed her into the kitchen. Geraldine was red-cheeked with the cycling, and still breathless when I came in. My mother took both her cold hands in her own and shouted at her.

'That Larry's a bad boy. You know that, don't you?'

Poor Geraldine didn't know whether to nod her head or shake it. She rolled her eyes mysteriously. I could see the pressure of my mother's fingers and kept well out of it. But I was puzzled and curious.

'Tomorrow you'll stay behind at the hospital till your daddy comes for you. D'you hear?'

'You'll ask me first,' said my father. 'I'm not acting chauffeur every five minutes.'

My mother didn't leave go of Geraldine's hands, nor did she look at my father, but said with a cold quiet that chilled me, 'No man is interested in Geraldine. If that Larry's interested in her, then it's for only one thing.' When she finally let go of Geraldine's hands they had the white stripes of her fingers pressed in them, and the tiny moon cuts of her nails.

During the family prayers that evening Geraldine received a special mention. 'Let her not be led into temptation,' my mother whispered fervently. 'In her heart she's still a child. Let her always be a child in Yours.'

I peeped up. My father was tying his shoelaces, ready to jog down the lane and meet Uncle Rory for a Saturday drink. Terence, clean in his pyjamas, was yawning. My mother had her eyes shut tight and Geraldine had hers wide open. She beamed round at us all through her fingers.

'She's over thirty,' my father reminded my mother when she hung the rosary beads back up.

'She's a child,' my mother asserted. 'And always will be. Look at her now, won't you?'

Geraldine was brushing my hair. She had always done this for me at night, and I loved her to do it. She was the only one who had the patience to get all the tangles out. She sat back on her heels to admire the job when she'd finished, and tonight, for the first time ever, handed me the brush and leaned forward till her head was on my lap. I stroked her thin, greasy strands with the brush. I could see her pink scalp.

'Poor Geraldine,' I said, not meaning to. She rolled her head sideways to peer up at me through her fringe.

'Poor, poor, poor,' she murmured. She laughed, sucking back the dribble on her wet lips. 'Poor Dendine.'

'You can't even say your own name,' I said. 'You should have had an easy name, like Anne.'

'Lie Kan,' she echoed. 'Kan.'

As my father left my Aunt Bridget came bustling in for an hour's company and a quiet drop of Irish while Rory was out drinking, bringing in with her the sharp cold of the evening. She clucked when she saw that Geraldine was having her hair brushed, bent down and patted her cheek, lifting up strands of hair as if to marvel at its softness.

'Will you just look at this!'

'How's Rory's mother?' my mother asked her. 'Poor thing.'

'The old woman is knitting dishcloths,' Aunt Bridget said. She slipped her coat inside-out over the back of a chair to catch the fire's warmth. 'In the old people's hospital, and loving every minute of it. Whoever would have thought that now?' She eased off her shoes and stretched out her legs to the hearth, wriggling her grey old toes. 'We went to see her this afternoon, and there was a new girl in the next bed to her who was giving her visitor the divil of a time. 'Take me home, Katie, take me away home,' she'd say to the poor woman. 'I will, Mam. I'll take you home as soon as ever you're well enough to go with me.' 'That means never,' the old woman said, 'Cos ye've selt me home. Let God take me, or send me to hell, that's the only home waiting for me.' Well, the daughter was up to here with it, and I was near wailing myself, and that's the truth, when Rory's mother pipes up, the shrill old bird.

'Shush your ranting, woman,' she says, 'or there'll be no tiddlywinks tonight.' And the woman did shut up, that's what took me. Tiddlywinks, when there's her whole life on display there like washing on the line, her house and home gone, and nothing in sight for her but the full stop. Is this what we're reduced to, Nancy, good strong willing creatures that we are?'

My mother filled up her glass and sighed.

Geraldine stood up and pulled me out of my chair for bed. We cleaned our teeth in the cracked bowl together, taking it in turns to spit out the fizz of paste. Hers always had a touch of blood in it because she brushed her gums too hard. She seemed to fall asleep before I was in bed but during the night I heard her lumbering round the room and I sat up, surprised to see her fully dressed and pulling on her thick socks.

'Geraldine, where are you going?' I asked her. 'It's too early for Mass.'

She looked dismayed, caught out in an act of mischief, and then decided that she hadn't heard me. She crept out of the room as though I was still fast asleep and made every step creak on her cautious way downstairs. I heard the whine of the front door and ran to the window to see her jogging down the lane in her wellies.

My mother and father seemed to be a heaving bundle rocking together in their sleep. I didn't know how to disturb them. I went back into my room and dressed quickly, keeping on my nightclothes underneath. My mother whimpered across the landing; my father moaned.

I paused again at their open door and didn't dare speak out. 'Geraldine's gone,' I whispered. The bundle gasped some kind of pain. I ran away from it and out into the bitter cold of the night. The tide must have turned, changing the wind with it. I ran down the hill in the direction Geraldine had taken, and it wasn't long before I saw her squat figure stumbling in front of me.

'Geraldine!' I shouted. 'Wait for me!'

She half-turned, changed her mind, and lunged off the lane into the shadowed trees. I could hear her plunging through the undergrowth. 'Please wait, Geraldine!' I shouted. I could hear her laughing as I ran alongside her path, too frightened myself to follow her into that blackness, and afraid of leaving her there alone.

Then I saw Larry waiting at the far end of the lane for her, and I realised what it was all about. He ducked his head when he saw me, in that familiar mocking servile way he has, and I felt betrayed. Geraldine lumbered up behind me, panting from the race and laughing aloud. Larry nodded to her.

'So ye've brought your sister, have ye?'

'We'll go back now, Geraldine,' I said. 'She has to go.'

'Does she now? Is that so?' He held out his hand and Geraldine stepped forward like a shy bride and took it, and I in my foolishness hung back while they climbed over the stile at the side of the lane and went down into the fields. I stood with my hands over my face thinking of my sin at the communion rails and of my mother and father rocking in their bed, and somewhere out on the dark sea a late hunting gull taunted me with its grieving laughter. Feeling like a traitor myself I moved slowly to the stile and leaned on it, and there they were, picking their way down the field-track towards the strand. I climbed over and slithered down the track after them, and as soon as they were lost in the shadows of the bay I started to run, dry in my throat with thrill.

But they were not in the bay, hiding together in the silk-sand by the rocks. I saw them heading out across the wet mud-flats in a silver track of moonlight, Geraldine stumpy and slow and slurping the mud with her wellingtons, and Larry with his hand under her elbow easing her along through the sticky slime. He was carrying a bucket. I kicked off my shoes and plunged in after them letting the soft mud ooze up between my toes, and the brown water trickle after it. When I reached them Larry and Geraldine were squatting in the mud by a little channel dug into it, and he was whispering to her as if she was a child.

'This is where ye find them, tucked in the slurry-slime. Ye'll watch out for them spittin' off. There, look.'

He pointed to a froth of brown bubbles and eased his hand into the mud. When he brought it out again he had a cockle in his palm. Geraldine laughed and held out her hands for it.

'There,' he said, pleased. 'Now wash it in the channel and drop it in my pail.'

She swilled the shell again and again in the water, intent in her task, her lips pursing together, her wellingtons sloshing quietly as she swayed.

'We'll have the tide back in at this rate,' he told her. 'Drop it in the pail and look for another.'

She did as she was told, reluctant to let go of the tight-frilled white shell in her palm, letting her hand linger in the murky pail water.

'Look,' he pointed. With a gasp of pleasure Geraldine reached out to the spittle and drove down her fingers. She brought them up slowly as though the mud made them heavy, as though it would drag her down and she would wallow there. When her fingers sucked at last out of the slime and came out pale and silky in the moonlight, and when she kept her fist clenched over her find so he had to lean forward and gently prise open her hand, finger by finger, stroking the mud off each languorously, till he eased his own fingers into her hollowed palm and crooked out the white shell and held it up between his lips and hers, in all that time that seemed like infinity he never took his eyes off hers, nor did she look away from him.

'Geraldine,' I said, uneasy, locked out, and she laughed and broke her look away from his and dived her hand again and again into the mud, scooping and swilling, scooping and swilling, so the mud spattered her arms and her face with the frenzy of her movements and the cockleshells clattered into the pail like the chipped bones of ancient men. And suddenly she'd had enough.

She put her hands onto his shoulders to heave herself up, and steadied herself against him as he stood up too. The light was changing, streaked pink and lemon like the little button shells I used to collect as a small child. Larry's pail was heavy and he leaned slightly to one side as they half-slid like skiers through the slime till they reached their own scooped steps in the cushions of moist banks by the shore. I followed them and it wasn't until I sat on a stone to rub the sparkling dry sand off my feet and to slip my shoes back on that they acknowledged me. In all that time it had been as though they had never noticed me at all and I was an eavesdropper at a deep and intimate conversation. Now Larry dumped the pail onto the sands and still without looking at me held out his arm for me to join them.

'You go back up with your sister,' he told Geraldine. 'And get yeself clean and dry for work.'

As I approached them he cupped her face in his big muddy hands.

'And did ye enjoy it?'

She laughed up at him and he turned away from her, picked up his pail and stumped off over the sands to the slipway sheds. We hurried back home. I had a thousand thoughts whirling about in my head, yet I was aware of a calm kind of stillness about Geraldine that I'd never known before, even in the way she walked, and in her soft and steady breathing, in the white silver silk of her face in the early light, and in the kind warmth of her eyes as she glanced across at me. How I would have wished her to know that peace of mind again.

We slipped as quiet as cats into the house and up to bed and lay muddy and silent between our sheets till my mother's shout would give us leave to fill up the cracked bowl and wash away our crime. The next night my father met her on the way back to work, and although she came home on her bicycle he drove behind her, and she rode into the yard and came into the house without saying anything. I was sitting doing my homework at the kitchen table and she came over to me and pulled my maths books over towards her, and sat poring over the lovely patterns of numbers as though she could understand it all, or as if it was a book of stories that said something to her. After night prayers my mother locked the house doors on the inside which she had never done before, and let us see her doing it. She took the key upstairs with her. Geraldine bit her lip and tried to turn the door handle, first to the front door which goes out to the yard and the lane, and then the back door where the wellingtons and raincoats are kept, and as though it was a puzzle to be solved she tried the windows too, and the doors again, and again.

Nobody said anything about the matter, that day or ever. I had no words with which to enter her sorrow and share it, though I stood by her the nights she opened our bedroom window and leaned out, and out again, as though leaning out would bring her so much nearer to the wet silk-soft of the cockle-beds and to Larry's fond laughter. But whether she ever saw him again I never knew, or daren't ask her. My father or my mother or sometimes Uncle Rory would see her to and from work as though she was an infant starting school, and she closed herself up away from us all, even from me. Child as I was for my years, I saw her as a woman of mystery and sorrow, and that gave her, poor simple thing, a kind of dignity for me.

And then, in the freakish spring tides of the equinox four members of the cockle-gang were swept out to sea, and one of them was Larry. It was the first time a tragedy of this sort had happened in our village. One of the bodies was never found, ever, and must be rocking now jammed by a fist perhaps between boulders deep below that sea, and turned to bone. And two of the others, a husband and wife, were found together nestled in a sandbank pool the next morning when the tide had gone quiet. They were found by the rest of the cockle-gang who'd gone out searching for them, and it's said they were couched together and cupped in each other's embrace, and that it was quite a lovely thing to see in the shallow green water in early sunlight, and that they were difficult to separate. There seemed to be a kind of grim satisfaction that it had happened like this and the cocklers finding them in this way went silent and prayed for their souls, and some of them would have them left there, sanctified in their marriage bed, but it was felt in the end that it would have been a startling thing for children to come by unawares if they wandered out as far as the sandbanks, or would be made unholy by people going out there to pry.

My mother and I watched them being carried home. We stood at the stile and could only just make them out, blank figures on the streaked strand, while the grey sea licked back away to the horizon. Years later I dreamt about them, but in my dream the couple became Larry and Geraldine, and the funeral procession was their wedding ceremony. When I woke I cried because it hadn't been.

Days later Larry was found, dumped at last by the tide up near the slipway. He was recognised and claimed by his father, and very quickly removed. My Aunt Bridget, telling us this at the tea table, said that several girls in the village would be mourning for him now, and quite a few children would never see their father again. I glanced at Geraldine but it seemed that for the day she'd forgotten who he was, and was far more interested in squeezing tomato seeds, which she hated, through the gaps in her teeth, and picking them out to add to the pyre at the side of her plate.

Chapter Eleven

It was a hot day in late July, languid and velvet-still. We had early Benediction that day in chapel, our last before the end of term. Next year I'd be one of the fifth years. I knew my parents would want me to leave after that, and I had no idea what I wanted to do with my life, which was a deep coursing river with ripples and eddies and satin streaks. I no longer wanted to be Father Carolyn's housekeeper, that was for sure.

I stayed behind after Benediction that day waiting for the priest to come out of the vestry again so I could give him a message about my mother's lupins, but I never saw him. The truth is that sometimes when I was in the chapel praying I would go into a kind of daydream that was almost a sleep, eye-open, till the crucifix rocked above the altar and the candle flames blurred to long points and the silence was a rowdy clamour in my ears. I would suddenly come to and would have no idea how long I'd been like that. Sometimes I'd find

Mother Joseph staring at me, wondering, and I'd be embarrassed and out of place, and would walk away with my feet like sponges because my legs would have gone to sleep with the pressure of my kneeling.

That happened on that July day, and I was sure I'd missed him. I went outside, wincing at the slow agony of the blood in my feet beginning to move again. The sunlight smarted my eyes after all that sleepy darkness. Noni and Biddy were in the rose garden waiting for me.

'There you are!' said Noni. 'We thought you must have sneaked away home, or something. Are you coming down the garden with us?'

I nodded, pleased. I was shy of them these days. We didn't spend much time together now. In a strange way I always felt they were older than me and knew more of the world. We walked together along the path that led off from the rosary walk, cool green as it was with the speckle of laurel leaves.

'You're always in chapel these days. The nuns'll have you, you know, if you're not careful,' Biddy warned me. 'Mother Mary Cecilia. I can see you now. You've got just the right face for it.'

'She has, hasn't she?' Noni stopped and put her hands in a V against my cheeks, cupping my chin. 'She's just made for a wimple.'

'Oh hush, you two!' It was a game we'd played since we were first years, when the nuns were beautiful and romantic creatures and we had desperately wanted to be chosen to join them, imitating their ghostly glide and the demure fix of their eyes just to be ready when our time came.

'If I joined the order,' Biddy said, 'I'd be a kitchen nun. I know my place. On my knees I'd be, scraping spuds. Think of all the souls I'd save.'

'They'd never have you, don't fancy yourself,' said Noni. 'You talk too much.'

'Well, and they're not having me, either,' I said firmly. 'I'm not cutting off my hair for anyone.'

Noni ran her hands through my thick untidy hair, smoothing it back to my head and holding it there. 'You'll get that terrible hair cut before you set foot in my convent, Mother Giddy Cecilia!' she croaked. I tried to shake her hands away and at last she let them drop, dragging her fingers down until my hair was loose about my shoulders. She arranged it so that it fell even on each side. 'But you have lovely hair,' she said simply, as if she'd never seen it before. 'Biddy, tell her about last Saturday.'

'Wait when we get to the hurley field,' Biddy promised. They each took my arm and we began to run, jogging unevenly on account of our different heights.

'That man might come.' Noni began to giggle.

'What man?' I asked, looking from one to the other of them as we ran, a child between two grown-ups.

'Oh him!' panted Biddy. 'I'm not troubling myself about him. I'll pray for him to Saint Jude. He's a hopeless case all right.' She looked at Noni over my head and laughed out loud. 'The size of his thing!'

'What man?'

'Oh, only some halfwit who hides in the hurley field and watches the girls. Let's stop here.' Noni flung herself down in the long grass at the side of the field. 'Yum yum!' she mouthed at me. I half-smiled and turned away from her. It didn't seem funny any more.

Biddy flopped down next to her and rolled her socks down to her ankles. The garters had made a red sweaty ring below her knees. She laughed up at me and unbuttoned the front of her thick striped cotton dress, tucking the collar under. You could just see where her pale breasts began to curve. 'Gorgeous, aren't I?' she sighed, glancing down at herself. 'Ripe as peaches!' She pulled the front of her dress a little lower, swelling out her breasts. 'Ready to burst!'

'You're disgusting!' laughed Noni.

I turned away, hot with a strange, deep pain as Noni began to unbutton her own dress. 'What does he do?' I asked, my voice thick, gazing away from them.

'Oh, forget him,' said Noni. 'He's just a pervert! Tell her about Saturday, Bid, when you had to stay board.'

'I will if she'll lie down. She's keeping the sun off me.'

I lay down on my side next to Noni, turning my back to her. She reached an arm across and tickled the back of my neck, twisting and untwisting strands of fine hair around her fingers.

'Cessy,' began Biddy. 'Have the boarders ever told you that they have to share their room with a nun?'

'I know that.' I was conscious of Noni's fingers, gentle and rhythmic. Sometimes we would write messages on each other's back, letter by letter, enjoying the sensation of it, not bothering about translating. Now her fingers were like flies on my flesh, a delicious irritation. I closed my eyes. 'She has a screen round her bed though, doesn't she?' I said, dreamy.

'But she never goes to sleep. Honest! I think she stays awake all night, praying for all their souls. She must. When I had to stay over we lay awake for hours listening out for her to start snoring so we could eat the Mars Bars I'd brought in. Oh, hours! Then Mary Keenan sent me a note daring me to climb up and look over the screen. Can you imagine it!'

'You never did it!' I crooked up my knees, curled up for the storytelling.

'She did!' Noni shrieked. 'She did!'

'I don't know how I dared, honest to God I don't. I got out of my bed and I lifted a chair over to the screen and I climbed up on to it without a sound. And then, very slowly, I straightened up till I could see over the top. And there she was, sitting bolt upright on the edge of her bed, and staring right at me. I nearly screamed out loud. Honest to God, I nearly died. She was fully dressed except for her head-dress thing, and her hair was short and spiky. She looked like a chicken, just so. Her head was too small for her body. And I could see her white scalp. And the way she just stared at me!'

I felt my own scalp creep. In my mind she was Mother Rose, wax-faced in the moonlight. 'Oh, Bridget,' I whispered. 'Whatever did you do?'

'Nothing. Not one thing. She never said a word, and neither did I. We just stared at each other and then I lowered myself down and crept like a mouse back into my bed.'

'And put your head underneath the pillow,' Noni reminded her.

'I did.'

'Poor thing,' I said, surprising myself.

'Poor thing! Poor me! I'll never forget that as long as I live, I can tell you.'

'They do wear nighties though,' said Noni, after a pause. 'I know that for a fact, because I'll tell you this. My mother told me about a convent orphanage school that got burnt down in the night and do you know why? The nuns wouldn't be rescued in their nighties. But it wasn't the nuns who died, she said. It was the poor orphans who were on their knees praying. My mother says that was carrying modesty too far.'

'When I get married...' Biddy stretched herself luxuriously. 'When I get married I'll wear a nightie that you can see right through.'

'For your wedding dress, Bridget Murphy?'

'Not at all. I wouldn't waste it on the congregation. It would be for the Big Night.'

'Who would you marry, Biddy?' I asked.

'I don't care who he is as long as he's a great lover,' she sighed. 'I don't care how poor he is.'

'I don't think I want to get married.' I said. 'I don't think I like the idea.'

'That's only because you're young for your age,' Noni suggested. 'Suddenly you'll grow up and then you'll want a husband. It's nature.'

'Well, I'll tell you what I think,' said Biddy. 'I think we've all got husbands already. Chosen for us. I think we'll be walking about one day not even thinking about men and we'll see him and know he's the one.'

'As if he was part of me,' sighed Noni. 'I know you, I'll say. You're the one. Isn't that incredibly romantic!'

'It is,' I admitted. 'I think I'd quite like that.'

We closed our eyes in the benediction of hot sun. Insects droned round us. Biddy started to hum, a low husky breathing that had no music in it at all. Noni's tickling fingers trailed away and lay limp and warm against my neck. Birds rustled underneath the hedge.

'Who's this, skulking under the bushes?'

We were jerked awake by the voice, all three of us sick to the stomach.

'Hell's bells, it's Rosebud.' Noni and Biddy heaved up their socks and rolled over, kneeling into the hedge to pull out their collars and button up the necks of their summer frocks.

'What's this!' Mother Rose asked me, her fine spray of spittle sprinkling my face as I blinked up at her. 'Just look at you, sitting brazen with your frock above your knees.'

'I'm sorry, Mother.' I struggled to stand up, dizzy with the sudden awakening.

'Oh, Mother.' Bridget turned round, buttoned up, cool. 'It's so hot, Mother. And it's the last day of term.'

'And no panamas on your heads! Look at that terrible hair of yours, Cecilia Deardon. When will you get it cut! You'll get insects in it and all sorts, goodness knows. Will you get it seen to in the holidays? You're one of the big girls next year, for goodness' sake.'

'Yes, Mother,' I said. 'Sorry, Mother.'

'And fasten up your cardigans, all three of you. Mercy on us all, you're not children any more. Don't you know that?'

The woman stumped past us, on her way to pull up weeds from among the mounds in the nuns' burial ground. I followed Noni and Biddy back up towards school. My stomach was weak with a deep sense of shame and dread; there was a weight of sin in me that I couldn't understand except that it was to do with a soft adolescent womanhood that turned my limbs to liquid and my flesh to air without any conscious prompting from me. It was to do with the sin of Eve, that was what I knew.

A slim young nun approached us. I had never seen her before. She had her head bent and her eyes closed in prayer as she walked. Biddy grasped Noni's arm and turned round to me.

'It's her!' she whispered. 'The nun with the head!'

Noni shrieked a laugh and Biddy pulled her into the laurels, out of sight. The nun approached and passed me slowly. For a second her eyes looked at mine, but she didn't see me. They were as grey as smoke, I noticed. I heard the whisper of her prayer and she bent her head again. And I felt cold; the juices in me turned to ice at her grey unseeing glance. For she was in a trance, and all our giggles and prattle were floating bubbles, catching sunlight, bursting into air.

Chapter Twelve

After that day the summer retreated into a violence of rain and wind and rain again. The soil in our little garden was swilled to mud and my mother's lupins were battered to the ground. The fuchsia trailing from the wall looked like spatterings of blood.

'It's a sore worry, so it is,' my Aunt Bridget said. I noticed how small her eyes were these days, as if they weren't taking in much light at all, and how her lips were clamped in a slit. 'These are desperate times, all right.'

I would hear anxious farmers talking together along the lanes, and my mother and father mulling it all over at the table, but we were all right, it seemed, so none of that worried me too much. For all that, dismal weather seeps into you. We all seemed to be forever bickery and depressed. My mother complained that Terence and I got on her nerves now the holidays had started, and when Geraldine had her week off work she gave up the housework altogether and followed my father round our smallholding. I would watch them from the window sometimes, two small figures in their old brown clothes, laughing together with the rain soaking into them. I had never known them to be so companionable. But the trouble with all this was that they both came in at night hungry and too weary to cook, so it was mostly left to me to fend for us all; and I was a dreamer, apt to let the potatoes boil dry and the bread burn in the oven.

'You'll never get yourself a husband if you carry on like this,' my mother told me, scraping away the burnt bits over the hens in the yard. 'Not till you shape up.'

'I might not want to get myself a husband.'

'Stuff and nonsense. What else is there for a woman to do?'

She was fifty during that summer. 'Will you just look at the sight of me,' she said, watching herself in the mirror and propping up her loosening chin with the back of her hand. 'I'll never be frisky again, Francis, d'you know that?'

'I do,' my father agreed, pretending to read the newspaper but glancing up and down at her like a small bird pecking, 'and you're growing stout these days.'

'Oh Daddy, she's not!' I said, angry with him.

'Ah, but don't I love a bit of flesh to grab hold of!' he laughed. She shook his hand away as he leaned over to try to pat her stomach, but I could see her face and I knew the hurting there.

'Don't you like being fifty, Mam?' Terence asked, his small face tilted up in the questioning way he has.

'Not much I don't,' she said. She had moved away to the window and was staring out at the wet lane that twisted from one small village to another, and at the damp, dun fields. 'It would be fine if I had something to show for it. But it's a long time, fifty years, a long time if you've not done a great deal with them.'

'But you've had us,' Terence said, in a small put-on baby voice, and she turned round and buried her face in his hair.

'I have,' she said. 'And thank God!'

Aunt Bridget, who would be eating with us that evening, pursed her lips. 'I'd like to know what greater thing there is in life Nancy, than to have the love of God and the love of your man. And to have the love of children too is beyond hoping for. We're here for a mortal time, what room is there in life for more than all that?'

'A bit of comfort, maybe,' my mother said. 'A bit of difference.'

'I fail to see what else money or good fortune could seek than what you have already.'

But my mother's eyes were again on those grey, rain swept fields with the lapwings paddling their oar wings over them. She closed the curtain over, making the flames cower down and smoke billow into our room, choking us.

The next morning Uncle Rory drove up to the house in an old car he'd borrowed for the week from a friend who'd gone to Lourdes on a pilgrimage. He beeped the horn outside to make us run to the windows and came with a jaunty whistle into the house.

'Where's my two beauties?' he called. 'I've come to take them out to see the world.'

'In that thing?' my mother was doubtful. 'And will it go up the hills, Rory?'

'Have you no sense of fantasy?' Rory asked her.

'I wouldn't trust you to follow a straight line on a bicycle, let alone in a motor-car.'

'Which is why you're not invited to come.' He bowed down and kissed her hand, making her blush and laugh aloud. 'Queen of the morning though you are.'

'Then it's the other two beauties you're after!' she said. 'My adventuring days are over are they, Rory, before they've even begun!'

Geraldine didn't want to go. Her perverseness makes her into a small animal, hunched up and hiding, head tucked into her knees, rocking herself. I put on my raincoat and stood holding hers out to her, impatient with her because I didn't want Terence to be invited instead. She wouldn't even look at me.

Uncle Rory squatted down on the hearthrug next to her, putting his head against hers, and sang to her:

'The rain blows cold and the wind blows free

And the fair maid sings this song

Oh bring my true love home to me

I have waited for him long

I have waited for him long.

It won't be the same without you,' he whispered to her. 'Come on Queen Geraldine. Say you'll come.'

She rolled her head sideways on her knee and peeped out at him, and he held his arm up to me for the coat. Then he slipped it over her shoulders and took her hand to help her up. Meek as a child she let him lead her outside into the lane and up to the car.

'What d'you think now?' he called over his shoulder to my father. 'Will this do for the little princess?'

Geraldine allowed herself to be handed in to the back seat and looked out at us through the window, unsmiling and afraid.

'You sit next to me,' Uncle Rory told me. 'My eyesight isn't good enough to read the road signs.

And then the fair maid did set out
Her true love for to find
She searched the land both north and south
For she was out of mind
For she was out of mind.'
My throat tightened to join him in his singing.

He took us first to have a cheese sandwich in a bar that he knew, which I think was what my mother had been afraid of. It was smoky and loud and I felt uncomfortable there in a room full of men. Rory stood at our table and joined their company, listening to a curly-haired man who was lilting at the bar as if he was at the dances, his tune light in his throat. Uncle Rory cheered him and bought him drinks, and had one himself. His mouth slackened as he drank and his talk grew louder and boastful.

Geraldine and I sat in our silence nibbling our sandwiches and picking up the crumbs of grated cheese bit by bit off our plates with the tips of our fingers till there was nothing more to pick, and we were forgotten children.

One of the other men at the bar started to sing in the liquid, melancholy way drinking men have, and he turned to Rory and pointed a finger at him. Rory scraped his wild tawny hair behind his ears and planted his feet firm and stood with his glass clutched in his hand and sent up his peaty voice. I felt a tickling of nerves in my stomach at the sound of it, longing again to sing with him, dreading the thought of being asked to. But I was never asked these days.

'The pale moon was rising above the green mountains,' he began, and the men at the bar sighed and nodded, and when he came to the last line, which he drew out and held down soft as a whisper, he put his hand on my sister's shoulder. 'Where first I met Geraldine, the Rose of Tralee.'

Geraldine's eyes shone with the light of nervous laughter as she looked from one to the other of the men, willing them to recognise her as the star of the song. On his last note Uncle Rory set his glass down on the table and without even acknowledging the applause he went out of the bar, with Geraldine and me behind him.

And now the sun had come out pale and watery through the clouds. With the cold stout warming up inside him Uncle Rory announced that the outing to see the world had really begun, and he ran us to the next shop to buy lemonade and chocolate biscuits and apples in case we never spotted civilisation again, and we set off.

By late afternoon we came to a place that was the furthest away from home I had ever been before, and he said that we must stay there till the sun set, it would be a glorious sight from the west. We parked the car in a muddy lane and walked to the edge of a field of barley, where it just seemed to run out of earth and fall away. Deep below us the brown sea churned, mothering the ragged rocks.

Uncle Rory stood at the very brink of the cliff and opened wide his arms. 'And when the sun dips down below our sea, guess where it goes to?' he said, having to raise his voice a little because of the water's noise and the wind. 'America! Think of all the waves between us and there, and the uncountable little drops of water, the miles and miles of ocean, the rocking shells. The fishes and whales and porpoises, Cecilia, think of that, and the tiny grains of sand. And it's just a touch of eternity, just a touch.'

'Does it not frighten you, thinking of huge things like that?' I asked him.

He looked down at me. 'Not at all,' he said. 'This is what puts you in touch with God.'

'More than praying?'

'It is a kind of praying.'

Geraldine shouted out to us from the far side of the field. She had wandered back to the lane where we had parked the car and which led down steeply past a farmhouse and half a mile or so to a tiny bay. When we came to her she was crouched down, her knees crooked so her skirt formed a tent that trailed into the mud. She dabbed up her skirt and showed us what she was sheltering.

'Well, look at the size of that divil,' My Uncle Rory laughed. 'Where does he think he's going, so far from home?'

The crab was the size of his palm, and nutmeg brown. It flailed its claws like a boxer, shielding its fleshy parts, trying with frail jabs to defend itself against our prying fingers, and lashing out an attack. Geraldine put out stubby fingers to pick it up and it bobbed away from her, lumbering and dainty on the tips of its pincers, dancing.

'Careful!' I warned her. 'It'll eat you up!'

It lowered itself down and waited in our silence till it thought maybe we had gone, then raised itself up on its points and tilted off sideways at high speed till it came to rest at last underneath the instep of Uncle Rory's shoe. 'Why the divil!' he laughed, pleased. 'But I'm not stopping here all the night to keep the gannets off your back.'

'Should we not take it back down,' I suggested, 'and put it in the sea?'

'Who's brave enough to risk their fingers to do that? Geraldine, you do it.'

Immediately Geraldine crouched down again on all fours, clucking to the crab as if it was a hen or a cat, trying to coax it into her outstretched palm. She put her face sideways down on the path to peer at it. 'Stop that!' I told her. 'It'll have your lip.'

At last Uncle Rory unlaced his shoe and took it off. He lifted it up and delicate with his long fingers he prised up the crab from where it had cowered and held it out at arm's length. Its useless pincers clawed air. It bubbled, hopeless. He waved it into Geraldine's face and she dodged back, screaming laughter.

'This creature has no power,' he said, holding it out again. 'No power at all. I could drop it from here and it would shatter to smithereens on the path. Should I do that, Geraldine?'

'No!' she shouted, alarmed. She covered her eyes with her fingers.

'No, I shan't do that,' he said. 'Because I am a greater being. I am a God. And I will save the life of the crab.' He poised it over the mouth of his shoe and dropped it in, and then hobbled down the lane displaying the toe hole in his green sock. We scrambled over rocks that were prickly with limpets, and him whistling grimly all the time, and came at last to a deep rock-pool. He let Geraldine dip his shoe towards it, and the crab slithered its way out and drifted down into the green water. Within seconds it had disappeared.

'Don't let my shoe in too!' Uncle Rory warned. 'Fancy. He doesn't even know or care who rescued him from death.'

'He probably thinks you were death,' I suggested. 'He was quite happy till you picked him up.'

'Well, I hope he's learned his lesson. A fellow his size should know better than to try to escape from his element.'

As he bent down to fasten up his laces an old woman came towards us, seeming to grow out of the rocks.

'It's a fine soft day,' she called out.

'It is indeed,' he said.

'It's a grand place to bring the young ones to,' she said, and then when Geraldine turned her face away from the pool, where she'd been lying all this time with her hair dangling in the water, she realised her mistake. She looked round. 'I've my own daughter here somewhere, with her children. They love to spend summer here, the little ones. They live in London, you see,' she added, a touch proud of the fact. 'But that's no place to bring up the children.' She eased herself onto a rock, her skirt wrinkling up as she did so, and she perched there looking for all the world like a weathered mermaid waiting for the tide to come back in for her. 'I come down here every evening of my life,' she told us. 'Just to watch the day ending on the sea. It's a grand sight. Look at it now.'

The water was white satin with a rush of salmon in it where the sun spread down. A small boat was making its way back to the shore.

'That's her man, bringing home the spoils of the sea for his family. He's not from this country, of course.'

She waved to a young woman and two young children who were clambering over the rocks towards us. 'There's Maire,' she said. 'My girl from London town.'

I noticed that Maire had let her legs go for the summer for they were hairier than my mother's and I knew there were ways of curing that with creams and suchlike. She was not at all what I would have expected from someone who lives over the water in London, not like holiday people I'd seen at home. She kept her eyes cast down most of the time she was with us, while her loud-voiced children squirmed round her faded skirt and stared at us. My Uncle Rory, who is never shy, did most of the talking, and seemed to want to quiz the life out of her, but she never raised her eyes to him once. Now and again she glanced across at Geraldine in the way curious people do, and my sister beamed across at her. Uncle Rory wanted to know how she liked things in the big city.

'I like it well enough,' she told him. 'Though it's always a good rest to come away from it.'

'Tell him about the birds,' her mother urged.

'Oh, the birds,' Maire laughed. 'Everyone knows about the birds, Mam.'

'Indeed they don't. I never knew they had birds in the Big City,' her mother said. 'Did you?' she asked me. 'They make a terrible lovely racket, Maire was telling me.'

'Well they do right enough,' Maire agreed. 'When you come out at dusk there's birds by the thousand, fluttering by the thousand, swooping about in the gutters and wires and round the buildings and all. Such a row they make, it'd make you laugh.'

'Is that so,' Uncle Rory marvelled, though he'd been to many a big city in his time before his back got sore, and must have seen birds there.

'Just starlings and sparrows.' Maire narrowed her eyes, watching a flock of oystercatchers poking their bright bills into the mud. 'Nothing special. It's just the noise they make.'

'And there's more pigeons than people.' Her mother nodded at me. 'Imagine what a sight that must be.'

We went silent, imagining it for a moment, while the children shrieked away from us and ran to the tide's edge. The little boat came in with a scuff against the sand and the children splashed round it. Their father's London voice came over to us. I badly wanted to ask Maire if she missed the sea when she was away from it, and to tell her that I had a brother who lived in England now, and that I even knew people in our village who had come all the way from Italy, so far from home. But I didn't know where to start, and could only keep my head lowered and help Geraldine to pop bladder wrack pouches while I listened to my uncle and the old woman gossiping away as if they had known each other for years.

I had never met strangers like this before, to pass the time of day with. When at last we turned to go the old woman and her daughter came up to the sand-track with us. The woman gripped my hands.

'You should all stay till the moon's full up,' she told me. 'Did you not see the statue of the Virgin at the top of the lane?'

I nodded, though I hadn't. Her stare fixed me.

'When the moon comes out and you're praying there, the virgin nods to you.' The old woman's voice was proud. 'That's our miracle.'

'Have you seen it nod?' I asked her.

'Many times. It's a great comfort to me in the winter. And Maire has seen her too.'

Maire turned away from us and went to join her family. 'Only now she lives in London she won't admit it,' the woman whispered to Uncle Rory. 'That's what travel does for you. Keep them at home if you can. Keep your girls safe.'

Berlie Doherty

Chapter Thirteen

It was when I was standing at the front of a boat that ploughed and lumbered over a chaotic sea that I told my mother about the nodding statue. It was all in an effort to make her feel better. I was queasy myself; my throat was swollen and had opened up in readiness to receive what seemed to be the solid mass of acid drops working its way up my gullet from the very pit of my stomach. She looked ghastly to me, whey-faced and cold with sweat, and I persuaded her to come up on deck for air, drenching as it was, convinced that so long as we could see which way and how often the ship was pitching we could settle our blood and flesh and bones and bile to the same rhythm. But she sat with both hands underneath her on the bench that was set out for better days and kept herself rigid, her lips loose across her teeth, concentrating on the chaos of a stomach awash, and no doubt offering it all up against some future sin.

'Mam,' I said.' Did I tell you we saw a nodding statue when we had our outing with Uncle Rory?'

As a matter of fact it was a lie. We had passed the statue in the car but had not stayed behind to watch it nod. Uncle Rory said that the roads were littered with shrines just as good as that one, and indeed we had our own statue just above the church, but it didn't nod, that was the only difference.

'I'm not saying that statue won't nod,' he went on, 'But I'll just mention that it has been said abroad by some people that if you look at anything for long enough in the moonlight it would nod to you, or weep, or wink. A cow would do it,' he added. 'Or a tree, or even the post of a gate, but especially something that had a painted face with eyes that looked like a real woman's. If you were a simple person, or in a receptive frame of mind, it would. And besides,' he said. 'I've a raging hunger in me now, and a long way between me and my supper.'

I looked over my shoulder to Geraldine and saw that she was as disappointed as I was.

'Have you never seen a nodding statue?' I asked him.

'I've seen a virgin that cries,' he told us. 'And that was a wondrous thing to see, Cecilia. Real tears weeping from the blue eyes. And there's a true, true story of a wicked heathen who wanted to remove a blessed virgin statue and the local people would not have it taken away. So do you know what he did? He ordered it to be smashed up.'

'What a terrible thing,' I said. 'And did they do it?'

'They did not. The man had to do it himself. But let me tell you this, as soon as he raised his hatchet and struck his first blow into the statue's side, blood began to pour out of it. He kept on smashing, and blood flowed all round him, soaking into the earth he stood on. It's true, it's true. And the heathen repented and had a church built on the very same spot.'

We sat back, satisfied, and watched the walls that looked like thick lace with their unruly balancing of boulders unwind from us, and the blue hills dissolve away to night.

But the next evening we had placed the little statue that was in our bedroom in the window alcove in the full moonlight, and had knelt there for an hour or two giggling and praying and watching for the nod. Nothing happened, and I knew why. It needed the close swish of the sea, I told myself, and bitter air on our cheeks. We were too comfortable with lino under our shins. It should have been grit or pebbles. We were too sinful maybe. But then I looked at Geraldine and thought, she can't sin. She has the mind of a pure baby. All she has committed is original sin, and she can't help that, it's Eve's fault. Dear God, I thought, that's another sin I've just committed, thinking that. No wonder the statue won't nod.

But I told my mother that I was pretty sure that the statue in the shrine had nodded to us that night as we drove past it in the car, because that was the sort of story she loved to hear, and it was nearly the truth because we had the testimony of the old woman anyway. She opened her eyes briefly to watch the pale blown seagulls and then closed them again.

I concentrated again on the activities of my stomach, the contents of which had become separate and lemony. My throat had a taste of brown slime. I lurched across to the rail and saw Liverpool, the clocks and towers, the Liver and Cunard buildings, the solid architecture of business and prosperity. It was a gladdening and quite beautiful thing to see. I gulped down the last buttons of gristle. 'We'll be all right now,' I told her. 'We're here.'

We walked round for half an hour or so in the port enclosure till she felt she had her land legs back again. I suggested to her that we should get one of the taxis that were coasting up and down, keeping us in sight. The idea of that brought back her strength.

'We will not,' she said. 'It's just idle decadence to waste good money on cabs like a film star when there's ample buses about.' When we found a bus that said 'Dingle' on the front our spirits rose. 'The Dingle's sure to be a wild and lovely place,' she told me. 'If it's anything like Ireland's.'

But Liverpool was not a bit like Ireland. We swayed on our top deck through street after street of terraced houses with red bricks grown grimy, and dark dredges of smoke in sluggish trails, and youths lounging together against walls, kicking the heels of their boots down on the pavements. We thought we would come out into green fields soon, and blue hills in the distance, but we didn't. The green fields were locked away forever on the other side of that brown, heaving sea.

We had nothing at all to say to each other now. Twelve hours ago we had left home in a pitch of laughter, caught up in the excitement of the brave and obvious whim that had brought her into my room to get me out of bed and packing immediately, and which had left Geraldine standing pale and bewildered at the top of our lane, biting her lip and waving us out of sight.

'Don't!' my mother had warned me then, though I'd said nothing. 'She'll be just fine. She'll have to manage without me some time, when I'm dead and gone. She'll have to learn.'

And all I could think of as we sailed along on the swaying bus down the streets and streets of terraced houses was how Geraldine shouted out her songs while she helped my mother at the sink, and how she clapped her hands to the jig of my Uncle Rory's whistling, and how the soft playing of fiddles made her put her head to one side and laugh. Would she still sing and dance when my mother wasn't there in the room to glance across and smile at her. And would she be like Mad Sean, who had danced out there in the churchyard on his mother's grave the very night of her burial, shouting up a lunatic hullabaloo that should have brought all the dead to their feet?

My mother grabbed my arm and pulled me from my seat when the conductor shouted up the stairs to us. 'We're here,' she said. She pulled from her pocket the letter that she had read and read on our journey in order to memorise the address. There was rain here just as there was at home, and as we jumped off the bus we splashed our calves in the puddles. We were wearing our best coats and shoes, both of us.

The house was tall and thin in a long row of Victorian terraces, quite smart at one time my mother said. Steps led down from the pavement to basement rooms, and in the dark well a skinny cat arched its back and spat at us. I peered at the names on the bells and was pleased to see that it wasn't the bottom one I had to push. Imagine living underneath the ground, and having a window that only caught sight of people's ankles as they hurried past. My mother tried to do something with her hair.

'Do I look dreadful?' she whispered.

'No,' I said. 'You look better.'

'I feel dreadful.' She turned her back on the house.

We didn't hear the bell, and had no idea whether it had sounded, and were too nervous to try it again. I pulled my mother's arm when I heard the trudge of feet in the passage. The door was opened by a young woman who stared at us in disbelief.

'My God,' she said. 'So you came.'

'Yes,' I said, timid, feeling childish.

My mother still wouldn't turn round.

'Well, he's out,' the young woman said.

'Will you ask us in?' my mother said in her new muffled voice. She looked worse than when she was on the boat.

The woman went back into the house and we followed her. The passage was musty and scuffed, with plum coloured tiles criss-crossed with tiny and grubby white and blue ones. It echoed with the sound of a tired baby crying. The room was just off the passage and as we went in the crying baby presented his red face to us as he tried to pull himself upright in his cot. He slipped down again and clung to the top rail of the cot with one hand, swinging round and howling as he bumped his way down. His blue sleeping suit hung damp around his crutch. His nose was running and his hair was matted. He looked as if he'd been crying all day.

'And is this Mark?' My mother went to the child and crouched by his cot, shushing him to a questioning silence. His breath shivered as he stared at her. The woman sank down onto a worn settee and felt round for her cigarettes. She offered the packet to my mother, who refused with pursed lips, and to me. She lit her cigarette and sucked it in deeply, hollowing her cheeks, parting her lips as she breathed out the smoke. It hung in a blue haze round her. I was still standing by the door and didn't know what to do with myself. The only armchair had a sprawl of clothes on it, waiting to be ironed. There were two straight chairs at the table, which had some plates with left-over food on; egg-yolk in a swill of cold white grease. It would be rude to sit there as if I was expecting a meal to be served up at any minute. Yet I couldn't sit bumping up against her on the settee.

So I stood, still foolishly holding onto the suitcase that Aunt Bridget had lent us, while my mother dandled the wet and staring child up and down in his cot.

'You got our telegram?' she said. 'Telling you we were coming?'

The young woman took in a long last desperate suck of her cigarette before squashing it out on a saucer. 'You obviously didn't get mine,' she said. 'Telling you not to bother.'

'Not to bother!' my mother repeated, shocked.

I tried to hide the suitcase behind my back.

'What's the point. He's working day and night and I'm due any minute.'

'But that's why we've come,' my mother said, never leaving off her jigging of the child. 'Good heavens, when we got his letter telling us you were about to have another child and we'd not even seen the first or met you, and we don't even know your name for goodness' sake...'

Her voice was rising to a pitch. Perhaps she would tell her next that when we mentioned her every night in the family prayers she was called 'that woman over the water...' and that my mother spoke of her as if she was some kind of temptress, a Mary Magdalene. I felt like crying. My mother hardly ever rowed except in sudden temper flares with us at home, and here she was raising her voice to a stranger. I'd wanted Michael to be there and hugging me and swinging me round, and I'd wanted his baby to be soft and sweet and tidy and tucked up in clean sheets.

'...But if they won't come to us, I said to Cecilia, we must go to them.'

'You won't catch me crossing the Irish Sea,' the woman shuddered.

'Well, I only have sympathy with you there.'

'God ridden country. It's only fit for priests and fairies, what I hear of it.'

My mother was intent on freeing one of her fingers from the child's fisted grip. 'I brought my insides up on that crossing,' she said. 'And we had one hell of a journey to Dun Laoghaire.'

The young woman said nothing. She was intent, it seemed, on scraping a whitish patch off the shoulder of her jumper.

'Cecilia,' my mother said to me. 'Could you make me a cup of tea?'

'Help yourself,' the woman said. She waved her hand to the washbasin that was in the corner of the same room, by the table. Washing-up soap, a tin of toothpaste and nappy-rash creams cluttered the space between the taps. I carried the suitcase over with me and set it down beside a pail of yellow-brown nappy water, and was reminded briefly of the time my Uncle Rory had had to wash down his own mother.

Later that night we were both awake in the cramped and lumpy double bed when I heard Michael come home. I heard his surprised voice in the other room, and hers, tired and listless in reply. I nudged my mother but she pretended to be asleep, so I put on my school coat over my pyjamas and went out to greet him. It was only then that I realised that we had been given their bed. She was hunched up on the settee with a coat over her, sleeping now, and he was buttering himself some bread at the table.

'Hello, Michael.'

He grinned at me, not his old wide smile. I went closer to him. 'Wherever are you going to sleep?' I whispered.

'Don't you worry about me,' he said. 'I'm a cat. I'll sleep on the clothes line. Besides, I'm out again at six. It's hardly worth taking my boots off for.'

'But you must sleep.'

'I'll doze in the chair, when I've eaten this.'

'Are you pleased to see us?'

He tousled my hair and winked at me, but there was no smiling in him. 'You'll be grand company for Joy. She's only two or three years older than you, did you know that?'

'Joy!' my mother repeated drowsily when I reported this back to her. 'Misery, more like!'

Mark woke the house up at five, and my mother was out of bed like a shot and putting the kettle on to make up a bottle for him. She shooed Joy off the settee and sent her to take her place in the bed next to me. Her feet were like lumps of ice. I was worried about having to make conversation with her but within seconds she was in a deep sleep. I could hear my mother chatting to Michael as he got himself ready for work, and I wanted to be with them, sharing it. I was shocked to hear her opening the door some time later and to realise that I had fallen asleep next to Joy.

'Creep out,' she told me. 'And let the girl get some sleep.'

She had cleaned the place up, done the ironing, and washed and dressed the baby. He sat propped up against cushions on the settee making happy noises. My mother put her face up to his and he laughed back to her. 'He's a rascal,' she told him. 'When he's clean. He's a scallywag.'

When Joy got up some hours later all her self-possession had gone, though she didn't have it in her to thank my mother. She padded into the kitchen and sank down on the settee next to Mark, rooting under the cushion for her packet of cigarettes.

'I've been told to rest,' she said. 'I've got high blood pressure, and the doctor said...'

'Do one thing for me,' my mother said, 'and throw away those damned cigarettes. It's a wicked thing to smoke with a baby inside you.'

'You're going to tell me it'll turn out black as smoke next,' Joy laughed, but nervously. 'That's what the woman upstairs tells me.'

'Blue more like,' my mother said. 'And then you'll be sorry.'

Joy ate the breakfast my mother had prepared for her in silence while Mark chuckled and I cleaned the cooker and my mother scrubbed the floor. She went back to her room to get dressed, waiting for my mother to put a sheet of newspaper over the wet lino so she could step onto it. 'You don't have to do that you know,' she said with difficulty. 'Besides, it'll soon get mucked up again.'

She did look young then, younger than me even, with her nightie stretched tight across her swollen stomach and her bare feet pink with cold and her hair tousled. And my mother just grunted with a grim kind of satisfaction and kept on scrubbing grey froth.

Later that day Michael called in for a few moments with a mattress someone had loaned him, and a golden eiderdown with tiny feathers poking through.

'I'll give it a good hoovering,' my mother said. 'It might have fleas.'

He crouched over little Mark and swung him up in the air to make him laugh. He kissed Joy with his arms round her and she wriggled away from him. 'Don't,' she said. 'You make my neck ache.'

Michael laughed down at her. 'You poor little mite,' he said gently. 'You're so small!'

'Eat, Michael, before you go,' my mother told him, but he shook his head.

'I'm due back now, Mam. I'll be home around midnight.'

My mother followed him to the door. 'Do you have to work so late?'

'Mam, this is the first work I've had for months. I've got to take it.'

'Your wife's more important. You're working all the hours God sends and you're wanted here.'

'I'm taking time off when the baby's come. I've got to make up now.'

My mother looked back into the room, at the two of us silent in our chairs, arms folded, while the baby snored lightly in his cot. 'She's only a child,' she said. 'Whatever possessed you both..!'

He bent down to put his finger on her lips, and then the driver of the van hooted and he went off, whistling.

My mother came back in to us, shaking her head, and joined us in our silence. Mark whimpered in his wakening.

'Take him out for a walk, why don't you,' she suggested. 'Fresh air will do you both good. Cecilia, you go too, while I make us all a good old stew.'

'I couldn't eat stew,' Joy said.

My mother raised her eyebrows at me and nodded towards my coat, and I put it on. She lifted Mark out of his cot and made a fuss of dolling him up in outside clothes, and at last and with a deep resigned sigh, Joy put on her own coat and pushed the pram out. I had to help her down the steps with it. We walked along quickly in a fresh drizzle, saying nothing. I had no idea what to talk to her about, and she was preoccupied, and Mark was asleep again, so we walked round the wet streets without a word between us till we were nearly back at the house again. Joy stopped to ease her back, putting the flat of her hand against it.

'Does it hurt?' I asked, and she laughed. 'Are you scared?'

'You have to take things as they come,' she said. 'What's the point of being scared? It's going to happen anyway.'

'I suppose so,' I said. 'I suppose babies always come out eventually.'

'How old are you?'

'Nearly sixteen.'

'You look miles younger. You should have your hair cut. Honestly, it'd put years on you.'

I was conscious that I was holding back my wet hair as if she was about to scalp me. I put my hands back into my pockets.

'It must be the bloom of virginity,' she laughed. 'Blooming virginity! We all know what good that does us.'

I hated her for mocking me. I decided then to tell my mother that I was going back home. Michael could take me to the ferry and I could ring up Father Carolyn from Ireland and he would tell me how to get back home again. I wanted Geraldine. I was missing her.

'I feel a hundred years old,' Joy said. 'Two years ago I was thinking of going to college. Look at me now. I'm going to live it up when I've had this one, I can tell you. D'you know, I wish I'd been a man. Don't you?'

I shook my head, wondering at this strange thought.

'You will. I've all this to go through. Women are always the ones to suffer. We're cursed.'

She rocked the pram, angry, as Mark whimpered. 'From the time your periods start, you're cursed. Have you started yet?'

'Yes,' I said, blushing. 'Weeks ago.'

'Well it's all pain from now on. Pain and mess. Having babies, and milk coming out of you, and blood every month till you're neither use nor ornament.'

I was deeply shocked, and she could tell. I hated her for the way she smiled at me, making me young.

'I wish I was a man, any day. Your Michael doesn't know he's born.'

'It was Eve who brought all that on us. You can't blame Michael.' I was made bold by her brittleness, by her sharp words. One day she would cut herself, that was what my mother would have said.

'Eve!' she laughed. 'That's right. Blame Eve, poor sod. I'll tell you one thing. I don't believe in God, but if there is one, it'll be a male.'

Her blasphemy shocked me. I had never heard anyone talk like this before. She would be struck down, surely. 'Michael thinks the world of you, I can tell,' I said, to appease her and make her think of other things.

'Michael is all mouth, like all you Paddies,' she said. 'All things are possible as far as that man's concerned. He doesn't know what he's talking about. Babies, and getting to college, and America, and the rainbow's end. All on a navvy's wages. He's talking out of his arsehole. Trouble is, I believed him. I was as daft as him, once.' Mark squawked himself awake and she rooted round in his pram for a rattle. She shook it in his face, making him blink. 'And trust him to ask his mother to come over at a time like this. Fancy her coming! Must be mad, the pair of you.'

'He didn't ask her to come.' I watched her as she rocked the pram backwards and forwards, making the baby bump about and howl even more. I hated her. 'He just wrote home to say the new baby was due.'

'And Mummy comes running like a happy little worried hen.'

'What about your own mother?' I asked her. 'Would she come?' We started walking again while Mark in a fury kicked back his blankets and flapped his fists on the pram sides.

'My mother keeps well out of it. She's got more sense. As soon as I walked out the door, that was it. She's having a great time, and she's not likely to let on to anyone that she's a thirty-nine year old grandma. Good for her, that's what I say. Great. She gets on my nerves anyway. I wouldn't want her around fluttering her false eyelashes at Michael.'

She tutted in exasperation as she tried to tuck the blankets round Mark and he kicked them off again. 'I don't believe in mothers being responsible for their kids all their lives. Why should they? They part with them when they give birth to them. Trouble is, no one wants to take them off their hands. Here.' She let go of the pram handle. 'Want to have a go at pushing him?'

'All right,' I said.

'You can push him home. I'll see you later.'

She walked away, a thin short figure with a strange ungainly spread in front of her that made her rock slightly as she stepped off the kerb and crossed the road.

'Don't you love Michael?' I called after her.

'I bloody do and I bloody don't,' she said, without looking back at me, and climbed onto a waiting bus for town.

Chapter Fourteen

'What I want to know,' my mother said after our silent meal that night, which Joy hadn't touched, 'is this. Do you and Michael go to Mass?'

Joy had left the table and was standing by the mattress that Michael had brought, holding a sheet to spread over it. She had trouble bending and my mother sighed and went over to help her. 'Did you hear what I said?'

Joy stared at her, her face taut. She seemed to hold her breath and squeeze herself. Her voice came out in a gasp.

'Mass!'

My mother looked round at her sharply.

'It's nothing to do with you,' Joy said. Her eyes were glazed. She was concentrated in on her own breathing. 'Mass has nothing to do with us.' She heaved her breath in again, her hands pressing deep into the base of her spine. My mother straightened up.

'How long?' she asked.

'Every few minutes.'

'God Almighty.'

Joy grunted. 'Hurts.'

'Do you want to lie down, Joy?'

It was almost too much effort for her to nod her head. 'Can't though. Can't move.'

As soon as she spoke there was a rush of liquid down her legs, a flood of it, clear and faintly sweet-smelling, spattering onto the scrubbed lino and nosing across it.

'The waters.' My mother's voice had the tremor of panic in it. She looked round, distracted, her arms out to steady Joy who looked as solid and immovable as a cathedral, reaching down to a pain deep within herself. There was an envelope on the mantelpiece with a telephone number on it and my mother grabbed it and shoved it into my hands.

'Get the midwife here, for God's sake.'

'Is the baby coming?' I asked, shocked, scared, but a sudden bellow from Joy sent my mother back to her and me running out into the hall, out to the front door and onto the pavement, and then back in and up the stairs. I hammered on the door of the upstairs flat. Joy was bellowing still. The woman took minutes to open the door, hours it seemed, and stood with her black cardigan draped round her shoulders and grey hairs like cobwebs drifting down from it. She only wore her bottom set of teeth, I realised.

'Have you got a phone?' I asked.

'You're not using it,' she grumbled. 'I've told her, there's one down the bottom at the pub she can use.'

'It's a matter of life and death,' I told her. I wanted to shake her as she peered and chewed. 'Her baby's coming, any minute.'

She looked interested. She took the note from me and held it close to her face, squinting at it. 'Fancy that,' she said. 'Wait a mo, chick.'

She opened a drawer in her hall cupboard and rooted round in it, bringing out a pair of scissors and handing them to me. 'You might need them,' she said, and then she ran, her feet slopping out of her slippers, her cardigan flapping. 'Tell her to hang on!' she sang, as she lifted up her telephone receiver.

The baying noises that were coming from Joy echoed round the passage as I ran downstairs and back into the room. Somehow my mother had got her onto the mattress, though she wasn't lying down but sitting back, propped up on pillows and cushions pushed across our suitcase, her legs drawn up and her knees apart, and a towel loose across her - to keep her warm I thought at first, though afterwards I realised it was for decency. My mother was crouching down by her with her sleeves rolled up as if she was about to scrub the floor again, and Joy was grunting and gasping like an animal in great distress.

I brought towels and Mark's newly ironed nappies and my mother shoved them round Joy's legs. I could hardly bear to look at her. She sat with her head sticking forward as though she couldn't lay it back for the life of her, and her mouth was stretched in a grin that showed all her teeth and gums, and the veins bulged in her neck. She kept gasping and gulping as though she couldn't help herself, as though she didn't know anything about the noises she was making, and my mother was bending over her scarlet straining face and coaxing her as if she was teaching her words.

'Wait now, wait now, wait now, hold on.'

'Can't!' Joy burst out.

My mother knelt back for a second on her haunches and closed her eyes, and I knew that she was praying.

'All right now, Joy.' She knelt up again and clasped the girl's clenched hands. 'We'll be all right. Bear down. And push with me. Push with me. PUSH!' as if she needed telling.

Under the tent of towel I couldn't help seeing how the darkness between her legs opened and winked and opened again, I couldn't help watching. I was drawn to this slow wink and must have stood there with my mouth open like a bird's and the kettle bubbling and spitting onto the gas flames behind me. There was the split again, like an eye opening, like the peep of a chestnut in its shell, and more of it, and more, and the winking open came more often and wider, something like a bulb glinted round and hairy and nothing could stop me looking now. My mother was crouched with her hands spread out to receive it, and there was blood and slime, and Joy gave one last long hoarse bellow, and the dark bulb spread out and bulged through, crown first, and lifted itself up, and up into air, till I could see the eye creases and the nose and the mouth, the purple shining crumpled face and matted hair, of a baby.

My mother's voice was caught in a kind of tight sob. 'The head's through,' she whispered. 'Rest a bit.'

She had the baby's head cupped gently in her hands now, as if she was guiding it, but of its own accord it seemed to turn over onto its side and thrust out first its top shoulder, and then the other, and then all in a second it was out, slithering through like a fish.

'Girl!' my mother said, hoarse, and stayed with her head tilted back and her mouth open across her teeth.

'Is it all right?' Joy asked weakly, and my mother came to her senses, though her eyes were still wet. She lifted the baby up, little frightening purple-blue thing that it was, and as she did so it gave out a cry and opened its eyes and stared round as if it was taking in its world, every colour and fibre of it, every atom.

'Perfect!' my mother laughed, and I laughed too and ran forward at last to look at it, and as I touched the tiny bud of its fist it opened out like a flower and grasped my finger. My mother wrapped it round with a towel then held it out to Joy, who smiled and put up her hands for it.

I hadn't noticed till then the long gristly snake of a thing that hung from its middle. 'What's that?' I whispered, thinking at first that something terrible was wrong with the baby that my mother was too scared to mention.

'That's the cord of life,' she told me. 'The baby's still attached to her mammy yet. There's a bit still inside Joy that will have to come out soon, the second birth, and then the cord will have to be cut away.'

'That's what them scissors were for. Do it now.' We hadn't noticed the old woman from upstairs who must have crept in while everything was happening and who now stood over the mattress in her hairy cardigan like the evil fairy at a christening.

My mother shook her head at her and turned her back on Joy. 'They could bleed to death,' she mouthed. 'The midwife will do it right.'

The midwife arrived just as the second birth was coming through, and this time it was a liverish-looking lumpy thing like a jellyfish. I only caught a glimpse of it but I wasn't interested. I only wanted to kneel by Joy and look at her baby.

I was devouring it with my eyes. Joy was trembling uncontrollably while her legs were being washed down, as if she was cold to the very marrow of her bones. Even her teeth were rattling. They took away the mound that was propping her up and lowered her head down to rest on a single pillow, and then someone's hand came over and gently eased her clothing from her shoulder till her breast was bare, and tipped up the nipple till it was close to the baby's mouth. And it searched round like a hungry bird and fastened its lips round it as if it had found home. Joy closed her eyes then, her body still, her face as quiet as a young sleeping child's, with just the corners of her mouth working as if she was the baby, sucking milk from her own mother.

We were all drinking tea when Michael arrived, and the soiled things were steaming in a boiler. He was a stranger in a room of women, and I'll never forget the look of tenderness and bewilderment that came over him as he knelt by Joy and she smiled up at him. He tucked back the towel to look at his baby's face, and it was clean and sleeping by now, and already looking like a real person. 'Pleased?' Michael whispered, and 'Yes,' Joy smiled.

I hardly remember going to bed that night, but I do remember waking up when at last my mother came in, and lying awake and wondering while she undressed herself and knelt in the dark to pray. When at last she tipped herself onto the mattress I didn't know how to tell her what I wanted to say. I wanted to snuggle up to her and have my hair stroked. I wanted to be wrapped round and rocked.

'Mam,' I whispered. 'Did I hurt when I was born?'

She was so long in answering that I thought she must have dropped off to sleep without hearing me.

'Mam?'

'You did hurt,' she said. 'But not in the way you think. You hurt a lot.'

We left Liverpool at the end of the week. The storms had settled, and the sea was a gentle brown wash. We went straight up on deck, leaning over the rail to wave down to Michael and Mark.

'I'm glad we came,' I said. 'But I'm glad we're going back now, too.' With a guilty rush I realised that for three or four days I had forgotten Geraldine, and my thoughts went back to her now, standing with her hand to her mouth at the top of our wet lane.

'I'm glad too,' my mother said. 'Though I never expected all that fun. I've never seen a baby being born you know, and there I was, knee-deep in it. It's a great privilege. A rare thing.'

The ship's hooter blasted as it slid gently away from dock and out towards Liverpool Bay, churning a foam of cream around her.

'I'll tell you something, Cecilia.' I could hardly hear her in the scream of gulls. 'The birth of a baby is a kind of miracle, I'd say.'

And I saw then as I see now the long, untold line of women who have carried me into life. I see them squatting, long skirts hoiked above their thighs, and I look away aghast. How clearly their cries come to me in the darkness, like the gathering of beasts, like the bleating of lambs.

Mother Agnes, Lamb of God, how clearly I remember you.

Chapter Fifteen

September was to be the month of my sixteenth birthday. I went back to school holding deep inside myself the birth of the baby. I would not have known how to talk about it. Yet my intentions now were fixed and fervent, as I walked near the chapel on my first day back at school. I was going to be worthy of my name. I walked on my own in the chapel garden that was drenched with the scent of late roses. The choir was practising plainchant. I loved the rise and fall, the figured dance of it, and the sibilance of the girls' voices hissing like swift skates on ice.

Noni came out to find me at the end of the practice.

'Cessy! Guess what!' she shouted. 'The old dragon's gone!'

'Rosie?'

'We've got a new music nun.'

'Rosie's gone?'

'They've retired her. Oh, she's sick, the new nun said, or gone blind or something. They've put her out to grass in a field, like the old donkey that she is.'

I could not take all this in. Something was being lifted away from me. 'What's the new one like?' I asked, but my thoughts were on Mother Mary Rose, her strange hatred of me.

'Oh, she's lovely,' Noni said lightly. 'Her name's Mother Agnes. She's really young, and she giggles a lot. Imagine that. Giggling in chapel! She's a heathen.'

I could not imagine it. I heard the cackle of rooks in bold echo round the altar.

'And Cessy, I asked her if you could be in the choir. She said you're to go down to the music room at lunch, if you're still wanting to.'

I pretended to be cross with Noni for not leaving me to ask for myself. Yet I knew that nothing would have brought me to ask this great thing for myself. I couldn't understand the slow fear in my limbs when I went down to the music rooms after morning lessons, or the cold blood in my stomach. I would have liked to talk to my Uncle Rory about it first.

Mother Agnes hardly glanced at me as I came in, but sat playing the piano. I recognised her as the young nun in the grounds at the end of last term and guessed that she had only just taken her vows.

'Just sing me a few of these doodles,' she told me, and nervous, I reached for the notes. They were squashed flat inside my shaking breath. She smiled round at me. 'There's no need to be frightened,' she said. 'You're as white as a daisy, look at you. Are you ill?'

I shook my head, miserable. I couldn't explain the terrible trembling that came over me, though I remembered Joy, legs spread wide, being wiped down and comforted by my mother.

'Try again,' she said. 'Deep breaths now.'

I faltered through the notes, sound hardly breaking through the fog of my breath.

She took her hands away from the piano keys and edged round on her stool, frowning up at me. 'You don't have to be in the choir, if you don't want to be. Nobody would force you.'

'No,' I said.

'Would you rather leave it then? If it worries you like this? I don't mind.'

'Yes,' I said. I wanted to cry, deeply ashamed.

I went to the refectory and sat by Noni. She glanced at me and I shook my head. She pulled a face, and the matter was not mentioned again.

But then a few days later Mother Agnes came into the classroom to collect for the missionaries. She laughingly teased money out of all of us, giving us photographs of black children in exchange.

'Come on now girls, two and sixpence. Two and sixpence, that's all I'm asking for. Two and sixpence to buy a little black baby. Have you seen these photographs of them, girls? My goodness, you rich girls have more than two and sixpence to spend on yourselves in a week!' She came to the desk that Noni and I shared and rattled her tin at us. 'Come on now, Veronica, you look rich enough. Empty your pockets.'

'I've only got my tuck money, Mother.'

'That'll do fine. Fish it out.'

Noni, pretending to grumble, pulled some coins out of her pocket. She separated them into two piles and put the smaller into the tin.

'And what's that other?'

'That's my dinner money, Mother.'

'Pop it in then, there's a girl.'

Mother Agnes laughed with us as Noni did as she was told. She was given a photograph of a smiling child. 'There you are now, pin that in your desk and always think of the little ones who don't have as much as we do. Isn't he lovely? Girls, I know of a little girl in the first years who has six babies already! Come on now, turn out your pockets.'

I slid Noni's photograph in front of me, touching the wide smiling lips with my finger. I looked up, surprised, to find Mother Agnes standing in front of me.

'And where's yours?'

'I don't have any money.' I could feel myself blushing.

'No money! Not even your bus fare?'

'I come on my bike.'

I couldn't look at her. I'd failed her again. I'd failed us both. She passed on, grave now, collecting pennies and distributing photographs. She paused at the door.

'Does anybody here bring sandwiches for lunch?' she asked.

I put up my hand.

'What could you do for Veronica?'

'I could share them with her.'

'Would you say that again?'

I stood up and repeated it, red-faced, for the rest of the class to hear.

'You've a very nice speaking voice,' she told me. She riffled through the photographs and hesitated over one. She put it on my desk. The baby was thin. It had an old man's face. 'I wonder when this baby last ate good food?' she said. 'Would you pray for him?'

'Yes please, Mother.'

'You have a musical voice.'

I had no idea whether she'd recognised me. That lunchtime I gave Noni all my sandwiches and hovered near the music rooms till I heard the piano. My blood banged. I went to her door and tapped on it.

'Come in,' she said.

I stood by her, foolish.

'Well?' she smiled.

'Could I sing you one of my uncle's songs?' I asked her.

'You could.'

I sang too fast, as she sat with her head bowed and her hands in a still fold in her lap, and I'd pitched it too high, but my voice filled out the low notes and the high notes took themselves off to echo boldly in the tiled corridor outside. My breath had gone by the end of the song.

She laughed up at me. 'Good girl! You have a lovely voice.'

'Thank you,' I said. The trembling had started all over again now. She must notice.

'Don't thank me. Thank God.'

And what was I to do then? I stood, foolishly smiling, not knowing whether to keep my hands dangling at my sides or tuck them into my pockets. 'What's your name now?' she asked me, smiling back.

'Cecilia Deardon.'

'Cecilia! It's no wonder you can sing, then, is it!'

She turned back to her piano and began to play, losing herself in her music. So I was dismissed.

'Could I be in the choir?' I blurted out.

She nodded, not opening her eyes. 'Pop along to the practice after school tonight, Cecilia. See what you think.'

And at last I was in the choir, at last, in my fifth year at the convent school. I sang with them for the first time during first Friday Mass the next month. Mother Mary Rose sat downstairs with the other nuns, bent low, not standing or kneeling to the responses but crouched forward on her bench, and as I sang I felt her ice-cold hand on me, I closed my eyes and saw the white face of her disapproval. I held my voice where I could just hear it among the other singers, rejoicing in it...

Gloria in excelsis Deo...

Glory be to God on high, and to the music that exalts him... At last I was a part of the huge cosmic ceremony in praise of the creation of life.

One day as I was leaving the chapel with the others Mother Agnes caught up with me and walked along beside me. 'Do you know, Cecilia,' she said. 'I can hear your voice among all the other girls.'

'Can you?' I was mortified. In a choir there should be no such distractions.

'I don't mean you are singing too loud. I mean there's a different quality altogether to your voice. I think I'd like to give you singing lessons,' she said, and stopped to look at me. 'If you'd come to me.'

I went straight to my Uncle Rory's that evening. My father was there too, helping him with some digging, and I ran round to the back to join them and to blurt out my news.

'Singing lessons!' Uncle Rory said. 'Nobody needs to teach you to sing, you know that Cecilia. You can do it already.'

'But perhaps she means my voice isn't really the right sort for a choir, and she means to tone it up,' I suggested.

But he shook his head, mystified. 'If it was piano lessons or maybe even the fiddle I would understand, there's probably things to learn there that you can't pick up on your own. But not singing. That's a natural. I'd like to see someone teaching a bird to sing.'

'Well,' said my father. 'As long as it's not going to cost us anything, maybe there's no harm.'

'You didn't say that when I could have had piano lessons,' I reminded him.

He looked sad then, remembering perhaps the day Michael left the family. 'Didn't I? I don't remember.'

He and Rory were levelling out soil in the back garden that had been such a riot of overgrown brambles and seeding dandelions and willow herb. They set back to it, while my Aunt Bridget watched furtively from the window making sure it was done the way she wanted it, though nothing in the world would have persuaded her to get her own hands dirty.

Uncle Rory leaned on his spade after a while of silent digging, and drove down his heel to stroke away the clogged earth. 'This is what I think,' he said. 'Some things should not be cut into shapes and patterns. Hedges, for one,' he dug again, flinging the soil in moist lumps behind him. 'And poodles. And singing voices. There's no sense in any of that.'

But I was determined to have those lessons, intrigued as I was to know what they would be, and besides, drawn to Mother Agnes. And I was prepared to speak up for myself these days, even against my uncle. 'It's part of education,' I said. 'That's what all learning and thinking is. If we didn't cut our thoughts into shape we'd never stop our minds rambling.'

'What shape?' my uncle roared. My father clicked soothing noises in his throat, hating this kind of talk, mistaking Uncle Rory's extravagant ways for argument and rowing. 'Who says what shape it's to be cut to, that's the thing. Who says?'

'The people who know better than I do!' I suggested, surprised. 'Scholars and people who've put their lives into thinking. If we all had to start from the beginning every time there'd never be any progress, would there? We'd always be just catching up with the last generation, and never getting any further than them. There'd be no new ideas.'

'What scholars?' He struck against stone and flung down his spade, exasperated. 'Name the scholars we have to thank for their generous endowment.'

I knew then that my father was right after all, and that this was argument. My thoughts swam like disturbed fishes, lost for a hiding place. 'Thomas Aquinas.' I had plucked the name from a cave in my memory.

He laughed out loud, his head turned up, his hands spread out to mock me. 'Thomas Aquinas!'

'He was a thirteenth century monk,' I gabbled. 'He based his theological writings on scientific knowledge... and on Aristotle...'

'I have heard of Thomas Aquinas!' he roared. 'I have heard of Aristotle the Greek!'

'Well, they were great scholars and thinkers who influence us today.'

'And I don't care what they thought!' His rage alarmed me. 'Is that all they can teach you in that place? Oh, they teach you sewing too, I forgot.'

I watched him, bewildered. He stooped down to pick up his spade again. He dug with vigour, his words snapping out of him. 'That's what I don't like about you going to that convent school. You're in the hands of a bunch of prejudiced and superstitious women who'll have all your thinking stitched up like the little embroidered altar cloths they're always making.'

'That's a terrible thing to say, Uncle Rory.'

'I don't like nuns.'

'It's no concern of yours where the girl goes to,' my father said, his voice quiet and level and cold, and Uncle Rory laughed again, hunching himself up with his knees bent together and his head bowed in mock servility. 'No your honour, it ishn't.' he said. He touched his forehead. 'Oi forgot my plashe, your honour. Oi'm shpeakin' out o'turn sho Oi am.'

My father turned away from him. Rory allowed his old fond smile to creep back.

'I thought you were proud that I go to the convent school,' I said. 'You always made me think you were.'

'I am,' he said. 'Very proud.'

Aunt Bridget called through the window that there was a pot of tea waiting for us all. My father went in ahead of us.

'Just don't get like your aunt there,' Uncle Rory said quietly to me. 'She's like a nun. She thinks that way, and she won't open up her thoughts to anything that hasn't been told her by the nuns. Her brain is a set of drawers marked good and bad, right and wrong, white and black. She knows where everything belongs.' He was laughing, but it didn't seem too funny. 'It's not good for a woman. It's not good for married life.'

For all that, I would go to my singing lessons. I was aware that my Uncle Rory wasn't interested in trying to understand what they meant to me after all, and felt strangely rejected. What I did understand was that I was to make my own way in this matter, and that it was my father who seemed to be quietly pleased for me. He had a kind of cautious pride in the knowledge that I was to do something that no one in the family had done before.

'Take no notice of your uncle,' he told me as we walked home together. I was pushing my bike, enjoying the sound of the wheels whirring. 'I'll tell you something, Cecilia. When you stopped singing he could have cried, big man though he is. He's blamed the convent school for that, year after year. He won't forgive them. So, I don't think he'll ever trust the nuns again.'

'They're all right Daddy,' I said. 'The new nun is beautiful.'

'Good.' He smiled down at me. 'I don't mind what you do, Cessy. You know that. Be happy while you can, that's the thing.'

'Aren't you happy, Daddy?'

'Oh, I am, right enough. I am.' He took the bike from me and started to ride it, 'You're a lovely girl,' he called out, leaving me to chase after him.

By the time I arrived home he had told them all, and they sang out loud as I came in through the door. My mother in her full heavy voice shared a popular song routine with Geraldine, laughing and breathless as the words went wrong and as they ducked the top notes. I could have helped them out but I didn't. I was amused and uneasy with the plainness of their voices, and ashamed of myself for that, yet I was too nervous to join in and that shamed me too. I pretended I didn't know the words. And I pretended to enjoy their song and rewarded it with applause as they bowed, hot-faced, in the middle of the kitchen.

'Will Cecilia be a great singer one day?' Terence wanted to know. 'And be rich and famous?'

'She can dream!' my mother laughed.

'It's as well she can.' My father had sunk into his deep chair by the fire, and had his back to the cavortings. 'If we didn't dream we'd be animals.'

'But animals do dream,' said Terence. 'I've seen them. They twitch and smile, that's with dreaming.'

'Indigestion,' said my father.

I squatted down on the hearthrug, close to him. 'I don't know,' I said. 'I think they have ripe old memories that they must slip into at times. That must be what dreaming is.'

'Oh, I think that's dangerous talk.' My mother, out of breath still, flopped into the chair opposite my father.

'Why, Mam?'

'Because if they're dreaming they have souls, that's why. That's what I'd say, Cecilia.'

'But they do have souls!' protested Terence. 'Only there's no Original Sin in them.'

My father shushed him through his teeth. 'If you don't understand things, don't talk about them,' he warned. 'Then you can't be in danger of saying a sin.'

'Anyway,' said my mother. 'Better not to have those sort of dreams, Cecilia.'

'I haven't. It was Terence who said it.'

'Why shouldn't she dream of being a great singer, Mam?'

I laughed at his earnestness, the way he tilted back his head a little when he was so serious, but my mother was pensive after her gaiety. She leaned back in her chair, her hands vee-ed to her chin and her mouth set in an odd line of sadness. 'Because dreams make us grieve, Terence. They're out of reach, those sort of dreams, to people like us. Maybe it's better to live a life without dreams at all than to be forever pining and regretting.'

The turf sods were damp and made our air bitter with acrid taste. I had learned to breathe from the top of my lungs so its spongy atoms wouldn't make me cough. So my breath came shallow and light, and my eyes prickled with the sharp juices. We were in a mist as my father's looming shape leaned to the hearth to ease back the sputtering sods and to prise one of Geraldine's logs under it; coaxing generous light from the lick of flame that tongued it.

'If we don't have our dreams to escape into,' he said in his light, quiet voice, 'then there's no chance of tomorrow, Nancy. Think of that. Today would last for ever. There'd be only yesterdays to think about. God help us with our yesterdays.'

My mother tutted. 'We could waste our life in dreaming.'

'We'd waste it if we didn't.'

That night in our bed Geraldine fingered my hair and crooned to me. The thoughts in my head were spinning out like sparks from a log, flaring in darkness. 'Geraldine,' I whispered. 'I do want to be a great singer one day. I do.'

She laughed, contented in her drowsiness. But my mind was set now on what I must do. Not a second of my singing lessons was to be wasted. All my waking moments would take their energy from them. And I would sanctify them with daily Mass, I thought, turning my head on the pillow so I could see the white blazing disc of the moon. Every day's renewed promise would blaze for me like the offered Host.

Chapter Sixteen

But the dawn was drenched in drizzle. My mother and Geraldine and I struggled against the rain, an early sea wind fizzing the sharp sand against our cheeks; and the sunrise was a pale yellow fuzz like the stain of nicotined hairs on my aunt's upper lip. Rain drummed on the roof as we knelt in front of the Virgin's statue after Mass. My mother lent me some pennies to light a candle, and I wondered how my prayers could ever find their way up with its flame, through all that drowning air. I went straight to school after church and was hungry all morning because I had fasted for Communion. My stomach was empty, like the gape of air in a poorly-kneaded loaf, yet I didn't give myself time to go to the refectory for lunch. I wanted to be at my lesson early, and I would offer up my hunger for the starving child in the photograph. All the same, I bit off a rind of my cheese sandwich as I was running down towards the music rooms, and swallowed a lump of it whole. I could feel it lodged in my chest all afternoon. When I pushed open the door to Mother Agnes' music cell she had her back to me. It was gloomy with the natural light of a sunless day coming through the high small window.

'I'm here, Mother,' I began.

The figure turned and I saw my mistake, because it was Mother Mary Rose who was crouched over the piano, her claw fingers hooking out of her black fingerless mittens, her white face pocketed with skeleton shadows, her angry eyes searching without sight.

'Who is it,' she asked, peering, groping out her fingers towards me. 'Do you want your lesson?'

So she had slipped up like a small cat retracing its routes, away from the chaos of her retirement and back to the habit of her music. Mother Agnes had followed me into the music room and switched on the light. When she saw the old nun hunched there she ran to her and knelt on the floor to put her arms round her.

'Dear God, what's this?' she said. 'Up and dressed and out of your cell, Mother? What are you thinking of?'

'Somebody's got to do the music,' Mother Rose said in her new hollow voice. 'I can't just let it go, just like that. It needs seeing to.'

'I'm seeing to it. The choir's fine, it's all fine. You mustn't worry about it now.'

'It won't be the same,' the old nun wailed. Her eyes seeped. 'It's my job, so it is.'

I turned to go away from the horror of it, but Mother Agnes put out her hand to me. 'You'll have to help me back with her,' she told me. 'How she got up here God only knows. She can't walk on her own.'

Mother Rose held up her fists in triumph. 'On my hands and knees like a baby I did it,' she crowed. 'Up the stairs, and down the corridors. Crawl, crawl, crawl.'

'And did nobody see you?'

I saw a dog once, slinking along in the shadows of our lane, his head hanging and his eyes glazed. And when my brother Michael had gone to kick it I had pulled him back by the raw hem of his jumper. 'Why kick a dog?' I had said. 'It's not a dog when it's like that,' he had said. 'Dogs shouldn't behave like that.' Further down the lane the children from another house had chucked stones at it and we had all run after it then, jeering as it slunk and cowered, as it rolled its yellow eyes and lowered its head again and limped away into the shadows.

I stood on one side of her and Mother Agnes the other, and together we lifted her from the piano stool. She had a sickly sweet smell about her. I could have carried her, I think. There was no substance to her, beneath the folds of her habit she was as flimsy as a bird. She trotted her feet along nimbly as we half-lifted her along the corridor. Her mouth dribbled and her eyes did too. We reached the refectory and had to go through it and along the corridors to the study, stared at by girls gone silent. At the end of the study was the door that led to the nuns' quarters. My throat was dry as we approached it. When we came to the door Mother Agnes steered us to a chair and propped Mother Rose onto it. The old nun was gasping. Her grey hands fluttered on her lap, trembling round for the comfort of her beads. I lifted them up to her.

'Cecilia will stay with you,' Mother Agnes told her. 'I'll fetch Mother Ignatia to take you to your cell.'

'Cecilia? Cecilia who?'

'Cecilia Deardon, Mother,' I said. Yes, I am worthy.

'I remember the day you were born, Cecilia Deardon.' Her mouth pursed round in a grim line, and her eyes searched round for sight of me. 'I know you.'

I said nothing. I sat listening to the rasp of her breath as she whispered her prayers.

'Pulled you out,' she said suddenly. 'I'm not a midwife, I told them. There's sin here.' Her hands relaxed on her lap. Slowly her fingers edged along till they came to the last bead. 'Glory be to the Father, and to the Son,' she crooned. 'And to the Holy Ghost. Amen. Call her Cecilia, I told them.'

And I felt then as though the old dog had turned round and cursed me. I sat with my head bowed until Mother Agnes came to take her, and returned again from her cell; but it was too late for my singing lesson, and anyway, hadn't all the joy of it turned sour for me, like the thick curdle of bile in my throat.

I wanted to speak to my mother about it when I came home from school that night, but I watched her instead. She and my father were forking up potatoes from the back field. I saw how her body had a soft plumpness these days. Her cheeks were defined because of the hollows of the flesh sunk below them, and her eyes had a kind of misty blue. Her hair was full grey, but she still wore it loose around her shoulders. She would try to pin it back, but always by the end of the day it would have slipped out free.

The soil they were forking was heavy with water, and she worked with a flowing and rhythmic intensity that was quite different from the vigorous jerks and plunges that my father used. He was all angles, like a tree, stiff-trunked and branch-bent. But she was my river, pouring over stones, flowing, flowing, and her hair loosening and drifting, and her misty eyes laughing.

I took my school books out of my bicycle basket and went upstairs with them. I sat where I always did, on the deep sill of the window that looked across our field and to where the lane wound behind and, beyond that, to the green-brown tide. I could still watch my mother from there. I tipped the books onto the sill beside me and turned them over and over. There was no pleasure in them for me that day. I had to write a history essay on the Gaelic tribal wars against the Tudors. I recited the facts aloud. In 1541 King Henry VIII of England proclaimed himself King of Ireland. Among the chiefs to resist him was Shane O'Neill, and his aggressor was another Irish chieftain, O'Donnell, for it has always been and will always be that the Irish are at war with the Irish, and that was something my Uncle Rory had told me many times, that it is our curse, he says. And here was the bit that made my skin grow cold for the picture it painted of men beaten down and dying for their beliefs, the bit that told of the vanquished men creeping out of the corners of the woods and glens on their hands and knees, looking like 'anatomies of death', for that was written in Spenser's poetry, and he told how they spoke like ghosts 'crying out of their graves'. I closed my eyes to see it, allowing the sounds of outside to tumble away so I could grieve for them, for the race of men cut down like corn in the summer fields. And inside their hovels their women would be waiting for the men who would never be coming home to them, and some of them would have their men's life in them and would give birth in their grieving, lustily bellowing as their babies were wrenched into air like potatoes plucked out of the earth.

I opened my eyes in a sweat of terror. My mother had stopped digging and was leaning against the far wall talking to someone. I could hear her laughter, and recognised the laughing replies of Father Carolyn. She pointed up to my window and he stepped back where he could see me and waved up. I watched him coming up the lane to the house. I snapped shut my book of Irish history and hid it inside my bag, ashamed and frightened of the emotions it had provoked in me. He called my name as he came into the yard and I ran downstairs to him.

When I was a child I used to kiss him.

'Cecilia,' he said. 'They've been telling me at the convent school what a clever girl you are.'

'Have they?'

'Oh, they have. And they're expecting great things of you. Great things. And so am I.'

I wanted to know what kind of great things, but daren't ask. He settled himself loosely into one of the straight chairs, with his fingers spread out on the tabletop, and yawned. 'Well now, I've been saying to Nancy that I can give you extra help in the Latin, if you need it.'

'Thank you, Father.' I loved Latin. I liked the sense and order of its constructions, and its clean sounds, and the chimes it made with the English language. I loved Irish more, though I knew it best for songs and poetry.

'Mind you,' he leaned forward to me and whispered. 'She's been telling me that you have it in your mind to be a singer now, and not a scholar.'

'Oh no,' my voice fluttered with my effort to laugh. 'One of the nuns took it into her head to give me singing lessons, that's all.'

'Free?'

'Yes, Father.'

He cocked his head to one side, smiling at me. 'Then don't say that's all, Cecilia. The good nun must think very highly of you to give you this for nothing. They like this stuff.' He rubbed his thumb against his first two fingers. 'For the

Church. Thank God for your gift and for your opportunity of improving on it, I'd say. And Cecilia, nothing, nothing in the world would give me greater pleasure than to hear you singing one day at Mass. Will you do that for me? Ask your music nun to teach you something specially for me, for God, of course, in God's name, to be sung at the Mass on St. Cecilia's day. How about that now?'

'Father,' I said. 'Why was I born at the convent?'

He was still smiling at me, his silly lipless smile, shuffling himself up from the table and coming across the room to me with his arms stretched out to hug me. And his smile stuck in his perplexed face. He was like a wooden doll with a painted smile. My mother opened the door and leaned against the jamb while she kicked off her wellingtons. Mud spattered onto the floor tiles. She stooped to pick up the bin-lid where the potatoes chunked together, and rose up again, her tired smile turning quiet as she looked from one to the other of us.

'It was Mother Rose who told me,' I said to Father.

'Oh God, no,' my mother said then, deep in her throat. 'Oh God, no.'

Father Carolyn turned away from me and took the lid from her. He carried it across to the table and laid it down as gently as if it had been full of eggs. My mother's neck-strings were taut. She clutched at her hair to tidy it with her soiled hands.

'Why was I?'

'I wanted you to be born there,' Father Carolyn said. He kept his head lowered, as if he was counting the potatoes and deeply interested in the shapes of them. 'I arranged it for you.'

He turned to my mother and put his hand over hers to comfort and reassure her. Her mouth twisted in the effort of a smile.

As he went out he passed my father on the threshold and shook hands with him as if he'd just come from Mass. There was something old about him then, and something that seemed surprised by it, and sad.

But my blood was boiling cold in my veins. I couldn't look at my mother. I ran upstairs and back to my window-seat and sat with my back to the ravaged field and the sea in its green spasms. I took out my catechism and read it out loud, too fast to listen to the words, making no distinction between the questions of dogma and the answers or pausing at full stops or commas, but spitting out the words like an endless roll of bullets from a rifle, gabbling out a vocabulary of nonsense till Geraldine came up to me teasing and laughing and took my book from my hands and pulled me downstairs to eat with the family.

Chapter Seventeen

When we passed the chapel on the way to the art block we would sometimes hear the nuns singing. Their voices made a kind of sweet wailing, such a woman-child sound that it would hurt you if you let it, hearing it in the bell of your memory years on. But now in that bird sweetness was another sound, full and ripe. It made me think of the deep moan of the wind when the tide's coming in; it made the other voices banshee wails.

I would not have gone for my singing lessons after all had Mother Agnes not met me in the corridor and walked down with me herself. We sat in the quiet cell while she riffled through sheets of music. The light of the afternoon was lemony on her skin. She glanced up at me, aware that I was watching her, and I felt myself blush.

'You're a handsome girl,' she said. 'Do you have any sisters?'

'One,' I said, surprised. 'Her name's Geraldine.'

'And is she as pretty as you?'

I bit my lip. 'She's different,' I said.

Mother Agnes watched me gravely, making me feel uncomfortable, and out of my foolish embarrassment I said, 'Do you?'

'Oh yes,' she smiled. 'We're all sisters here. Now, here's the music I want for you. You might know it already. I'm going to sing it through for you, and then we're going to learn it step by step.'

I couldn't watch her while she sang. I was timid to be sitting in a cell with a nun who was singing just for me, and in such an unashamed, boastful way. I hoped she'd get it over with before any of the others passed. Her voice breasted the cell and overflowed it. Her soft notes trembled the hairs on my neck, making my sweat cold, and her full notes swam in my head and my ears and my throat, seeming to be not sound but inhabited air. Sometimes my mother would pretend to be an opera singer and let her voice out loud, but it was full of sharp edges and breath and had no real music in it. But this was a voice of passion, too rich for the slight figure bent over the piano keys. The song was 'Ave Maria'. It didn't sound like a holy song to me. It sounded like a love song. I tried to close my ears to it, wishing it away.

When she finished singing the air in the cell hummed with the memory of her voice, like a charge of electricity. She kept her head bowed and her hands just raised above the keys, as still and lost as if she was in a trance, and I was locked out of this. Then she seemed to let her whole body sag. She was tired. She turned round to smile at me.

'Well?'

'It's lovely, Mother. But it's too hard for me.'

She shook her head. 'It's a long time since I've sung like that. You must have inspired me, Cecilia. Now, I'm going to take you through the first phrases of it, that's all. Just to try out your voice.'

She was business-like again now. She tapped out the melody in single notes on the piano and listened impassively while my thin voice piped through them. It hurt my head and my throat. Then she put me through some exercises, making me put both my hands flat above my waist while I breathed slowly in and out, telling me to fill up my lungs to the very bottom so I could feel my hands being pushed out, and then to ease out my breath and let my hands sink into the hollow. I did this again and again till I felt I would faint. She made me sing scales to ooh and ah and mee and mo and I was just beginning to forget my nervousness at hearing the echo of my voice when she closed down the piano lid and put away her music.

'That'll do fine,' she said, as I hovered by the door. She glanced up at me. 'And did you enjoy it?'

'Thank you, Mother,' I said. 'It was hard. I don't know really whether I can manage it.'

'Next time we'll start with the scales, but I think it's nice for you to know what you're aiming at.' She burst out laughing at my stricken face. 'Don't look so frightened, Cecilia! You'll sing! One day you'll sing like me.'

I wandered back to class in a daze, dizzy with the deep breathing she'd made me do and with the high head notes I'd sung for her, and hearing in my mind, louder than any of the classroom voices, the rich full sound of her singing.

But I told them nothing of this at home. I spoke only when I had to these days, and this was because I had become suddenly so awkward with them that I had nothing left to say to them. My mother seemed to notice and yet not to; she spoke to me as she had always done, but with a kind of restraint as if I were an invalid and had to be treated gently. And she was the one I could least respond to. I was ashamed and angry and hurt with a swim of suspicions that I had no name for. It seemed to me that my father was gentler with me than he'd ever been, but I was not going to be wooed by him.

'Cecilia,' he would say. 'Come on and tell me all about these singing lessons of yours.'

I would just shrug and say, 'They're all right, Daddy,' and I would not look at him, because to talk about them would reduce them, and would bring Mother Agnes swaying down, down, to stand firm and matronly among the slow moving crowd of adults that darkly bordered the fields of my days. She was not like them.

'Cecilia,' my mother said to me one day. 'Cycle down to Mass with me this morning, would you? I don't feel like going on my own.'

I had thought of not going at all, not even on Sundays. In that way I would be able to avoid Father Carolyn for ever. I could attend Mass in spirit but not in flesh, out of a sickness in my heart which God would surely understand and forgive. Father Carolyn would worry about my immortal soul all right, and be punished by thinking that on his account I was committing mortal sin. But then, when my mother sidled up to me in this sheepish way and asked me to go to Mass with her I thought this would be better, and that I would brazen it out in church, not sitting with her but right on the front pew and staring at the priest with cold eyes that he must notice and be discomfited by. So I went, and throughout the Mass while I was staring at the priest I was aware of the eyes of the statue of the Blessed Virgin staring at me. After Mass I lit a candle to her, and was cold in my heart because my mother hadn't done the same.

'Holy Mother,' I whispered. 'Be my true mother. Holy Virgin, make me worthy...'

Her white alabaster face and china blue eyes stared down at me, and I fixed my eyes onto her familiar face; and into that image came the face of my mother, that Magdalene, sweating and laughing as she had been at the birth of Joy's baby. She was brown with the sun and wind and cracking in white spider lines round her thin mouth, and she was loose-fleshed under her chin, and hollow-cheeked, and her eyes were faded green; and bent into her was the white face of Mother Mary Rose, heaving at a fleshy fish thing, and my mother's face again, straining. I willed back then the flawless virgin face, and with it came the pale sound of nuns singing, then the luscious ripeness of Mother Agnes' voice, and inside that my mother's, with all its spread of lusty coarseness.

The candle sputtered into its wet wax. I had burned it out, and I was late for school.

After our singing lessons Mother Agnes and I took to walking round the rose garden for a few minutes, 'to let the music settle' as she called it. She had a way of walking with her arms crossed and her hands tucked into the loose folds of her sleeves, and I found myself doing the same, working my fingers inside the ribs of my cardigan, jerking them free again when our walk was finished.

'Tell me about all your boyfriends,' she said to me on one of these walks.

'I don't have any,' I said to her, surprised. 'I don't really like boys.'

'Oh,' she laughed. 'You will. You will, Cecilia. I'm surprised they're not fighting at the door already for you, with that marigold hair of yours. Believe me, you'll be married and with an army of little ones at your feet in no time.'

I was shocked that she should think this, and that she should be able to talk to me with such intimacy. I looked at her sideways, daring.

'Did you ever want to get married?'

'Not me!' She bent down lightly to pull off a flower-head. It resisted, and she left it hanging from its bruised stem. 'I had five brothers, can you imagine! What on earth did I want with more men in my life? Besides, I was only your age when I entered.'

A bell rang inside the chapel, and that was the signal for her prayers. She began to walk away from me briskly, and I had to run to keep up with her.

'Mother, did you always want to be a nun?' I asked her.

'Oh yes, always, always,' she laughed. 'It was all I ever dreamed about.'

I watched her as she slipped through the side door of the chapel to join the other nuns, and wondered what there was left for her to dream about, now she was initiated.

Chapter Eighteen

Midwinter, and deep frost outside. A strong fire blazing, and our shadows in a dark dance across the ceiling. That was the night my mother and I came together, briefly. Terence was ill, and we were sitting up with him. He seemed to have taken a cold that wouldn't leave him, that was all, and then it seemed that the cold had gone to his chest and was maybe bronchial. But on that night in a spasm of coughing he went blue and still and I believe he almost died.

My mother and I were the only ones in the room - Geraldine was already in bed and my father was out with Uncle Rory. We had made up a bed for Terence on the settee by the fire so he'd be warm day and night. The two hard chairs were pulled up with their backs against the settee so he wouldn't roll off, and my mother and I were sitting in them, she reading a thick romance and I daydreaming that Mother Agnes had come to live with us. Terence's racked coughing and sudden quiet jolted us both. My mother pushed back the chairs and rolled him over onto his stomach; then she began pummelling his back, her mouth working in a grinning line.

'Shall I go for someone?' I asked, frightened.

'No, God help me. Don't leave me,' she panted.

So I stayed with her, scared out of my wits almost, watching her as she beat her fists along the line of his spine like a drummer intent on a rhythm, and when my father came home he hovered like a stranger in the doorway, his hands dangling and useless by his sides.

'What's up?' His voice was strangled in his throat.

'He can't get his breath,' my mother shrieked out at him. 'The boy's slipping away.'

My father crossed himself and stood with his head down and moaning in the doorway. I went to kneel by my mother. I pressed my hands over hers and as if we were kneading bread together and she a child again and learning from me we rolled and rocked into the small of his back, our teeth gritted against the ache of it. My mother grunted 'That's it, Cecilia, that's it, that's it,' with her voice thick in her throat. It was as if we had the rhythm of the languorous surge of the tide and knew no other movement but this. Her hands under mine lost their separateness and became my own flesh and bone, her gasping breath torn from me, and all sense of time and essence was dissolved. And then Terence started to splutter and she lifted away her hands like Mother Agnes lifting her hands away from the piano keys, and mine came up away from hers, weightless. She turned him over and he lay with his head back and his eyes open and wondering and scared, a dribble of slime bubbling from his mouth, and she laughed and crooned and nestled him against her with her eyes closed and I drew away to let my father in.

Next morning my Aunt Bridget was knocking on the window at dawn, waking us all up as we dozed by the dying fire in front of Terence's couch.

'I heard the banshees last night,' she told us. The morning air was cold on her.

'You heard no banshees,' my mother told her.

'Oh, I did so. There's tragedy, I told Rory, but he wouldn't let me come. Is it the boy?'

'Shush!' my mother said. 'He's sleeping sound, and don't you go scaring him with your talk of banshees when he wakes up.'

'I get prickles all over my flesh when I hear them,' Aunt Bridget went on. 'Such a cold queer wailing in the night. I said to Rory, it's the boy.' She pulled back Terence's blanket and peered at him. 'Look at the darling, fast asleep. I tell you Nancy, while you've all been dozing and snoring here I've been on my knees on the cold floor, praying for his life and listening to that wailing in the night.'

Afterwards I wondered how I could have touched my mother's hands like that, in such a familiar way. I watched her as she worked next day in the kitchen making a broth for Terence; how briskly she chopped and pared the carrots and skinned the onions with the blade of her knife.

'Do something!' she said to me sharply.

'I am,' I said. 'I'm doing my homework.'

'No, you're not. You're irritating me.'

She dropped the knife suddenly and let it rock on its round wooden handle. With her hands red and slimed with onion juice she scooped up the chopped vegetables and tipped them into the pot.

'We used to be such friends, Cecilia,' she said, not looking at me.

I said nothing.

'Then tell me. You can tell me. Ask me, for goodness' sake, if there's something you want to know.'

'There's nothing I want to know,' I said stubbornly.

Later she shouted at my father because he slopped the soup she'd ladled out for Terence.

'You're a goat, d'you know that?' she yelled with the raw edge of her voice. 'A clumsy goat.'

He took her hands in his strong ones and held them down at her sides. 'What's the matter with you these days?'

'She is,' she said hoarsely.

I went out of the house. Geraldine was gardening. She was tackling brambles with a spade, and when the roots of one refused to give she dropped her spade and bent down to grasp the spiked stem with her hands. She grunted as she pulled, her head back and her teeth bared, and still it wouldn't give way. I circled her waist with my arms and steadied myself up to her and we both heaved, and when it snapped we tumbled backwards together, Geraldine screaming with laughter. My father came running out of the house to see what was happening. He tried to haul her to her feet, pretending that she was too heavy for him and staggering and panting so she dropped back again and again, grown weak with laughing.

'You'll have the girl sick!' my mother shouted from the house.

He looked over Geraldine's shoulder to me as I sat with my knees hunched up. 'Now you be nice to your mother,' he told me. 'She's unhappy.'

'Are you my father?' I asked him.

Geraldine screamed again.

'What was that?'

'You heard. You heard.'

His face closed up. Geraldine began to sag away from him. It pleased and frightened me to hurt him.

'Why would a baby be born in a convent if it had a father?'

He turned away then, letting Geraldine's fat fingers slip through his till she lay on her back. She tilted back her head to look at me, tears of hysteria dribbling back into her hairline, her face blotched and swollen, her body heaving with laugh sobs.

'Shut up!' he shouted at her. 'Stop your idiot hollering!'

I thought he was going to kick her, the brute way he moved over to her, but he jerked up the spade and drove it time and again into the earth, time and again, spattering the soil like loose rain as he slung it to one side, and long after the bramble root was exposed to its last fine hairs he still dug, while Geraldine gave out her shudderings and I sat, quiet and apart, watching him.

Mother Agnes took me into the rose garden after my next lesson. She had been very light-hearted that day, laughing when I made mistakes and clapping when she was pleased with me.

'Come on outside now,' she said. 'I've a present for you, you've done so well.'

She broke off a rose head and gave it to me. 'There. I've been watching that one opening out day after day, a mid-winter rose, just waiting for it to open right out, and today I thought, it's perfect! Today I can give it to Cecilia, if she's a good girl!' she laughed.

'Thank you, Mother.' I took it from her.

'Don't thank me. I didn't cause the rose to grow, and I didn't give you that voice of yours. I'm so pleased with you, Cecilia. Every week your voice has been growing stronger and more certain, like that small rose. Can't you feel it happening?'

I twisted the rose round in my fingers. She moved lightly from one bush to another, letting her long skirt sway.

'I love it here, d'you know!' She looked up at me, her eyes shining. 'Peace and joy and beauty, all in one little garden. Every minute of every day I thank God that He brought me to live here.'

'You always seem to be happy.'

'I think I am. Yes. I've a great deal to be happy about, after all.'

'Mother, what's it like for you all, living here together?' I asked her. 'Don't you all get fed up with each other?'

'What a question! We're sisters. We love one another.'

'Well, I wouldn't like it at all. I couldn't bear to have people round me all the time. It's like that in our house. I can't get away from anyone, and we're always rowing these days.' I let the rose stem roll in my palm. 'I sometimes think we hate one another.'

'Oh Cecilia, don't you ever say that.' She pressed her hands over mine and took back the rose. 'I'm going to put this under the statue of the Holy Mother for you. She'll watch over your family. Besides,' she smiled, 'you'll not be wanting to carry a rose with you to your mathematics class!'

I watched her from outside the chapel as she went in, genuflected as she crossed the aisle, and stood on her tiptoes to slip the rose into the vase under the statue of Our Lady. She came out still on her tiptoes, a little girl with her finger to her lips.

'Always remember she's your mother,' she whispered to me. 'Pray to her with your troubles. And by the way Cecilia, there's someone very special to mention in your prayers. Mother Mary Rose.'

Something surged in me. 'Is she dying?'

She nodded, fingering her beads as though to keep in touch with them was to release her own prayers.

'I can't pray for her,' I said. I matched my step to hers as I walked. 'I suppose that's a sin, isn't it?'

'You think too much about sin.' She shook her head at me, mocking my graveness. 'If you're not careful it'll take a hold of your life and rob you of your joy of it.'

'But that's not wrong, is it? I thought we were always supposed to be aware of the sin in ourselves, always. That's what the Church says.'

'Oh, She does. We are all born with original sin in us.'

'And the Church says we're 'inclined to evil from our very childhood.' Evil, Mother.' She glanced at me, as grave as I was now. 'It makes me dizzy to think about it,' I said. 'How can you tell little children that they're inclined to evil? Don't you think Catholicism is a negative religion?'

She drew in her breath and held her lips pursed like a whistler.

'And that's a sin, too, to say that about the Church. Oh Mother, the more I think about it the more worthless I am.'

'You mustn't think that now, Cecilia.'

'Mustn't! There you are, you see!'

I'd never had these thoughts before. I was lightheaded with them. They were taking me to dark places. 'I must not think I am worthless, because God has made me in his own image and likeness. So that's another sin, thinking that. I'm trapped in sin, Mother. I can't get out of it.'

She had stepped away from me and stood with her hands ballooned out in an orb of thin fingers, tips touching, and as she spoke the orb spilt and came together again as she tapped her finger ends together with each new thought. 'God is in you too, remember. Always remember, Cecilia. He is good. He is Love. In His love lies happiness.' The orb became invisible as she spread out her hands. 'Surrender yourself to that happiness.'

I turned away from her. 'I don't understand your happiness.'

'You do too,' she said softly. 'You do too. It's so simple. If I do something because it's good to do it, then it makes me happy. Like teaching you to sing, Cecilia. You can see that, surely?'

'But what if you do something because not to do it is evil?'

'All right. It would strengthen me, yes, and I could offer it up to God, yes I could, as I offer up all my thoughts and words and deeds. But it wouldn't of itself create happiness…'

'So it's not as good?'

'How can it be?' She came round to me, smiling. 'Cecilia, how can it be?'

I looked away from her again. The sun blazed through the trees like amber window-lights, half blinding me. I wouldn't close my eyes against it. I let it smart and sting till the sharp outlines of the branches blurred to a watery smudge. 'Then I think you're wrong Mother. I think you're wrong to expect happiness out of the things you do for God. Pain is surely a greater offering. The way that doesn't bring you happiness. That's the greater way.'

Our walk was finished. Before she left me she inclined her head slightly, without smiling to me. 'I think you should talk to your priest,' she said. 'I should like you to do that for me, at least.'

And so natural to me was my sense of guilt that I knew I had committed a great sin by saying all that to her. I had hurt her, but there was more to it than that. She was a nun, and older than I, and my teacher. It was wrong for me to say all that to her, in that way, in such haughtiness. But I was right. And yet I was wrong to allow myself to think even in my head that I was right.

There were confessions to be held in our chapel the next afternoon, and in class I asked permission to go to them, which was in itself an act of humility as our regular confessions for upper school were held on a different day. Mother Philomena gave me permission, but told me to see her after school for extra practice with geometry. I didn't mind. That would be a punishment, because it meant I would have to cycle home in the dark. I went into chapel with the younger children and knelt down on the floor while I was waiting for my turn, not even granting myself the comfort of the wooden kneeler under my calves. I whispered my sin to Father Carolyn in the dark womb-cell. His listening breath rasped through the grille.

'Beware of the sin of intellectual pride,' he told me. 'Ask your Holy Mother the Church to guide you.'

'Yes, Father,' I said. 'Forgive me, Father.'

So the burden of guilt was lifted from me, and I stilled my dancing mind. I crouched down in front of the statue of Our Lady to say my penance, listening to Father Carolyn's whooshing sneezes as he made his way back to the vestry. The whispering and coughing of small children distracted me, and I turned my head from time to time to make out the bent figures at the back of the chapel. I knew Mother Agnes would be there soon, and I wanted her to see me in my humility. I saw her come in with her class and shush them into their benches to wait for Father Carolyn to return to the confessional, and then I felt her quiet presence behind me as she waited to light a candle. I moved to make room for her, and she knelt down briefly next to me to watch the candle tongue its small flame steady and to send up her prayer with it. I was aware only of her. I kept my head down, my face tucked into my hands for intensity. Dimly I was aware of her movement back down the aisle, and then I knew that she had left the chapel. My penance prayers were not completed. I made the sign of the cross and followed her out.

The door to her music room at the end of the corridor was ajar. I hovered outside, waiting as she leafed through her sheets of music for her to notice me. She did, and pretended not to. I could see that. When she was ready she looked up to me, her face glowing.

'Well now, Cecilia?'

I went in and perched myself on the edge of the spare stool. Class bells were ringing for the change of lesson. I was out of place here now.

'Mother,' I said. 'There's something else I don't under-stand.'

She clapped her hands. 'Dear girl, there's plenty of things I don't understand, right enough. And never will do, poor simple creature that I am. I can accept that in all humility.'

I lowered my eyes. 'But it worries me.'

Feet and chairs scraped in the upstairs room. I should be there.

'Sure everything worries you, Cecilia. It always will do, too. Now go on. Try me.'

'Well,' I breathed in deeply, as a singer should, letting the air spread down to the bottom of my lungs. I was cold with nervousness. 'It's about martyrdom and virginity, Mother. I don't see how they can be entirely good.'

'Not entirely good!' She stopped rustling through the piles of sheet music and sat down, leaning forwards slightly, her hands clasped in her lap. 'What's this you're saying?'

'I was just thinking about what you said yesterday. About creating happiness for people in what you do.'

She nodded. 'So?'

'Well, if that's the case, then sacrifice has to be wrong.'

'Does it!'

'It does, because it's negative. Doing without something that has been given to make you happy must be negative.'

Don't smile, Mother. Understand me. Take these infant steps with me.

'That is what I understand from what you told me yesterday.'

She spread out her hands in a useless gesture.

'But also, Mother,' I said slowly. 'I think sacrifice must be easy.'

'Oh! Easy, is it?'

'I think so. I think some people actually enjoy making sacrifices, and therefore it's wrong.'

'Wrong to enjoy?'

'That's what I'm saying, Mother.'

'That's what you're saying.' She nodded just as if she was agreeing with me. 'Believe me, for some of us sacrifice is very hard. Consider the sacrifice the members of this community make every living day. We have given the whole of ourselves to God, for the rest of our lives. Is that easy? Is it?'

'Yes! It is for you! It makes you happy.'

Yesterday you were a girl in the garden, dancing. Deny it, Mother. Deny your dreams.

'And you feel you could sacrifice things so easily?' Her voice was cold.

'I have only one thing to sacrifice. I could sacrifice my singing,' I said.

She relaxed. 'Your singing?'

'I could. What if I said I would never sing again?'

'But that would be wrong. Very wrong.' She stood up abruptly. Her girls were filing past the door, their confessions done. 'Your voice is a gift. To deny yourself the use of that gift would be wrong.'

'It would not, Mother! I enjoy singing. I love it more than anything in the world. To offer my singing up to God is easy. But to give it up now would give me the greatest pain I could imagine. Think of it, Mother. Think what a great, great thing it would be to be able to offer up that pain.'

Chapter Nineteen

I had a deep need these days to be with my Uncle Rory, and as soon as I was free of my housecleaning jobs on Saturday I cycled off to see him. Many things were tangled, and I felt he was the one who would be able to clear my way through. He had been to the house the evening before with my Aunt Bridget but there had been no talking to them that night. I had gone into the kitchen from the yard when they were all four of them talking together in a kind of weary arguing way that I seemed then to have heard many times before, but they went silent when I came in. I knew then that the talk had been about me. I stood uncertain in the doorway. My aunt pressed together her hands almost as if she was about to pray, and I thought how old she looked just now. I had slipped past them then like a ghost in the house, guilty of something perhaps, and appearing not to see them just as they appeared not to have seen me. I had gone upstairs to my books and had heard the sharp edge of their voices, but when I was called down with Geraldine and Terence for evening prayers my uncle and aunt had gone.

So next day I set off to see him. The door was closed but I found him sitting at the bottom of the garden, leaning back against the remains of his old den. I thought at first that he was reading, and then that he was asleep. I propped my bike against the washing-pole and sat down next to him, ready to wait, and saw the empty bottle at his side. His jaw sagged down as I watched him, and his breath snagged in his throat. As I leaned forward I could smell the stale sweetish whiskey smell about him. He had white streaks now in the yellow tangle of his hair. His chin was an ash-gold fuzz. If I'd been younger I'd have taken a long strand of grass to tickle him with, and would have pretended it was a spider.

'Come on now, Uncle Rory,' I whispered. 'This is no place to be sleeping.' I was a little afraid. His mouth pouched open in a rasping snore. I must have sat nearly an hour watching him, not knowing what to do. But soon the chill of January crept over me, and I knew I couldn't stay there any longer. I shook his arm but he snored again loud and sharp and tilted over onto his side. I moved the bottle so he wouldn't fall on it, and as I went over to collect my bike I realised that my aunt was in after all. She was sitting at an upstairs window, staring out like a white wax doll. She must have heard me trying the door earlier, and must have watched me sitting in the cold with him all this time.

'Aunt Bridget!' I shouted. I ran to try the door again. 'Let me in!'

There was no answer. She had bolted the door on the inside. I hammered on it again and stepped back to wave up to her. She had gone from the window. I waited by the door, and heard only the silence of an empty house.

'Aunt Bridget! Are you ill?' I shouted. 'Aunt Bridget, please!' There was no answering, and I pictured her white and afraid of something, hunched up on the edge of their bed perhaps where she could watch over the untimely sleeping of her drunken husband. Later when I was gone she would maybe creep out and scoop him up somehow and drag his heavy, stupid body into the warm.

So I wheeled my bike away and cycled on and past the turning to my own house and down to the village, unwilling still to go back home. There was a commotion going on near the church, sharp cries like the shindig gulls make when they've spied fishing boats. It was coming from the pond, and when I cycled round to it I saw that it was surrounded by a dozen or so older girls from the parish. I recognised them all, though I didn't know them all by name. They were in a great excitement over something. Some lived in at the hospital, and some at the Big House belonging to the Caravelli's; kitchen girls and the like. A girl was standing in the very middle of the pond, half-drenched to the skin, and screeching at them all in a language I didn't understand. They in their own language were shrieking back at her, and at first I thought it was a game they were playing; but there was no laughter in it. I recognised the girl, too, from church, because she was dark and very striking and it was said that she had recently come to the Big House and was Italian, like the owners. Her long blue-black hair gleamed in strands like the feathers of magpie wings. And she stood in her fine Italian clothes in the middle of the muddy pond where animals come to drink, holding up a velvet purse-bag to keep it dry, and her mouth was a black screeching O. The girls surrounding the pond linked arms and circled slowly round it, taunting her with their jeers and kicking out at her as she tried to scramble out of the water. She with her free hand scooped up water and swished it round at them. In the distance a couple of village boys leaned against a shop wall and laughed.

I had to stand on tiptoe to peer through the jostling circle, and all of a sudden I realised that Geraldine was there among the hospital girls, arms linked, shouting along happily and excitedly with the others. I left my bike against the paper shop doorway and ran to her.

'What's happening?' I asked.

Mary Keagan, one of the girls linking with Geraldine, stopped shouting for a moment to lean back and put her mouth to my ear. 'That's the Italian whore! Didn't she go and sleep with Eileen's young husband last night, brazen as you like in the old sheds, and Eileen at home with sore tonsils!'

The Italian girl tried to stagger out again, and the village girls like baying dogs thrust out their chins at her. I yanked Geraldine's arm free of Mary's.

'Come on. Home,' I told her.

'Ah!' she pleaded. She tried to hitch her arms back into Mary's and Maura's again. I pulled her away.

'Where's your bike?' I demanded.

She jerked her head towards the grocery shop, her attention still on the fun. She raised her fist and shouted at the Italian girl, her eyes bright, loving it all. I pulled her over to her bike and helped her to tuck her skirt back into her corduroys.

'Now you're to stay out of this, d'you hear me, Geraldine!' I scolded her. We wheeled our bikes quickly down the street and mounted them at the end. 'There'll be a fight later on I've no doubt, when Patrick Logan gets home. The girls will make the boys fight him in the street. You don't want to be mixed up in that now, do you?'

She nodded, sullen.

'You do not,' I assured her.

The roar from the girls made us turn round. The beautiful Italian girl had managed to crawl out of the pond somehow and was running barefoot to the Big House, her shoes in one hand, her velvet bag in the other, her wet hair clinging to her like strands of seaweed. It seemed to me that the boy Angelo had come down to the gates and that he took her hands to comfort her, but I couldn't be quite sure of that.

'That girl has done a bad thing,' I told Geraldine as she panted up the hill beside me. 'But it has nothing to do with you.'

All the same she flung down her bike in the yard and ran in front of me into the house bright still with excitement, and my mother had to calm her down by sitting her in a chair and rocking her gently with her arms round Geraldine's shoulders. Throughout my life I had watched her do this with Geraldine. And I sat down through the meal and all evening, and never took my eyes off my mother.

When we knelt for our prayers at the end of the day my father led the rosary as always and then my mother said the special prayers. She thanked God especially for making Terence well again. He crept over on his knees still, grown boy that he was, and wriggled through till he was between her and my father, so like the two of them that he seemed a mockery of them both, with his young pale skin and his greeny eyes. I could tell by his fine black hair that he would go bald early, like my father.

'And thank you God for the good job you've provided for Geraldine, and for the wonderful opportunity you have given Cecilia, and bless Michael and his children and help him to see your truth again. Amen.'

'Amen,' my father said, with a tremor to his voice. He leaned over and kissed her hair.

'You should have prayed for my Uncle Rory,' I told her. 'Because he's a drunkard, did you know?' She looked at me sharply. 'And for my Aunt Bridget,' I added, 'because he's turning her old and silly. She won't open the door of her house to her own family.'

My mother tutted, chocking together the rosary beads in her palm. 'Never you mind about that,' she told me, her voice suddenly rough in her throat.

'And for the Italian girl who slept with Paddy Logan last night,' I dared.

'Don't you say such things to me.' She was deeply shocked, and I was pleased then, with a warm guilt inside me, knowing that I had hurt her.

And during those prayers I had made up my mind. I kept my thoughts in my head till my next singing lesson. I was quite calm about it. As I went to the music room I could hear Mother Agnes playing soft and lovely chords on the piano. I walked there slowly and stood by the doorway, knowing how her face would look, how she would be listening to what she was playing with her head tilted back and her eyes closed, the way my mother sits at church listening to Father Carolyn giving his sermon.

'I know you're there, Cecilia,' she smiled, without stopping her playing, and with her eyes still closed. 'Come on in. I've found a lovely new motet for you. It's just right for your voice, I know it is. Listen now.' And she started to sing before I was ready for the passion of her voice. I stood with my head back against the doorjamb, wanting to run away from her. I broke into her singing.

'I've come to tell you that I'm not going to sing today.'

She brought her hands calmly together. 'Is that so?'

'Or any day. I'm not going to sing again. That's what I wanted to tell you.'

'I see,' she said quietly. I drew away and she raised her hands again and swung herself round to me on her piano stool. 'Dear child!' she blurted out. Then she regained her composure. 'Very well. If that's what you want. You must do it. It's your decision.'

'Yes, Mother. Thank you.'

'Oh but... it hurts me.' She stood up to come towards me and I backed away. 'You know that, don't you?'

My throat hurt. 'Isn't that good?' I asked her, defiant.

'Good? It's not good, no it is not. That you can cause someone else's unhappiness? Where's the good in that, tell me?'

I didn't want to talk about it. I wanted her to release me, easy. 'You can offer it up, Mother.'

'Thank you,' she said sharply. 'You'll let me choose what I offer up. And do you enjoy hurting people then?' She jolted her head back, willing me to look at her. 'Yes, you have it in you. I can see that. You deny yourself. All the time you deny yourself. And you're the one who enjoys making sacrifices. Isn't that so? Don't look away, my dear.' She grasped my hands, and I felt how hot and sticky mine were against her marble coolness. 'Don't you see, if to enjoy is wrong, as you will have it, then you're making your sacrifice for the wrong reason.'

'But you said sacrifice was good. You said so. That's what you believe.' I was shouting, with her hands still over mine. I could hear my voice echoing cold down the chapel corridor. 'Believe. Believe. Eve...' it said to me.

'You don't do it out of LOVE! Cecilia, you don't understand. Where's the love in a sacrifice like this?'

I snatched my hands away. She knew nothing about love, if this was what she thought of my sacrifice.

'YOU don't understand ME,' I shouted. 'You don't even try to. Just because it's not your way, you think it's not good enough, you think it's wrong. I can't do anything right, can I? I want to do my sacrifice my way.'

'Cecilia…'

'Forget it, forget it, Mother.'

She opened her arms out in a gesture of acceptance.

'It doesn't matter any more,' I shouted. 'Forget it. It's worthless. Leave it.'

'Come here will you. Don't go off like that now. Upset like that. Come on here. Sit down a little. There. Calm yourself.'

Shaking still, bewildered by my grief, I sank down onto her piano stool.

'There now,' she said. 'I do understand you. As I understand myself. But I fear for you, too.'

We waited in silence for a little. People were moving about upstairs; tiny mouse-scrabblings of feet. Soon the girls would be coming in for afternoon classes. The corridors would be full of their vigour. I bent down to pick up my schoolbag and my wooden handled hairbrush slipped out of the corner of it and skidded along the floor. Mother Agnes stooped down to pick it up, and stood trilling the teeth of it with her thumbnail as though it was a musical instrument, and as though she was trying to make up her mind about something. Then she moved behind me and very gently began to brush out my hair. I closed my eyes.

'You have such beautiful hair, Cecilia,' she murmured.

'Thank you.'

'Don't thank me.'

I timed my breathing to the stroking of the brush.

'*A woman's glory is her hair.* Who said that, would you think? Would it be a man or a woman?'

I leaned forward, letting the sound of her voice and the frooshing of the brush wash over me. They were like soft rainwater. It was a witch chant she was weaving, wooing me to dream, and I was lost in the spell of it.

'My father would brush out my hair for me like this when I was a little girl. Especially if I was upset. Not my mother, you know. My father. But then, I was his only daughter. He used to tell me my hair was the colour of midnight, and I, vain simple creature that I was, I believed him.'

I snapped out of my dreaming, jumped up, and snatched the brush out of her hands. 'You shouldn't touch me, should you?'

'Cecilia. I'm brushing your hair!' She was startled and bewildered. Red daubs flushed her cheeks.

'But you're enjoying it.'

'And who says I shouldn't enjoy things, for goodness' sake?' Angry now, she tried to close the door against me, but I in my strange fear and madness was stronger and wrenched it open.

'I do!' I shouted, liking the coarse echoings my voice made on the chiming tiles as I ran from her. 'I do, Mother Agnes. I do!'

Chapter Twenty

Throughout the next week I was like an artist or a cunning murderer; biding my time, preparing in my head and in my dreams the thing that I must do. Yet as the week passed and the hour for my singing lesson drew nearer my will nearly failed me. I dreamt that I was swimming in yellow seas, and that the golden-red strands of long twisting reeds wrapped themselves round me and tried to pull me down, so that I was drowning in their amber light, and that she reached down to save me, laughing. And in my dream our fingers touched, and I let mine slip away. Instead of going to my meal on the day of the lesson I hid in the cloakrooms, then when all was quiet I crept to the needlework room and found it open. I stole a pair of scissors and ran back to the cloakroom. I took out my brush and fluffed out the bright warm cloud of my hair, again and again. Then I swept it back and grasped the thick bunch of it and hacked it through. The scissors snagged and caught;

they weren't sharp enough. They jagged and tore and brought smarting tears to my eyes. I flung a handful of hair into the lavatory bowl and watched it redden and darken as the swirling water flushed it down. I chopped through again and again, just hacking in my blindness. Loose strands flickered over my face like feathers.

I slammed shut the lavatory door. As I passed the mirrors I closed my eyes.

'Cessy! Is it you?' There was Noni, sent down from the refectory in search of me. 'Your hair! What have you done to your hair?'

'Cut it,' I muttered. I tried to push past her, but she grabbed my shoulders and held me at arms' length.

'Cessy! Just now? It looks terrible. It's a fright, don't you know that?'

'I don't mind.'

'You're nearly bald on one side. You've cut it right to the scalp.'

'I know. I know.'

'It isn't even straight. Let me have the scissors. Let me see if I can even it up at all.'

'Leave it Noni.' I gripped her wrists, hurting her as I tried to wrench myself free. 'I want it just like this.'

'You can't do!' she wailed after me. 'Have you seen yourself?'

I ran on down the main corridor suffering the shocked and amused glances cast at me by the duty prefects. I kept on running till I reached the chapel corridor. Mother Agnes was playing softly, waiting for me I knew, hoping I'd come. I was trembling again now, with a spread of cold nausea under my ribs.

This is for you, Mother. I've done this for love of you.

She didn't look round, hearing me gently push open the door. 'I thought I might see you. Listen to this, Cecilia. I'm just certain I can tempt you with this. It's made for your voice.'

She was playing a version of the Magnificat. It soared up, note on note, peacock colours opening out. I broke into it.

'I don't want to sing.' Tight, someone else's voice that I couldn't recognise. 'I've told you.'

Look at me. Look at me, Mother. See. Your sacrifice and mine. See what I have done for you!

Mother Agnes sighed and closed down the piano lid, resigned. Her voice was cold as she turned.

'Very well. If you don't want…'

She saw me at last, and her hand went to her mouth.

'Dear God!'

She stood up. 'If you don't want to sing, I have other work to do. Will you go now please. Please, Cecilia. Go.'

I hadn't even thought about my family. It was my Uncle Rory who was the first to see me. I walked straight out of school that day from the music room with no thought at all of going to my class. I was in a kind of trance, floundering in some deep waters. I only saw my uncle at the last minute. He would have cycled straight on past me without recognising me, I think, but I lunged towards him, nearly knocking him off his bicycle and into the ditch. He let his bike fall and stepped out of it.

He stared at me for a long time.

'Who's been at you?'

'No one,' I whispered, my hands to my head to cover it up. 'I did it myself.'

'Yourself!' Anger and astonishment chased each other across his eyes, and brief mirth at seeing something ridiculous, and horror and tenderness. 'Your beautiful hair now.' He ran his palm over the stubble of my scalp. 'Your beautiful hair.'

'Uncle Rory,' I said, made calm by his softness. 'I need to tell you something.'

'What now, what?' He spoke gently to me, searching my eyes with his as if I was ill, or a little child again.

'About my daddy.'

'Your daddy?'

'I don't think he's my father.'

His face fragmented then; his mouth broke into pieces. Tears slid and glistened like snail tracks down his long and trembling jowls. They kept coming, squeezing from the corners of his closed eyelids, they slid and gathered in the cracks of his lips, and he sucked them in, and still they came. When he spoke at last his voice was high in his throat with a kind of small dog whine.

'Is that why you did this to yourself?'

'I don't think so. Please don't. Please don't.'

He wiped his hands across his face. The snail tracks oozed again. 'You love your daddy, don't you?'

'I do...'

'Well then. Well then.' He wiped his nose on the back of his hand and stooped to pick up his bike. He walked away slowly, shaking his head, letting out small yelps as if he couldn't help it at all, as if they were bursting out of him the way belches do, as if they would hurt him not to.

I walked on home and went past my mother and father in the yard. They raised their heads to look at me and called after me as I went into the house. I went straight up to my room and stayed there. Neither of them followed me. When Terence came home from school he ran upstairs to laugh at me and was called down again. Geraldine came home, and crept into the room with her headscarf. She wrapped it round my head as if she was bandaging me, and I let her.

But I was proud of my hair, not ashamed. I was proud of the statement it made of sacrifice and commitment. I went to school the next day knowing that the girls would be shocked and would laugh at me, and knowing also that their laughter would hurt, yet deep inside myself I held a thrill about it. It was an immolation. It would sanctify me. As I walked up the long drive to the grey convent school and into its perfume of polish and flowers I spoke to myself my words of offering:

Agnus dei, qui tollis peccata mundi...

Lamb of God, who takest away the sins of the world...

Mother Agnes. Your sacrifice and mine.

I knew that she and I would never seek each other out again.

My commitment to my sacrifice was absolute. I walked to Mass every morning, and from there to school with the communion host inside me. 'Now God, now,' I would say as I came out into the slow morning traffic. 'Let me die now, while I'm in a state of Grace. Take me now.' Yet maybe such a thought was a sin, to wish myself away from life before time. Maybe just by thinking that I had already lost my state of grace. I went straight to chapel as soon as I reached school, eager to pray and regain my state of grace. I spent my lunchtimes there, fasting. Make me worthy.

The boys of our parish used to gather outside church after Mass on a Sunday. Some of them would be altar boys who would have bundled up their surplices in the vestry quick so they could get out and meet up with their friends and their fathers. As soon as they could they would be slipping in through the back door and under the counter of the local bar while the front door stayed shut. And while they waited they watched the girls. I saw them flirting; the sly turn of their eyes, the wet-lipped smiles. Didn't I know the thoughts in their hearts. I dreaded walking past them.

'What happened to the head?' They called after me the first Sunday after my haircut. 'Did the moths get at you?'

I kept my eyes down.

'Is it sheep-shearing time already?'

Lamb of God.

One of them, the Italian boy Angelo Caravelli, ran along the path after me, his friends whistling him on. He bobbed in front of me. I remembered how we had danced together in the darkness under the trees, years ago; how he had touched and held me. I tried to turn away from his knowing laughter. The other boys were behind me on the path now, hounds after the hare. 'Are you short of some curls?' he asked me. 'Here, would you like some of mine?' He plucked up a handful of his black hair which bubbled like the head of a chrysanthemum. 'Do you want some, Cecilia?' He danced down the path in front of me, facing me, laughing over me to his friends.

'I do not,' I said, and that was my mistake, because as soon as I spoke to him he jigged towards me and back and round me, doing a strange cavorting dance with his arms and legs flinging out to the sides and all the people of the congregation, it seemed, turning round to look and laugh, and as I hesitated and then tried to break through his mad jiving I tripped up and fell forward. He caught me in both his hands, held mine, warm in his.

'What are you doing?' I asked, astonished.

He burst out laughing and let my hands and his drop to our sides, and in a second he was gone back to his friends. And I walked on quickly, ashamed of something that I could not name. It was a strange softness that was throbbing inside me. It was an elation. And I was afraid of this.

So after that I took to waiting in church on Sundays till everyone had gone. I knelt in front of the Virgin and whispered until there were no more sounds to be heard outside church than the mewing of gulls, and then made my way home alone.

Geraldine had been making a present for me, and she gave it to me one Sunday when I arrived home from church. I knew she'd been knitting something for me because I'd had to cast on the stitches for her and to pick them up when she dropped them, and yet I knew that it was meant to be a surprise for me because she would sit with her back to me while she was knitting, and would look furtively at me whenever I moved. She always sat as close to the fire as she could and when her hands began to sweat they'd make the wool stick to the needles. You could hear the squeak of it as she pushed the stitches along.

'What's that you're making, Geraldine?' I asked her once.

She glanced over her shoulder at me and rolled her eyes.

'Is it for Aunt Bridget, to keep her warm in bed?'

She giggled.

'Is it for Daddy, when he's out watching the moon come up in the fields?'

She laughed again and clicked on, her eyes slightly crossed in concentration, her tongue resting on her bottom lip so her spittle dropped down onto her knitting. And on the day she finished it she stood waiting for me in the kitchen, flushed with pleasure, and as I came through the door she crept behind me and slipped it over my head and turned me round to tie it under my chin. She squealed with joy and ran me to the mirror over the hearth so I could look at myself. What she had made for me was a baby's bonnet, pink smudging to grey, and my spiking hair sprouted through the holes.

'Let's have a look,' my mother said.

I turned round.

'You look like a piglet just off to market,' she chuckled.

I snorted and dropped down onto all fours, running at her.

'Don't!' she gasped. She clutched at herself to hold in her laughter. 'Poor Geraldine, and she's worked so hard at it too.'

I snorted again and turned round to rub my woolly pink head against Geraldine's legs. Alarmed, she backed away from me. My mother let out her laughter at last in great whooping gales, and Geraldine in pleased amazement crouched down to me to pat my bonnet. She tried to poke my hairs back in.

'Dear Heaven!' my mother said, wiping away her laughter tears. 'What am I to do with you now?'

It was like a party in our house that night. She sang as she scrubbed the potatoes, and when my father and Terence came in with armloads of carrots with their sharp sweet smell she made them wash their soiled hands and try on the bonnet in turns. I wore it throughout the meal to please Geraldine, and every time I caught my mother's eye she spluttered in silent hysteria into her food.

After prayers that night she followed me up to my room. I had asked her for a small bag and was packing it with my nightie and wash things when she came in.

'What's this?' she asked me. 'You're not thinking of going travelling are you, in your pink bonnet?'

'It's the retreat at school next week.' I said. 'I told you about it, Mam. We stay over at the convent for it when we're in our last year.'

'You didn't tell me at all.' She sat down on the edge of my bed.

'I did too. You didn't listen.' I turned away from her. Maybe I hadn't told her yet. I couldn't remember.

'Well,' she sighed. 'I envy you. I used to love the retreats when I was a girl. Peace and quiet for a whole week, mind. All that wonderful peace and quiet.'

I finished packing my things in silence. The laughter of the early evening rang like lunacy in my ears. She watched me while I got myself ready for bed, and I was embarrassed.

'You're a woman now, all right,' she said. 'I didn't notice you growing up so fast.' She touched my hand, making me timid, and kept her eyes on my face. She reached out and touched my head then, for the first time since I had cut my hair. 'Cecilia...' she began, and I waited for her to speak, knowing that I could too, and that she could make the ice flow, she could. But she drew away her hand and let her lips purse up. She had hurt herself.

'Don't be unhappy, Cessy.' She stood up from the bed, stretching from a great weariness. 'Enjoy your life.'

She went downstairs quickly. I sat for a long time. Geraldine came up and started washing herself, peeling off her clothes and discarding them at her feet, walking naked and unashamed while I turned my eyes away. But my thoughts were with my mother still. How simple a gesture it would have been to have reached out to stroke back the pale looseness of her hair. How easy then might it have been to talk.

And was her soul black with the sin of my birth? Was she to burn for ever for it in the flames of hell?

I flung myself back onto the bed, shocked and frightened. Perhaps, after all, my sacrifice was to be for her redemption. I decided then that my retreat would be offered up for her.

Berlie Doherty

Chapter Twenty-one

I was to spend five days away from home. For the first time in my life I would have none of my family round me. I was to spend my week in prayer and contemplation within the convent's silence, and my focus would be on the liturgy of the Church, the teachings of priests, and the mysteries inside the pale shadow of my soul. Our vow of silence was to be maintained day and night; we would live like nuns. I longed for it.

I felt strangely as if I was leaving home that morning as I set off, small pilgrim on a spiritual journey, with my nightdress and my rosary beads, my missal and my toothbrush. My mother and my father, Terence and Geraldine all kissed me goodbye and came to the end of the lane with me, but my silence had already begun. I walked to school that morning. It was late spring, and every note of birdsong and every glint of flower were fresh clear sparks in my head. As I approached the drive I met up with other girls, all with their bags, and smiled at them and shook my head as they called out to me in their excitement. There were to be no lessons that week. All the girls from fourth years up were on retreat, and all the younger children had a holiday. Only my year, the most senior girls, were to stay with the boarders. We smiled shyly and nervously to each other as we were led upstairs by the boarder prefects and shown our dormitory, vacated by the juniors. I glanced round the long room and chose the bed in the least favourable position, away from the window, nearest the draught in the door, and opposite the dormitory nun's screen. I sat on it to test the mattress, and was disappointed to find that it seemed more comfortable than my bed at home. Maybe, I thought, I'll slide out of it in the night and sleep on the floor.

We went down to the study which seemed to have been specially polished by nuns on their early morning duties, and were told to select holy books to read between prayers and sermons. These books were kept in the glass cases that surrounded the study. Most of them were leather-bound and the pages were brown and smelling of must. I chose the autobiographies of the two Teresas. One was the girl saint, who was always painted with lilies in her hand: the Little Flower, as she had called herself, St. Theresa of Lisieux. She was my Aunt Bridget's favourite saint because she had died young and consumptive and striving for perfection. The other was a brand new book. It was the life of St. Teresa of Avila of the order of the Carmelites, a visionary who had seen Our Lady. Mother Agnes had talked to me about her, many times, as intimately as if she had known her as a friend. She had told me that her passion and strength remained an inspiration to the church four centuries after her life, and also that she had died in a state of rapture. I walked back to my desk with my arms folded, hugging the books to myself, coveting them.

Mother Joseph strode in her manly way into the study and shook the hand bell to summon us to chapel. We walked in slow and silent procession along the corridors and stood lined up outside the chapel while the organ played. The visiting retreat priest walked up to the front of the procession, and we, agog, turned our heads to see him. There was a rustle of delight as we realised that he was a monk, that he walked barefoot, and that his face was thin and pale and starved-looking.

'Aesthetic!' Noni mouthed at me. I pursed my lips and shook my head. Ascetic, she meant, but I wasn't going to break my vow to tell her that. She nodded back to me. 'Aesthetic. Be-oo-tee-ful!'

When we had settled into our chapel pews he told us all that we were like flowers in the sight of God. We bent our heads, and he told us that already our petals were bruised.

'Every minute of every day,' he told us, in a voice so quiet that we had to strain to hear him, 'every second of every minute it is possible for you to sin, in thought, word, deed or glance.' We closed our eyes. 'Every second,' he repeated. 'Examine your conscience. What sin are you committing now, girls?'

We sat upright. We put our feet together on the kneeler. No, not the kneeler, that was for knees. We put them together on the floor. We clasped our hands. We put our palms together for prayer. We opened our eyes, looked at the crucifix on the altar, looked at the monk. We closed our eyes again, while he waited. What sin, we thought. Where? We had lost concentration. Maybe that was it.

The first two rows of girls were asked to stay behind for confession. The rest of us were sent away to prepare ourselves for midday Mass. We sat at our desks and stared at the statue of the Sacred Heart of Jesus that had been placed on the study teacher's raised desk. Mother Joseph and Mother Philomena paraded the rows between our desks, whispering their rosaries.

After Mass, where for the first time that day the choir opened their throats to sing, we were brought to silence again to eat our meal. Mother Joseph read to us from her favourite book about the nun in Red China while we ate the boiled fish and boiled potato that was to be our diet for the week. After the meal we paraded the grounds and the corridors with our heads bowed and our lips forming prayers. We walked gravely and lightly as the nuns did, listening to our voices in our heads, winkling out our sins and scrutinising them. We were forbidden to walk with friends, though as we passed each other we smiled self-consciously. I kept myself away from everyone, following the route Mother Agnes and I had always taken. I walk alone, I told myself. Throughout my life perhaps, I walk alone.

The monk's afternoon sermon was about our calling in life, which was, he said, to bear our husband's children. He talked about the Virgin Mary and told us that she would be our guide, always, in these matters. He begged us to consider in our hearts the virtue of chastity, which he told us was a state of moral purity and freedom from unholy intercourse. He told us to avoid passionate kisses. We shuffled uneasily in our benches. He walked out with his head down, leaving us to our prayers, while the nuns surrounded the Virgin's statue with lighted candles.

In our evening sermon he told us of the harlot saint, Mary Magdalene. 'She is not a virgin,' he reminded us. 'She sinned with her flesh, yet she was forgiven. She knew men, yet she became a saint.' I remembered then something that I had heard my mother saying to my Aunt Bridget once, some years ago. She thought I was not in the room. I had crept away with the words, savouring them, and puzzled. 'The saints all seem to be virgins or reformed whores,' she had said, 'There's none of them wives and mothers, except Elisabeth.' The monk told us then the story of how Jesus allowed the harlot to bathe his feet with her tears, and dry them with her hair, and then to anoint them with oils. You'd think it was a poem, the way he told us that. You'd think we were all asleep with our eyes closed and he afraid to waken us, so softly he spoke, so closely we listened.

Afterwards in the dormitory we undressed in the dark with Mother Philomena sitting in the doorway. She put on the light when we had folded away our clothes and knelt with us to say our prayers. As I lay in my bed I could hear the squeaks of girls giggling nervously into the darkness. They disturbed my thoughts. I tried to fix on them, to enter inside my head like a ghost of no substance, to wander about there in its chasms. I woke up suddenly in the grey dawn light and sat up in bed, mortified. I had meant to lie on the floor and instead like a sloth had slumbered in comfort all night.

I loved best to be in the chapel. There I felt at peace with myself. I didn't even try to pray. I closed my eyes and let my breathing become lighter and lighter till it was only a whisper of air in my throat, till I wasn't breathing at all, just being, till I had left my bone shell kneeling there and I had surrendered myself to essential stillness. When I came to, my flesh was cold and numb.

And outside in the sunlight I walked alone. I watched Noni and the others drifting together and I shunned them. They had ways of talking to each other, mouthing and miming. I didn't want my new wholeness to be entered. After Mass they bought holy cards in the study, and wrote messages to pass on to each other. They slipped them into each others' missals in chapel or posted them on the desks, like Christmas cards.

I bought some to take home to my family. One was a picture of a fat cherub holding out a lily to the Blessed Virgin. They were surrounded by roses and cloud wisps. Geraldine would love that. Another had the Christ child holding out his arms to a lamb. That would be for Terence. All the cards had gold pinked edgings and were printed in Italy. The saints had gold haloes that shone when you caught the light on them. I picked up the little pile that was waiting for me on my desk and glanced at them. Noni had given me one of Saint Ignatius Loyola, who was clutching his heart in one hand and his missal in the other. He looked like the visiting monk. I turned it over and read the back. 'Dear Cecilia,' she had written. 'Isn't this the most wonderful retreat of our lives! Isn't the monk the most beautiful creature on this earth! I'm in love with him. Are you as happy as I am? Noni. PS Pray for me.'

Biddy had sent me a picture of Our Lady of Lourdes, which was decorated with little blue bubbles containing the scenes of the fourteen Stations of the Cross. 'Dear Cecilia. I've put a rude question in the box for this afternoon's question time. Can't wait to see his face. It's not rude really, because I need to know. Urgent. Pray for me. Biddy.'

There was a third, and it was unsigned. I read it and glanced round to see if anyone was watching me. I could see that the same card with the same message had been put on other desks. 'Dear Cecilia. I've found out that Angela Pearson sleeps with boys. Did you know? I heard her confessing it. Wasn't she brave to tell?'

But I knew that already. I put the card face up on the desk and drew the book of Teresa of Avila towards me. It fell open at the page that I had already read and reread, but it was Mother Agnes' voice that kept coming through, and I closed my eyes to recall the day she had told me. I remembered now going into the rose garden with her on a day when the sky was a lumbering grey and the soil was turned to frost.

'Cecilia. I want you to do something for a girl in your class. Angela. I want you to pray for Angela Pearson.'

'Angela Pearson?'

Mother Agnes had lowered her voice. 'She sleeps with boys, Cecilia.'

I had been deeply shocked, and unable to look at her. I can see now the way the frost smoked where the pale sun touched it. That Angela could have spoken to Mother Agnes about such a thing. That such a thing could be spoken about at all, in broad daylight. That Mother Agnes could have told me. Mother Rose is dying. Angela Pearson sleeps with boys. The exams are coming soon. Pray pray pray. Everything will be all right. More things are wrought by prayer than this world dreams of...

'Will she go to hell, Mother?'

'She will, if she doesn't repent in her heart. So will you, if you do that thing.'

'Me, Mother? I wouldn't..!'

'Ah, don't be too sure now. Don't be too sure...'

It seemed that I had forgotten that we had ever had that conversation, and that I had deliberately pushed it away. It seemed that the sudden memory of it then filled me with guilt. What's it like, Angela Pearson? What's it like?

I tried to read my book. The words of my favourite passage danced like midges in front of my eyes. I put down my head on the desk. The words danced on. I knew them off by heart. Teresa was describing her angel, who came to her many times. '...In his hands I saw a great golden spear, and at the iron tip there appeared to be a point of fire. This he plunged into my heart several times so that it penetrated to my entrails. When he pulled it out I felt that he took them with it, and left me utterly consumed by the great love of God...'

Mother Joseph rang the bell for my row to go to confession before Mass. I started up from my desk in confusion, scattering my holy cards. My cheeks burning, I gathered them up and put them inside the page and closed the book. I put my mantilla over my head and walked quickly to keep up with the others.

'I have been guilty of impure thoughts,' I told the monk.

'Where?' he whispered into the darkness. 'Here, in God's chapel?'

'In the study,' I told him. 'Everywhere.'

I knelt in front of the Virgin to say my penance. Mother, ask God to forgive Angela Pearson. And to forgive me. To forgive the man on the hockey pitch. He knows not what he does. It was their fault for watching. Forgive Veronica and Bridget. It was my fault for remembering. Forgive me. I pray for him because he is a sinner. I pity him because he is sick. It is his curse. I fear him, Mother, because he is a man.

And above all, ask God to forgive my mother.

On the third day of the retreat I fainted in chapel. I had been fasting for two days, and had managed to spend most of the last two nights lying on the floor. When I came round there were anxious faces bending over me. I closed my eyes again in the swim of black blood. 'I want to go home,' I moaned. 'To my Mam. I want to go home.'

Mother Joseph sat me up and thrust my head between my knees. 'This is your home, dear,' she whispered. 'We are your family. And there is your mother, the Blessed Virgin. Pray to her, child. She's the one who loves you most.'

Chapter Twenty-two

It seemed to me that Mother Joseph was watching me all the time after that. I felt she could read the thoughts in my head. I withdrew more and more from the others. My silence was a white flame inside me. The days passed in a pattern of lines, from my desk to the chapel, to the rose garden, to the refectory, and again, and again, and to the dormitory, and again, like a slow silent dance whose geometry had no beginning and no end. Its rhythm gave my breathing its pulse. And yet there was an end to the sequence, and all the patterns of all the separate dances led towards this point, as when we all take hands and bow or curtsey when the fiddlers stop.

This moment was the receiving of the medals of the Sodality of Our Lady, which took place at the final Benediction of the week. It was granted only to a few senior girls, who were to treasure the medals for the rest of their lives. I was among them. I knelt down with the others at the altar rails, my head bowed, my eyes closed. I could feel rather than hear the slow rustling approach of the monk. His whisper bent towards me as he placed the blue ribbon over my head. The medal moved cold against me. I didn't touch it, or look down, but as we moved out of chapel in double file Noni touched my arm.

'Cessy! Look!' she mouthed.

She was interrupting my prayer.

'Nun!' she mouthed.

I frowned at her.

'Nun! Nun!' she whispered. 'Look at your medal, Cessy.'

I glanced down. The raised imprint of the Virgin was turned towards me, not facing out. I looked at Noni again, disbelieving. Throughout our school lives we had been told that if this happened it was a sign that we were intended to join the order of the nuns. It had been passed on from senior girls to juniors, it had been told to us by the nuns themselves. And on this day of days I had not remembered it.

'Hard luck, St. Cecilia!' Noni whispered, and touched my arm as she moved away. Something was spinning round, distorting images, shattering the known and the physical. My blood was cold inside me. Something like a knife was screaming in my head. It's a game, that's all. Not this. It's a game. Not this. My mind snapped shut, closed tight. No thoughts there. Refuse to think.

'Come here a moment, child. Come here.'

Mother Mary Joseph, hovering and beckoning from the doorway of her study. A spider. Her hand came across and closed, cold, over mine. My palms were sweating. I clutched the traitor medal in my fist.

She closed the door gently and I sat down on a chair near the window. I could hear the suck of sandals on the corridor, and the low notes of the organ playing out its last chords.

Outside in the garden some of the nuns were walking. Mother Philomena was there, with her sweet child's face. Mother Imelda, the mystic, who always walked out of the chapel backwards, blank eyes fixed on the tabernacle. The girls had begun to talk; the retreat was over. I could hear the waves of their voices. Mother Joseph was speaking to me. I couldn't listen. I focused on the two black figures bent in the garden and gradually my sickness and trembling ceased, the crystal stopped its spin. The low insistence of her voice worked its way into my consciousness.

'It's been quite apparent to us for a long, long time. We've been watching you, my child. Don't turn your heart away. We will all welcome you.'

Mother Imelda's gown was caught up in one of the bushes. She worked stiff fingers to free herself. Mother Agnes had come out into the garden now. Laughing, she went over to the old nun and leaned over to release her.

'You must not be afraid child. This is a most wonderful gift.'

'Mother. Please.'

I was watching Mother Agnes as she moved through the garden, as she bent low and held out a rose for Mother Imelda to see.

'You have courted Christ, my dear. He would have you for his bride!'

I flushed deeply. I looked down at my hands, how they clenched and unclenched in my lap. 'I never thought about it, truly Mother, truly.'

'Of course you never thought. None of us do, till we receive the sign. And today, your sign came to you, when you received the medal with the face of the Blessed Virgin Mary turned to you.'

'It's only a game though isn't it, about the medal? It's only a folk-tale. It's never true. Surely it's never true. Oh Mother Joseph!' Helplessness flooded over me. 'Please don't make me.'

'No one will make you. You will come because you want to. Because there is no other way.'

I still couldn't look at her. Outside now there were more nuns receiving the sunlight in their walled garden. Sparrows and finches were playing about on the dusty paths, lifting themselves up with sudden bright wing beats as the nuns approached them. House martins darted along the eaves of the convent house, swinging and drifting across to the fields beyond. The spider voice went on, and again the cold hand closed over mine.

'We will pray for you and with you, child. Pray to God that you will not turn your back on Him.'

I turned to her at last, to her kind peasant's face that was filled with love.

'Go now,' she nodded to me. 'And don't be afraid. Just remember that today God asked you to join his special children. Cecilia, my dear child, you will be so welcome if you choose to come and join us.'

Chapter Twenty-three

I said nothing of this at home. The only person I wanted to speak to about it was Mother Agnes. I don't know how I passed the minutes of the weekend. I know that I could not break my silence. 'What is it?' my mother kept asking me during our first family meal. I stared at her, almost not knowing her, till with a look that was half angry and half afraid she sent me upstairs with my plate of food. I think I may have spent the next day there, though I know I went with them all to Sunday Mass. 'Speak to her, Rory,' she said as we left the church all together, 'I can't get a word from her,' and he tried with teasing to coax me out of myself. I don't honestly think I was there.

On Monday I went straight to chapel. The choir was still practising. At the end of practice there would be five minutes before Mass started. That would be enough, at least, to let her know that I needed her to help me. The girls went down the stairs and Mother Agnes went straight out into the rose garden. I bent my head quickly. I knew she had seen me. I knew the eyes of the virgin were on me.

'My soul doth magnify the Lord...' I began.

The door from the rose garden opened and I knew that Mother Agnes had come back in.

'For He hath regarded the lowliness of His handmaiden...'

She walked slowly through the chapel, genuflecting as she passed in front of the altar. I even knew how long she would take to do that, how low her head would bend.

'For He that is mighty hath magnified me...'

She knelt in one of the pews at the back of the chapel, in its shadows. At last I stole a glance at her. She was watching me. 'This sacrifice is yours,' her closed face said to me. She crossed herself and bowed down her head. 'This surrender is your own.'

I buried my face into my hands. I pressed the black redness till it was right inside me and swirling round the bone-caves beneath my flesh.

Though I walk through the valley of darkness, Lord, hear my prayer.

So that night, I decided, I would speak to my family about it as soon as they were all there together. The words were in my head and well-rehearsed. I needed only a silence to pour them into. And that silence and the silence that came after booms in my memory every moment of my life.

That was the night when I left behind everything that I knew of my childhood. It was the night I left home.

Chapter Twenty-four

That night is trapped in the still pool of my memory as a painting traps its portrait subjects for ever. But however loving the painting, the flesh is never quite soft enough or powerful, nor is the breathing ever heard, or the tense and nervous hum that shifts the air between the figures. Neither can the painting ever show what happens when the figures move again, when the words that have to be said have been spoken.

But the painter can show the colours, and hold them fast. My mother's eyes are pale ash-green and the wisps of her hair are grey froth on the curved line of her neck. My uncle's hair has a lustre of flames to it as he bends forward to lift turf sods that are flaking white on the hearth. Aunt Bridget's yellow face is caught in the surprise of laughter, and my father's hand too is yellow as he reaches out to touch me. He is wearing the brown corduroys that I love to burnish with my fingers, stroking the piles to dark and light. He has a gleam of sweat beaded along the balding line of his scalp. In the deep sill of the window Terence sits, cross-legged, almost a shadow there but for the looming of his white face. And there is Geraldine, head bent, fidgeting with the gold fringes of the table cover, and she is wearing a lemon frock, a colour which does not suit her but which she loves. There is a scattering of orange flowers on its yoke, which she and I embroidered together.

A painter would catch the calmness of the scene, but not the monotone drip of the overflow pipe into the tub by the porch, or the creak of the peewit in the field behind the house; the low moan of the cows in the barn.

Aunt Bridget had been telling ghost stories, and had left a cold quiet on us, and it was into that silence that I spoke.

'I have been thinking,' I said, 'that I might go back to live in the place where I was born.'

That was when my father reached out his hand to touch me, and when Aunt Bridget gave out her laugh of surprise.

'And would you care to tell us what you mean by this?' my mother said at last.

'I have a vocation.'

You could have held the silence in your hands and known the weight and substance of it. No painter could have captured that.

'What a wonderful thing!' Aunt Bridget said. 'I knew it, Cecilia! I knew you had it in you!'

My mother crossed herself, dumbfounded. 'I had an inkling,' she said.

'I hoped and prayed,' said Aunt Bridget. 'I did.'

'You have no vocation,' said my Uncle Rory.

'Indeed she has,' said Aunt Bridget. 'She's as pious a child as ever I was, but I was not asked. Oh, this is a great thing to rejoice over. Should we not be on our knees praying our thanks?'

'We should not,' Uncle Rory said.

'I thought you were going to be a famous opera star,' Terence whined. 'I've told all the boys at school.'

'A good Catholic family would be pleased,' I told them all. 'Father Carolyn would be pleased.'

'Of course he will.' My father stood up then from his chair to come over and hug me. 'And so are we all. If this is what you want for yourself, we're all pleased for you. It is a blessing on our family.'

'So it is!' agreed Aunt Bridget.

'Please sit, Daddy,' I said. Surprised, he felt back for his chair and sat down again. 'What I mean is this. He will be particularly pleased; being my father.' My voice was cold and hard but even so it caught somewhere. My speech was floundering. 'Surely this is what Father Carolyn would want for me.' I stayed with my eyes cast down.

'So that's it,' my mother breathed.

'What's this about being your father?' my Aunt Bridget asked. '*Being your father*? It's Francis who has a say in this.'

'Father Carolyn is your spiritual father,' my mother said in a strange, quiet voice.

'God is my spiritual father.' I could look at her now.

'But Father Carolyn is your friend,' she said.

'Not my friend,' I told her. 'Not mine.'

My mother sank back into her chair, as though the life had gone from her. Her face was grey. She thrust forward her legs, showing how the heat from the fire had marbled her shins. She dragged her fingers through her hair. Her voice was ragged. 'So you think the priest is your father.'

Aunt Bridget drew in her breath and crossed herself. My father put his hand across hers.

'He as good as told me himself,' I said.

'He did no such thing. He is not your father, Cecilia.'

'Who then? Who?' My reserve was gone. My voice was as ragged as hers. In my emptiness now I did not want to know, but there was a naked perversity in me that would haul me on. My father had withdrawn from the table. Pale and deeply troubled, he had moved to sit on the window-seat with Terence. He put his arm round his son's shoulders and drew him close. Then, 'Go up to bed, Terence,' he said faintly, and was ignored.

'I have a right to know who my father is.' I did not recognise my voice.

A pan of boiling water hissed on the cooker. Aunt Bridget went over to move it and stayed there, a dim moth figure hovering.

'I don't know who your father is,' my mother said. 'And that is the truth, Cecilia.'

Her words were small stones. The fire spurted a late and ready flame. There was a startle in the room then that would have made your skin shiver.

Then the woman with the pale ash eyes said, 'And I am not your mother, Cecilia.'

I saw in my mind the grinning, straining red face of a woman giving birth.

'Geraldine is.'

And I looked down inside it to a woman-child, a mother-virgin, and such a lemon-skinned wet-mouthed weed-haired and simpering thing at that, such a tadpole half-life, such a green womb.

Chapter Twenty-five

When I walked out of the house they were all hollering. Geraldine, seeing herself the centre of some catastrophe, set up a howling such as I've never heard before, and in turns she was being petted and shouted at by the women. The two men were roaring at each other. And I walked out of this without being seen except by Terence. I walked calm and quiet out of the hullabaloo into the sweet night. He ran after me and held onto my hand. 'Don't go. Don't go, Cecilia,' he said.

'I have to, ' I told him. 'There's no home for me here.'

'Please don't go,' he moaned, understanding very little, but frightened for me and for himself.

'I have to,' I said. I ran away from him a few steps. I looked back just to see him standing at the top of the hill.

'Cecilia!' I heard later, a woman's voice wailing and far away.

The trees were black and comforting, and their whisper had a strange familiar sibilance. I walked quickly, thinking of nothing more but the counting of my footsteps. I had nothing with me. The convent house was a dark and looming shape. I thudded on the door and waited, thudded again. I was beginning now to feel cold. For a long time it seemed as if no one would come, and that I must make my way back to that other house or curl up under the shrubs and take my chance there, but eventually I heard a quick firm tread and recognised it as Mother Joseph's.

'Who is it?' she called through the door, out of breath with hurrying.

'It's Cecilia Deardon, Mother. Might I come in?'

She pulled back the bolts and stood arms akimbo, watching me as if she was weighing me up for purchase at the market place. 'We are at prayer,' she told me. 'The whole community is at prayer and will be throughout the night.'

'I'm sorry to disturb you, Mother.'

'Does your family know you're here?'

'Yes.'

'What are you doing, coming out this time of night to us?'

My throat was beginning to tighten. I held back tears. 'I had to come, Mother.'

'Something has happened to bring you here at this time.'

I shook my head, clenching and unclenching my fists in the pockets of my coat.

'I wanted to come.'

She stood aside, saying nothing, gave me no embrace of welcome, or blessing, showed no further curiosity about my arrival or about whether my decision had been made. She locked the door and led me through into the school and upstairs to the dormitory where I had spent the retreat. The younger children were in there, snoring softly and peacefully. She pointed to the one spare bed.

'Don't go waking up the little ones,' she whispered.

'Of course not, Mother,' then, as she turned, 'Could I not come and pray with you?'

'You could not,' she said. 'Not with us.'

I left my clothes on and crept into bed. I lay listening to the retreat of her footsteps down the stairs and along the corridors, and I heard the door that separated the school from the convent house close. Only then did I let out my breath. As soon as I drew the cold sheets over me my trembling started. I turned over onto my stomach and lay with my arms outstretched gripping the bar of my bed head, and it seemed as if every nerve and fibre of my body were charged with electricity. My teeth chattered in my head. My skin shivered as if it was silk loose and chill across my bones. I bit the wet pillow where my tiny voice splashed. I heard whisperings in the room, and the creak of the bed shaking under me. My fists flexed and loosened and flexed again on the bedhead.

Someone with light feet came and sat on the edge of the bed and laid her hand gently on my neck and kept it there, humming my name to me, till my rage of trembling ceased and I lay in a coma of exhaustion. And when I came to again she had gone, if indeed she had ever been. All the children were sleeping. I turned onto my back and watched the dawn. I could hear the birds starting up. With the light came a bluster of wind. I could see the great tall poplars swaying.

During the morning the wind grew into a frenzy with itself, like the gales of the equinox. The day-girls came in, laughing and red cheeked. A tree had come down in the drive, they said. They had had to clamber over it to come up to school.

'Whatever's happened to your school dress?' Noni whispered to me in the corridor as she came in. 'It looks as if you've slept in it!'

'I have,' I told her.

'Cessy, are you all right?' she asked me.

I shook my head. Old Mother Ignatia slapped me on the back of my neck as she hurried past. 'Pssh!' she said.

I left Noni and went down to the chapel. We had been told that there would be a special assembly before Mass that morning. I went straight into chapel and was alone there, at last. Gusts from nowhere sucked and flattened the candle-flames. The wind made a deep mad roar round the buildings; it could be heard tunnelled in the rose garden, ripping at shrubs. The two old nuns, Mother Ignatia and Mother Stanislaus, came in whispering and tried with the long poles to secure all the high windows.

I knelt in front of my statue trying to shut out all sounds.

'Holy Mother of God,' I prayed. 'Help me. Let me be your child, too.'

Her constant smile soothed me. Her arms were outstretched forever to embrace. 'Come to me, come to me,' she would always be saying. She was totally without stain, for all time: forgiving, unchanging, unquestioning. 'Please Mother, please Mother, please Mother.'

There were voices in the corridor. I could hear scurrying feet, and a man's voice, raised. The chapel doors were thrust open, and Father Carolyn hurried in. 'She's here,' he said. Outside doors must have been left open. Cold air swayed the flowers on the altar and round the statues on their high shelves. Candle flames leapt and guttered out.

Father Carolyn ran towards me with his hands spread open.

'Cecilia! Cecilia...'

At that moment the side door from the rose garden opened. Mother Agnes had been out there tying twine round the bushes. As she came in a gust of wind rushed in round her, hustling her robes. She turned to snatch the door before it slammed but the wind like a surging wave between two currents rose and swelled, and in the eye of its vortex the statue of the Blessed Virgin Mary rocked on its shelf. I leapt back as it toppled down towards me. It crashed down onto the wooden handrail of the kneeler, shattering out into long blue shards. The hollow head cracked open like an Easter egg. It rolled backwards and forwards, backwards and forwards, the calm forgiving smile appearing and disappearing, winking and hiding, winking and hiding.

Old Mother Ignatia darted forward at once, tittering. She held her hands across her mouth while she stamped on the skittering pieces as if they were ants. Mother Stanislaus hobbled into the sacristy and came back with a brush and pan. With tears in her eyes she hoisted up her skirts and knelt down to sweep up the remains.

'It's no laughing matter,' she hissed.

I knelt down by her. 'Can I help?' I whispered.

'You get to assembly, Cecilia,' Mother Agnes said. 'There's nothing you can do here.'

I ran past Father Carolyn, who was wandering, shocked, spotting fragments of statue splinter and easing them up on the ends of his damp fingers. Mother Agnes followed me down to the gym. The whole school had been called in. I squeezed into my place next to Noni and Biddy.

'Are you sure you're all right.' Noni whispered to me.

I shrugged. I was almost too tired to stand.

'Psssh!' came the nuns at the door.

'Girls!' Mother Joseph climbed slowly into her pulpit, gripping the sides of it to heave herself up. 'Dear girls. I have to report to you that during the night our beloved sister Mother Mary Rose was taken from us and has returned in peace to the Lord.'

Rosie!

And the nuns had been at prayer for her all night, not asking me to join them in their vigil. Yet I was closer to her than any of them had ever been. She had brought me into life. She had given me my name.

'I would like the girls of the choir to remain behind after assembly in order that Mother Agnes may rehearse with you a Requiem Mass - a fitting tribute, dear girls, to one who has given her life to the music that glorifies God. Let us pray, girls.'

After assembly I made my way out of the gym, but was overtaken by Mother Agnes.

'Cecilia Deardon. Where are you off to?'

'To class, Mother.'

'You may not go to class. You will take your place in the choir.'

'No, Mother, I…'

'I'll hear no more of it, Cecilia. Take your place.'

Her long steady look was without emotion. I dropped my gaze. 'Yes, Mother.'

'And here. Take this music with you.'

I took the sheet she handed to me.

'*Pie Jesu*'. This is an exquisite piece. Mother Rose's favourite. I think it would be a very nice idea for you to sing it for her. Don't you?'

'Do I have to do it?'

'Yes, Cecilia. You have to do it.'

Later that afternoon, when the long school day was finished I went back to chapel. All the statues were shrouded.

Where the Virgin Mary had stood there was simply a candle. The wind was a whisper of itself now.

I knelt for a long time, almost sleeping I think, yielding to the exhaustion of the last days that had seemed years of my life. The child Cecilia had slipped away. That was all I could be sure of. There were no words in my head, only colours, and the shudderings of firelight, and the traces of spent emotions. I was aware that someone heavy had come to kneel by me, but could not open my eyes.

'Cecilia,' Father Carolyn whispered. 'Come out of the chapel. I want to speak with you.'

I kept my head bowed.

'You do no good by hiding. Come on now. Come on.'

He pressed my hand as he stood up, hurting me. He stood at the side of the bench, waiting, his breathing thick and rapid.

'Come on.'

I crossed myself and obeyed him. He led me out of the chapel and into one of the music rooms. It was the one we had always used for my singing lessons. I looked round it, smelling its familiarity. There was a jar of blue delphiniums on the window-sill. Such intense blue.

Father Carolyn sat down heavily on the piano stool and leaned back with his elbow on the closed lid of the piano. He did not look comfortable, and must have tensed his arm to be able to hold himself in this position.

'Well?' he said.

I stood with my head bowed and my hands clasped behind my back. I had no idea what he wanted me to say.

'Your mother is very worried. Very upset.'

I frowned, trying to concentrate on this word mother that he had used.

He leaned forward. 'They all are. Everyone at home is grieving for you and praying for you. They need to see you. Won't you go home tonight and talk to them?'

I shook my head.

'Cecilia?'

'This is my home.'

'This is not your home. Child, if you wish to enter the novitiate, well and good. You must speak to Mother Joseph and to Reverend Mother about it. They are willing to receive you, they have told me that. There is great joy for you here in the community.'

'This is my home then.'

'It must be done properly, with the blessing of your family. It must be done with great thought and care. This is for all your life, Cecilia.'

'This must be my home. I have a bed here.'

He blew out his lips in frustration. 'You have a bed in the junior dormitory, I am told.'

I kept my head bowed. I was beginning to sway with weariness. Father Carolyn stood up abruptly.

'If you must stay here rather than in your own house I'll pay your boarder's fees for you. Here.' He fished inside his jacket and brought out some notes and laid them on the lid of the piano. One of them drifted down onto the floor. 'You can pay for yourself. You can have anything you want Cecilia, you know that. But you must talk to your family.'

'This is my family.'

I have no rememberings of what he said after that. When he left I sat down on the piano stool. He was blowing his nose in the corridor, loud brute snorts; I knew them well. When I knew he had gone I picked up the notes and studied them with interest. Never in my life before had I held money. In church I was passed a small coin which was hardly in my fist before it was dropped onto the collection plate. I had never seen the colours or patterns of a note of money. I bent down to pick up the stray note and fanned them all out. But my head was busy all the while with my other thoughts and for the first time that day I let myself enter them. Mother Agnes had spoken to me at last, weeks after my sacrifice. Was this then to be my new sacrifice, the Act of Obedience? I wondered whether this was my trial for the novitiate. If I would sing, would I be worthy? Or would my singing be a new taunt to the dead nun who had denied the music that was in me?

Berlie Doherty

Chapter Twenty-six

Anxiety about my solo sweated my sleep and distracted my waking hours. I saw the white angry darting face, the distressed fingers catching air, the hiss of hatred.

A message was sent to me in the study that my family had come to speak to me. I could not see them, I said. The child who had brought me the message stared at me, mystified, but when I shook my head she ran off to deliver my reply. I went straight upstairs. From the dormitory window I could see the four figures walking down the drive. The man had his arm across the woman's shoulders. The smaller, dumpy woman swung her arms as she walked. That was her way of pretending she did not care; how well I knew that way of hers, and how her face would be smiling, and her eyes puzzled. And the boy looked back at the convent house and then ran, head down, out of sight towards the gates. I could hear the pounding of his feet.

Early next morning a parcel was delivered for me. It contained my clothes and my blue rosary.

And at midday when I was walking in the drive I saw Rory coming up the drive on Michael's bike. My first thought was to hide, and then I turned to face him, in the middle of his path. He stood looking down at me, his legs straddled each side of the bike.

My question was so simple. 'Are you my father, then?' I watched his Adam's apple rise in his neck.

'Nobody knows who your father is, Cecilia, and that's the truth.'

A group of younger girls passed us. He waited till they had gone. 'I hope she loved him, whoever he was. I hope she enjoyed it, in her way.'

I looked away. 'I wish it was you.'

'Bridget and I wanted to bring you up as our own. We wanted that.'

I could think of nothing now to say to him. Soon it would be time for the Angelus. People would stop work in their fields to pray.

'Is there anything else you want to know?'

'Does everyone else in the village know about this thing then, except me?'

'Not at all. Nobody knew. It was all done for your sake, Cecilia.'

'It was not. Not for my sake.'

'Will you come home?'

I shook my head.

'Is there anything you want?'

I clutched the notes in my pocket. 'Money,' I said.

When the time came for the Requiem Mass, I led the other girls in slow procession behind the nuns. We walked in silence, our black mantillas covering our faces. When we reached the chapel we went up the centre aisle past the coffin of Mother Mary Rose. With shock I saw that the lid was open. Each one of the nuns in front of me stopped for a moment to take a last look at her and to say a whispered goodbye. Some bent to kiss her. I kept my eyes closed as I passed her. At the altar we genuflected and split into two lines to process down the side aisles, some to fill up the benches from the back, the rest of us to climb the choir stairs. Mother Agnes, in front of me, took her place on the organ bench and handed me my sheet music, then nodded to me to go back down and along the aisle and to take my place in the centre there so the nun in her coffin was between me and the altar. I could see her white wax face, and her still hands that were folded for ever. Footsteps cluttered round the chapel as the little ones came in last and filled up the front rows of benches below. The quiet organ notes thrilled on the air, a flutter sound.

The priest entered in his black vestments. The serving nuns took their places, heads bowed, and the congregation of children and nuns stood. The incense was blessed, and the smell of its sweet-spiced smoke in the thurible of burning charcoal stung my eyes and my throat. The priest moved to the right of the altar and the music for the Introit began. I stepped forward slightly, the sheet music trembling in my hand, and when the shrill bell rang and the figures around me bent their heads and I sang, I felt a calmness that I had not known for months.

Later, Noni and Biddy and I stood in the upstairs bay and watched the nuns. They huddled together like crows in the grey light, silently waiting, until at some soundless signal they came together in twos behind Reverend Mother to form the funeral procession. Wind lifted and lashed their robes, and leaves scuttled dry around their feet. As they moved forward they began to sing in the sweet quavering way nuns have, and their voices drifted up to us on the gusts of wind.

'*Dies irae, dies illa…*'

The slow black river of swirling robes wound its way down, down, and was lost from sight and came to us again through the bowing trees.

'I can almost see Mother Rose herself,' Noni said. 'She would be like a mangy old sheepdog, darting among her flock of black sheep.'

'Yapping at their ankles,' said Biddy. 'In time, Mothers, in time. Will you listen to me now!'

'You're a giddy goat, Mother Stanislaus! Won't you keep up with the others!'

'It's my funeral procession…'

'And I want you to get it right, so I do, so I do! Sing up, you little goose!'

'What do they remind you of?' I asked them.

The nuns had stopped. We could just see them, head down, flocking together now around the priest.

'Birds. With clipped wings.'

And so it was that I came at last to the forbidden place, holy of holies, the nuns' burial ground. The blank row of little flat stones was well ordered, protected by the evergreen trees and shrubs which crowded in on all sides. Beneath my feet the soil was moist, newly turned and tossed on the plain coffin of Mother Mary Rose.

I crumbled earth and scattered it across the fresh mound which bedded her. My wild thoughts were still at last. The anger and wretchedness and hate that I associated with her always had all dissolved. I felt only compassion for a cantankerous old woman who had died in great sickness. She was the same age as me when she first came here. Sixty-two years she had spent embalmed in the mystery of the Church.

Do you know what you have rejected, Mother? I whispered. And I felt as if I was speaking to my true mother at last. Do you regret the slow barren years?

Once an Italian boy gripped my hands in his, and left me to my tenderness. Once there was a virgin who was hollow. I don't understand your love. I don't understand your God. I have been beguiled. I have lifted the veil of the tabernacle and seen the gleam of trinkets.

I put my hands in my pockets and fingered the notes that Father Carolyn and Rory had given me. I knew already how they would be spent. I would go to Liverpool and stay with my brother. I would get a job and I would learn to sing.

I will be worthy, Mother. I will be worthy.

Part Two

Requiem

How long ago that seems. What arrogance of hope she had, that child that I was. How like writhing birth is the casting off of skins, the gasping swim to light.

Yet under the one glittering skin lies another. I should have known that.

I can smell my thoughts, they are so potent. I can taste them and hear their music. Especially that, rising and falling like the echoes of the sea in a shell.

Chapter Twenty-seven

I came to Venice like a child again, my hopes in my open hand.

Venice. That tricksy city.

In front of the station of Santa Lucia was a white open square. I had a glass of wine there while I watched the traffic on the Grand Canal. I wasn't expected here for two days, so there was no one to meet me. Good. I basked in the fleshy heat. All around me were stalls full of tourist junk, and the babble of voices in many tongues, and the fuss of pigeons.

'*Felice soggiorno*,' the waiter called after me as I tipped too many coins on the table. I am not a tourist, I would tell him. I am a working woman. I found the station for the vaporetto to take me along the Grand Canal, green with the reflection of the copper domes of San Simeone Piccolo. 'How beautiful it is,' I told the passengers next to me. 'How can a city be so exquisite? How can solid matter be so delicate?' They turned away from me, smiling at each other. Like a child I scrambled to be the first to disembark at the Rialto Bridge; and I wandered in a dream through narrow streets of high pastel houses and antique shops with their litter of dark paintings and decorated pots. Thin cats wound round my feet. Canaries hung in cages from high windows, spilling their song. Piano scales trickled through shutters. I stopped at a market stall. Cabbages were displayed like flowers; yellow, red, green, purple. I filled my bag with fruits. 'I don't want these,' I said to a child. 'Show me a good place to stay and you can have them.' He understood 'Show me' and darted in front of me, glancing back occasionally to make sure I was still with him.

'Zatterie,' he panted. 'Giudecca Island.'

'Lovely?' I asked him. 'Nice?'

'Lovely nice,' he promised me. He hung down his head, holding out his hand and looking up at me through his dark fringe. I gave him the fruit and he shook his head. I gave him money as well. 'Take them, take them,' I insisted. 'For Mama!' He scooped the fruits in his arms. 'How lucky you are to live in this beautiful city. Do you know, I have never been so happy?' He smiled at me, understanding nothing.

'Perhaps I can stay here now,' I thought. The idea frightened me. 'Perhaps I will make my home here at last.'

The child darted away as the ferry approached. I found a hotel with rooms that were dark and cool. I topped up a bath with perfumed oils and let my body slide into it. I leaned back, eyes closed, breathing in the scent. No more running. Peace now, peace. Without drying myself or dressing I wandered round my room unpacking my few possessions. So little to show for over thirty years. What had happened to all the moments?

I opened the shutters of my room and leaned out, as the Italian women did in their gossipings. Far below me people wandered backwards and forwards in the square like fishes drifting in shimmering water. Only two days ago I had left all my known friends behind, and the man who had asked me to share his life with him. Oh no, not that. I had turned, and turned, and turned again from that.

At mid-morning I came out of my hotel again into the heat. Huge ocean-going vessels loomed against a vivid sky. I took the ferry again and asked to be directed back to the Grand Canal. Voices splashed round me. People with cameras pressed against me, smiling apologies. 'I am not a tourist,' my smiles told them. 'I live here.'

I wandered aimlessly, like a drunken woman, and without knowing it I entered the piazza San Marco, and could have cried for its beauty. I walked through the square towards the basilica in a lilt of music from café orchestras. Always the flurrying of pigeon wings, and the rising and falling hum of voices, and everywhere, colour: the tall red campanile, the pale classical arcades, the green Byzantine domes and all those winking mosaics of the basilica.

Dazed with it all, I went inside. Mass was being celebrated at the central altar by an ancient priest. His voice hissed between the clatterings of footsteps. Visitors were asked to stand at the back until it was finished. The gloom pressed down on me after the light and bustle of the piazza. I looked round at the gilt and blue and greens of all the mosaics on the domed ceilings, and the huge dark paintings on the gold walls, the dark wooden carved reredos behind the altar, the patterned marble of the tilting floor, and it was like feasting beyond feasts. The priest's whispers flicked round me. I had to get out. The air stifled me. I tried to push through the crowds towards the entrance, and as I reached the doorway a family arrived, late for the service; a man and a woman, a girl in her teens, two small neat children clinging to her. The man held back the door for me to go through, and touched my arm. I looked up, and recognised him.

And it was a startling thing to see someone from my past when I was a stranger in a dreamed place. It was like seeing one of my family almost, after all these estranged years, and yet not seeing them. Not seeing them at all.

I went outside into the brilliance and sat in one of those bright café chairs drinking cold white wine and watching the lift and sweep of the pigeons and waiting for him to come out again from the basilica. Maybe I was mistaken. It must be more than fifteen years. When he came out I pretended not to notice until I felt sure he was looking for me too, and then with a kind of knowing dread I watched him say goodbye to the woman, a hand on each of her shoulders. I looked into my wine glass and glanced up again as he came over to me, his head a little to one side, his smile a surprised question.

'I think you are Cecilia?' he said.

'Yes,' I said. 'I am.'

'I am Angelo Caravelli,' he said. He held out his hand to me and I stood up.

'I remember you,' I said.

How foolish I felt, smiling like that, as we sat down together and he invited me to have more wine with him. I could smell his skin and a perfume on his hair or his clothes. We sat in near silence and smiled at each other. He spread out his hands and shrugged.

'So? In Venice now?'

And I laughed, as if he knew already about all my wanderings and had discounted them.

'I've just come today,' I told him. 'I'm going to live here now, I think.'

'Good. Very good.'

He poured out wine for both of us.

'Why Venice?'

'Why not?'

We both laughed. He leant back in his chair to seem easy, spreading out his hand on the table, his first and second fingers in a vee around the stem of the glass. His rings gleamed.

'Were they your family?' I indicated the basilica.

He counted his answer with taps of his hand. 'My wife. My three daughters.'

'Good heavens. Three children!'

He shrugged. 'When I was nineteen I was married. I was a boy, but I thought I was a grown man. You know what love is, after all.'

No, Angelo. I do not.

'And what about your families?'

'I don't have one.'

He tutted. 'In Ireland. How are your families in Ireland?'

An old hurt swelled up in me. 'Well,' I said. 'As far as I know.'

'Ireland is a long way away.'

'It is. Have you ever been back?'

'Not once.'

'And neither have I,' I told him.

He nodded slowly. 'I thought so,' he said. 'I thought so.'

We drank a little more wine. It was going to my head already. I was frightened of getting giggly.

'So Cecilia did not get married.' He raised his glass to me.

'Much too busy.'

'Never be too busy to get married. You must be busy with some person.' He put his head to one side and coaxed a smile out of me.

That night I recalled all this word for word as I lay naked on the top of my bed. I had opened the shutters after I had put out the light. Somewhere in the room a mosquito whined. I will have bumps all over me tomorrow, I thought. I switched on the fan and lay back again, loving the moving air on my flesh. I am too hot, Angelo.

He had ordered more wine. The sides of the glass carafe were misted. He poured some out for me, spilling a little on his fingers and then sucking them gently against his mouth, as if he was kissing them. A slow languor crept around in my limbs. I knew it well.

'I will be working here,' I had told him.

'Well then. We shall have many more meetings like this.'

Soon I would have to find the apartments of my employer, though she wouldn't be expecting me yet. I had met her in Lyons where she was staying in the same hotel as my small touring opera company. She was the English wife of a wealthy Italian jeweller, and we met because I spilt coffee all down her skirt and went mortified with her to her room to help to clean her up.

'It really doesn't matter,' she told me. 'It's a horrible skirt.'

'It's a lovely skirt.'

'I never wear it.'

'Well you should. It suits you.'

She stood in her damp underclothes and held the skirt out to me. 'Really, it would suit you much more, with your hair. You have it.'

'I really couldn't,' I said, astonished.

'Get it cleaned. I'll get it cleaned, and you can have it.'

'No, really. I couldn't.'

She sat down on her bed, her skirt a ball now in her hands. 'I'll be glad to go home,' she said. 'It's been one damn thing after another.'

'Are you on holiday?'

'Would you come here on holiday?'

'No.' I agreed.

'I'm the businessman's wife, if you know what that means.'

'Not really.'

'It means that I eat too much and sit around getting bored when he's at his conferences. You're with the opera group, aren't you?'

'Yes,' I said. 'We're halfway through a European tour.'

'You're good,' she said. 'It's the only thing I've enjoyed this week, anyway. You're the lead, aren't you? The prima donna?'

I laughed. 'Only tonight. Next week I'll be in the chorus.'

'That must be a drag,' she said. 'I'd want to be the star every week. Besides, you have such a gorgeous voice! What a pity to waste it in the chorus!'

I shrugged. 'It's our policy,' I told her. 'And I helped to form the company.'

'So you like it that way.'

'It's wonderful.'

'Is it really?' She stared at me intently, making me uncomfortable.

'We've been going eight years,' I said. 'It's been a wonderful time for me.'

'But you don't enjoy it now.'

'Oh, I do.'

'Eight years in the chorus?' she smiled.

'On and off.' I smiled back. 'And it's a good chorus.'

She nodded, saying nothing.

'We're like a family.'

'But you are not happy,' she told me.

No. I was not happy. I was afraid.

And she had said as simply as if she was offering me a meal, that she could give me a job in Venice if I wanted. A home.

'Yes,' I said. 'I'll take it!'

She laughed. 'Think about it!'

'I've already thought about it.'

'Tell me tomorrow,' she suggested.

Next day I told David, who ran the company and who was my closest friend, that when the contract ended I wanted to leave. He tightened the muscles in his face but did not look at me. I knew his anger well. I knew he loved me.

'When will it be?' he asked quietly.

'I know exactly when it will be. In September.'

'But I want you to play Tosca when we open in France,' he said.

'I know, David.'

'It's your part. You have always wanted Tosca.'

'Yes. I know. I don't want it now.'

'You were born to sing Tosca. You always said so.'

'Please, David.'

Let me go. I did not understand myself. Let me go.

'I don't understand you,' he said.

How could he have understood me? All I knew was that I was afraid.

'Cecilia,' he said, taking both my hands in his. 'I want to marry you.'

That was it. Now I understood myself.

I stood in the dressing-room for the last time exactly a week before coming to Venice and hung up my gown with its stains of grease-paint and its hem dark with dust, and shook out the wig of black gleaming hair. I covered my face with removal cream and wiped off the sweat of carmine and powder. My face gleamed pale in the huge mirror. I felt nothing. I picked up my little pots and tubes of paint, my brushes and powders, and let them chock together in the wooden box with the sliding lid that my singing teacher in

Liverpool had given me. With a nail file I had scratched my name into the varnish, long ago.

The women in the chorus had brought small gifts for me. I had known some of them for years.

'You would probably get Tosca next time round,' one of them said. The music surged like a fountain in me. It always will. 'Don't you want it?'

I shook my head, not trusting myself to speak.

'You're mad!' she said. 'Your wonderful voice!'

And next day David saw me to the station.

'I wish you wouldn't go,' he said. 'Now you've made me want to leave, too.'

He held my hand, as he often did. He had a way of rubbing his thumbnail with his first finger as if he was polishing it. I'd grown used to that. I used to hate it.

'I want you,' he said.

No, I thought. Not that.

'Should I come to Venice to see you?'

'No, David.'

Traffic noises bellowed round us as we walked. We had to shout.

'I hate it here.' I turned my face to him so he could read my words. I had hurt him. He was my only friend.

Already the company trucks had been loaded up for the next stage in the tour. Toulouse it would be, and then Amsterdam. Soon the unloading would begin, the dresses would be shaken out with their pungent smells of sweat and sweet grease. New rehearsals would begin on a strange stage in a dark theatre. The hotel would be too noisy, too quiet, the food would be awful. David would sit in a corner of the bar and be unhappy for a while.

He helped me up the high steps of the train and bundled in my luggage after me. I was laughing.

'Is this really all you have?'
I can see his face now, smiling goodbye, sad.
Is that really all there is? No, Angelo. I did not understand.

Chapter Twenty-eight

Andrea, my English friend, lived in a fifteenth century palazzo on the Grand Canal. From the outside it didn't look the home of a wealthy family. The stucco walls were crumbling and dingy; what had been a fresco design above the door was faded. It was surrounded by other, grander palazzi, with many windows and balconies, and carvings like stone lace. I had to go by gondola, rowed by two oarsmen. They pulled up at the poles outside her steps and helped me out.

Andrea's maid told me she was not at home, she had gone to the market to buy flowers. I could see behind the maid to a hallway that seemed to be walled in carved wooden panels. Triangles of light slanted across them. I decided to stand outside and wait for her. Canal traffic fractured the images of the ancient buildings; shouts and whistles and singing echoed across. I was a little nervous about meeting Andrea again; our meeting had, after all, been brief, and I had set so much on it, and on her warm generosity. Before long she appeared in a water-taxi, waving to me from a distance, and clambered out onto her steps with a young girl at her side.

'Cecilia!' She passed on her armload of irises to her daughter and came up to me with her arms out, kissing me on both cheeks.

'I came early,' I told her. 'Couldn't wait.'

'Come on in out of this terrible heat,' she said. 'Do you know, sometimes I long for good old English drizzle. Mind you, we get plenty of that in the winter here. You'll see.'

She introduced me to her daughter, Gianetta, who was a sallow, long-limbed girl of about fifteen, with hair the colour of yellow coins. She tilted her face for me to kiss her cheek. I was to be her singing teacher.

'There'll be loads more pupils for you by the end of the week,' her mother promised me. 'You've no idea how rich most of the people are round here. They all have beautiful daughters who are dying to be opera stars, isn't that so, Gianetta?' The girl rounded her shoulders and pouted.

'And do you want to be a singer, Gianetta?' I asked.

Again the girl shrugged. Her yellow-brown hair swung forward across her face as she lowered her head.

Her mother laughed and led me into the palazzo, which was dark and hung with huge old paintings. We went into a room with a carved ceiling and walls and heavy carved furniture. By the shuttered window an old woman sat in a straight-backed cane chair. Her hair was scraped to her skull and she wore a long black dress and shawl. Her dry hands fidgeted on her lap as I went over to her with my hand out. She looked dimly at me, mouthing prayers. I touched her shoulder, and bent down to kiss her dry old cheek. '*Buon giorno, signora.*' Her fingers cracked as she clasped and unclasped her hands.

'My husband's mother, the old contessa,' Andrea said. 'She doesn't take much notice of life these days. Can't speak a word of English, of course, and precious little Italian. Sit down, Cecilia.'

The chairs were all rigid. The house had a distinct smell of damp. I imagined its cellars awash with the waters of the canal. I felt that when the rains came it would creak and sway like an old ship, that it was a painted ark washed up from yesterday's shores. Three small children ran in to us noisily and hesitated when they saw me, then came to be kissed. Andrea's husband, whom I had met in Lyons, came in briefly with another man; they both offered their soft, ringed hands for shaking, then kissed everyone before going out, wishing me great happiness in Venice.

'I'm a stranger here, after thirty years,' Andrea told me. 'You will be made very welcome by the Venetians. I'll introduce you to all the people I know, and they'll take you into their homes and overwhelm you with Venetian hospitality, overwhelm you I'm telling you. They'll stroke you to bits with it! But you'll always be a stranger. Does that worry you, if you make your home here?'

'Not at all. I like my own company.'

'And that's something you'll never be forgiven for.'

A maid served us with iced coffee and pastries and stood arms akimbo in the doorway, staring at me. Her legs bulged from the bottom of her tight black dress and she wore thonged sandals that flapped as she walked.

'In Italian the word for 'alone' is the same as the word for 'lonely',' Andrea went on. Her youngest child sprawled across her knee as she drank, ruching up her good clothes with the heel of her shoe as she squirmed and wriggled. '*Solo*. It means the same thing. You'll never be allowed to be alone, because they couldn't bear you to be lonely. Can you stand that?'

I could not, I thought. Aloneness is a chosen state. 'After all,' I told her, 'I will have the privacy of my apartment.'

'You can try,' she laughed. 'You can try. Privacy. That's a strange idea here. Well, you tell me, Cecilia, do you want to live here with us or do you want your own apartment. You tell me.'

'I took a hotel room on Giudecca. I thought I'd look for somewhere there.'

'Good heavens, you don't want to be over there. We'll move you tomorrow.'

'I like it there.'

'I'll get you a place of your own. I don't blame you. These children would drive you mad. Utterly mad.'

She bent her youngest child over, sucking her face with noisy kisses. The child rubbed her cheek with the back of her hand and tilted her head back to laugh up at me.

'They're lovely,' I murmured.

'Not if you don't have children yourself. Do you have a family, Cecilia? No. I didn't think you had, somehow.'

I sat with my eyes lowered and hands clasped round the glass. The maid leaned over me and filled it up for me.

'Apartments are the very devil to find, I tell you. You need to get in by *raccomandazione*. You might call it 'pulling strings'.' Andrea laughed. 'Bribery or nepotism, it amounts to. You haven't a hope otherwise.'

The maid shouted at one of the children and slopped over to shoo them away from the pastries. She took one herself, breaking it up, sly, and offered half of it to the one who was crying.

'I have a friend who has a lovely apartment to let overlooking Rio di Santa Lucia. Really it's quite beautiful. It's just a pigeon spit from La Fenice - you'll be able to hear them tuning up from there. And San Marco is just round the corner. You'll get used to the bells, of course.'

'I don't know if I could afford somewhere like that,' I told her.

She waved her hand at me. 'Now you can stop that. She really needs someone to keep it aired for her, you know. And besides, my husband did her father a favour. That's how things work here. You'll soon find out,' she sighed. 'Contacts. Family contacts and 'good friends'. It's better than the Old Boy system, I suppose. Anyway, Cecilia, by Christmas you'll have so many pupils the thought of money won't enter your head.'

The old contessa bent over in her chair and spat onto the marble floor.

I walked back to the piazza, where I had arranged to meet Angelo. My tongue had stuck on the name Andrea as I had left her. I no longer knew what to call her. In my mind I told Angelo all about it, as one rehearses a speech in a play. I wondered whether he had a house with marble floors and whether he kept old parents cool in dark corners. I imagined him lifting up the youngest child and swinging her in the air to make her laughter echo in the house. Somewhere in a large kitchen his oldest daughter would make coffee for him, skimming the top lightly before she handed it to him to drink. I imagined the noise of all his children in the house, and him the centre of all their rioting. I did not imagine where his wife would be.

I should write to David, I thought, to chase away the criminal imaginings in my head, but I was comforted by the knowledge that I would not. I had left many Davids behind, and they had no more substance for me now than remembered dreams. And a man with a wife is quite safe. He is like a priest. He is untouchable, after all.

And I only agreed to meet with him that day because he had offered to show me round Venice, as anyone would. When I saw him again standing by the campanile I was afraid. It had crossed my mind that maybe this time I would not recognise him, or that he would change his mind and not wish to be lumbered with a grown woman who had been his friend when he was a little boy. He had not been out of my thoughts since he had touched my arm in the basilica. I remembered the whisper of leaves of long ago, and the child that I was tilting her face up to his for a kiss.

There was a hint of white in his dark curls, I noticed. He looked up and waved to me and, shy, I stood still so he had to come across, weaving through the family groups of tourists. He shouted to me that I was late. He put a hand on each of my shoulders and kissed my cheeks. I could smell his body.

'Can you speak Venetian?' he asked me.

'I can speak Italian a little. I can sing in it.'

'The whole world can sing in Italian!' He stood back and began to sing the familiar aria from *I Pagliacci*, holding out his hands theatrically, mocking his own good voice.

'Bravo!' I giggled. He bowed with a flourish to a white-faced couple who stopped to stare at him.

'I will teach you my language,' he promised me, 'because without it you cannot survive here. And I will polish up your Italian.'

'I'll need a lot of lessons then,' I said.

He spread out his hands and shrugged. 'Maybe you are very clever.'

I couldn't look at him. I stood beside him with my head bowed. He touched my arm.

'But today I will show you my country.'

We walked under the clock tower and through the Mercerie, bustling as it was with shoppers and sightseers. He taught me to ask for a pistachio ice-cream and the seller tossed the green blob from the cornet in his left hand and caught it with the cornet in his right hand without taking his eyes off me. 'Manchester United,' he said.

'I'm Irish,' I told him.

'I must go away now,' Angelo said. 'I have to do work, after all.'

'Thank you for the tour.' The ice-cream was melting already. I didn't really want it.

'It's not finished,' Angelo said. 'If you like I can take you further tomorrow.'

'I'm moving house,' I said.

'In the evening it will be cool,' he promised. He bowed his head and looked up at me. 'It is good to see you again.'

'I know,' I said, foolish. The ice-cream was running down my fingers, dripping round my feet.

'I have in mind for seven at night, at the same place.'

'Thank you, Angelo.' I said.

He bowed a little formally and walked away quickly through the shoppers. I tipped my ice-cream into a bin, watched by the seller, and licked my fingers. Even my toes were sticky now.

The next day I brought my bags over from the hotel on Giudecca and was taken by water-taxi to the apartment that Andrea had rented for me. I seemed to be surrounded by churches and convents. Nuns in cream habits were sweeping the courtyard as I walked through, so that pale clouds of dust floated round their sandalled feet. They nodded to me as I passed. A small boy who was playing in the entrance ran to them and was laughingly chased away. There was a well in the centre of the courtyard hedged in with a brilliant display of crimson and mauve nasturtiums in terracotta pots.

A maid opened the door to me, and in the hallway behind her a huge gilt-framed mirror showed me myself in my summer dress, the plants and the dust and the peering nuns behind me. She silently showed me round the green marble rooms, pointing to the bathroom, the bedroom, the kitchen, the lounge, putting her hand on the piano and lifting up its lid for me, demonstrating the opening and closing of the shutters, and showing me the door key.

I wondered whether she was mute, or whether my Italian remarks were totally incomprehensible.

'*Grazie*,' I said when she had finished, and without acknowledging me in any way she picked up her shopping basket and went out, locking the door behind her. I immediately unlocked it and left it wide open, and opened out the shutters. The walls were cluttered with poor paintings of Venice. I wondered about taking them down, but thought maybe they had been painted by the owner of the flat. And anyway, I had nothing to replace them with. Somewhere in London in the house of a singing acquaintance was a box with a few of my bits and pieces. I hadn't seen them for six or seven years. I certainly didn't miss them. Maybe there were some sweetheart letters there, and a photograph or two. It didn't matter. The walls of my room shimmered with reflections from the water. I could hear the swish of barges going past my window. 'It's wonderful,' I said aloud. 'It's all wonderful.'

At midday I heard the Angelus bell and almost stopped in my unpacking from a long-suppressed reflex. There would be people pausing in their rooms maybe and on the pavements in full sunshine; and far away in fields that rustled with the breath of the wind in the barley they would be bending their heads in prayer. I had forgotten. I sat down at the piano and lifted up the lid. I could play, but not well; enough. I tried the keys gently. I could still hear the bell of the Angelus, though whether it was in my head or outside my rooms I couldn't tell. I breathed slowly, trying to let in silence, and at last, almost without knowing that I was doing it, I began to play. I could see lemon light on white hands. I could hear the echo of whispers.

The girl Gianetta came in to my apartment without knocking and stood by the piano. I could hear her fidgeting, and looked up at her when I was ready. She came to me to be kissed.

I said, 'You do speak English, don't you Gianetta?'

She nodded.

'And are you looking forward to your lessons?'

She nodded again. 'My mother says I must tell you she has found three more pupils for you, to begin tomorrow.'

I felt a rush of nerves. 'Well,' I laughed. 'I will be busy, after all.'

'She says I have to come every day.'

'That's Ok. We'll just do a little, you know. We won't hurt your voice.'

She smiled at last. 'Hurt?'

'We won't do too much. Shall we start now? Shall I just hear the sound of your voice, Gianetta, to give me an idea?'

Goodness, I was more nervous than she was.

Mechanically she copied the arpeggios I played out for her on the piano. She had a pleasant, breathy voice. I would be able to do a great deal to improve it, that was for sure. Pleased, I closed the piano.

'If they are all as good as you, Gianetta, I am going to enjoy teaching the daughters of your mother's friends.'

I walked with her to the bridge. A group of girls were waiting for her. On the other side were some boys, leaning together, laughing, talking loudly so the girls would hear.

'Go straight home now,' I told her. She pushed her fingers through her hair and shrugged.

I had hours to wait.

That night I walked with Angelo along the Canale de San Marco. Water has such a peculiar bloom in late evening, a cast of silver across it, and such a hush about it. We listened together to the whisper of it round the poles where the gondolas nestled, and then in early darkness made for the Giardini di Castello. We no longer talked. My burst of early prattle about the apartment and Gianetta hung in my ears. He walked with his hands clasped behind his back, head bowed.

'I wanted to bring you here,' he said, 'because it is a place that is special to me.'

I wondered why, but daren't ask. I knew already that it was to be our sanctuary for many weeks to come, and that the walk back through shadowy canal passages to my apartment would become familiar and customary. Our footsteps echoed across the water. He is a married man, I thought.

'Tomorrow.'

'Tomorrow I will be busy. I have my singing lessons.'

'Then tomorrow you should begin your lessons in Venetian.'

'Just an hour.'

'Of course.'

That night I couldn't sleep. I lay awake on top of my new bed and heard the quiet sheesh of water, like a sighing in my head. Am I really home now, I thought. Is this it?

Two new pupils came in the morning with their mothers. The women stayed while the girls had their first lessons, and stayed on, talking and laughing, while I gave them coffee and did my best with my Italian. They seemed to have the day to spend with me, and when I told them I had a lesson with Gianetta in the afternoon they seemed quite set on staying on to hear her sing. They had always known Gianetta, they said. She came from one of the oldest families in Venice. Her father was a powerful man. My rooms rang with their voices. I gazed out of my windows at the rippled reflections. Someone in a nearby apartment was playing the piano. The sound was like another dimension of light on the water.

I wondered what the people in David's opera company would be doing now. They would be in rehearsal, perhaps. I had not used my voice since I had left them. I should be practising every day. What was I doing here, I asked myself, teaching the daughters of rich women?

'I'm very tired,' I told the women. 'I must sleep a little before Gianetta comes.'

Of course. They understood that. The heat was terrible for foreigners at the moment. They never came out after ten, themselves. I must come to their houses and meet their families. 'Of course,' I smiled, opening the door at last for them. '*Grazie. Grazie.*'

In the afternoon Gianetta arrived without knocking again, and came straight to my piano as I sat preparing the sheet music and making notes.

'I have brought Rosa,' she said.

Rosa lingered in the doorway. She wore a skimpy child's dress that was grown too short and tight for her. Her limbs gleamed like silk.

'Come in, Rosa. Have you come for lessons too?'

She didn't understand me, but flicked a nervous glance at Gianetta.

'Well, I'll hear you in a minute,' I said. 'Gianetta, you can sing a scale or two just to show her what we do.'

Gianetta was very quick and confident. I found a simple song to teach her, knowing that her mother would want to hear her sing when she got home, and would notice the daily progress. I had no way of knowing whether the girl liked singing or not. 'Maybe it's better not to,' I thought to myself, and had told myself that many times.

'Now Rosa,' I smiled. '*Il solfeggio*, Rosa.'

Again Rosa darted a timid glance at Gianetta. I noticed how her fingers fumbled with the hem of her skirt. Outside on the canal passing bargemen and gondoliers shouted greetings to each other. The girl's hair was lank and greasy. She is poor, I thought, surprised. There is no money here. And as soon as she pitched her first note and began to sing I felt that chilling of my spine that only music gives, when for a moment the blood runs cold as snow with it. I stopped playing, wanting to listen, and she faltered.

'Go on, Rosa.'

She hung her head. Her hair fell forward over her face in black loops. I wanted to smooth it back behind her ears for her.

'You can sing, Rosa,' I whispered. '*Tu sai cantare.*'

Rosa turned away. I could tell that she was shaking.

'You mustn't be afraid. Your voice is beautiful. *Hai una bella voce.*'

I looked at Gianetta. 'Tell her.'

Gianetta spoke quickly to her in a thick, clipped dialect. A half-smile flickered across Rosa's mouth. She put her hands to her face.

'My mother will pay for her if you like her,' Gianetta told me.

'Your mother is very good.' I wished Rosa would look up at me. She was a tiny, fragile thing in her thin dress and her hair loose and untidy. 'Come together again tomorrow, won't you? But soon I must teach you separately.' I felt a sense of urgency. What if the child never came again? 'You understand?' Gianetta nodded. 'You will come, Rosa?'

But the girl had given way to her nervousness and had glanced quickly at Gianetta and had caught the other girl's pursed smile. They both began to shake with silent laughter.

'Shush!' I said, half-angry with them both, excluded. The child put her fingers in her mouth and looked at me, guilty, her eyes still bright with laughing, and I laughed with her. She swung away from me, overcome.

'Sit down, the pair of you,' I said. 'I'll sing something for you. Rosa, one day you will sing this. Tell her that, Gianetta.' The girls whispered together in their chairs. I knew they were laughing again. I looked away and sat with my hands poised, taking in my slow, deep breaths. Their murmurings dissolved away from me. I began to sing, and it was not in the way I had been singing all these years. I had forgotten this. I made a tiny sound with my voice and held it where it could just be heard, just there, cradled. The room was a silent well and the sound was a point of light in it. And then I poured colour in it so that it soared and spread, so the air was drenched in it. For years and years I had not sung like this. This is not for you, Gianetta with the hair like yellow coins. This is not for you, Rosa of limbs like darkened silk.

When I had finished singing, the girls had gone.

'And now you are a happy person,' Angelo said, and I agreed with him. I was.

'But I've been happy since I came to Venice,' I told him.

He shook his head. 'Not true. You have a sadness.'

Our Italian lesson for the day was finished, and we were walking away from our café.

'I will go very slowly with Rosa,' I told him. 'It will be quite wrong to push her.'

'Is she so good?'

'She has a wonderful voice.'

'Can you tell now, from a few little squeaks you have heard?'

'She has a quality. One day she'll be a singer. She has to be.'

'And what about you?'

'Me? I'll stay here to teach her.' I was quite sure of that now.

'Of course. But you. Have you a 'quality'?'

'I believe, once, somebody thought I had.'

'And it went away, no?'

Oh Angelo, don't press me like this. How the music surges in me still. 'When somebody has that kind of faith... it's a kind of love. It's an inspiration. You become what they want of you.'

'So simple.'

'I think so. You do it for them.'

I felt I should ask him about his family, and did not know how to. I formed sentences in my head and left them unspoken. They were trivial. Perhaps he would ask me to his home. It would be a courtesy. It would be a gesture of hospitality and friendship such as the women had made, and I would accept. He did not ask me.

When we reached my apartment I told him that my Italian lessons must stop for a few days.

'Why?' he asked, surprised.

'Because... I must prepare a lot of music for my pupils.'

'But not in the evenings?'

'In the evenings I must rest.'

He tutted. 'Then you don't like the time you spend with me.'

'I do. Of course I do.'

'Then why not come?'

I had no way of explaining to him. 'It's better, that's all.'

'No. It's worse,' he said. 'I like to be with you.'

I shook my head and turned away abruptly. Inside my room, with the closed door behind me, I heard him begin to walk away. I locked the door. I had a dread inside myself. I did not understand myself.

I was nervous all next day in case Rosa didn't come. She arrived with Gianetta and hovered in the doorway till I took her arm and brought her in. I let her sit through the whole of Gianetta's lesson then sent the other girl away. I took her through her breathing exercises and scales. She had a voice that soared, and yet she was afraid of it. How well I understood that.

'Do you love singing?' I asked her.

'*Sì,*' she said, a little doubtfully.

I told her to come again tomorrow, and she shook her head.

'The day after?'

Again she shook her head.

'When, Rosa?'

'In a week.'

Next week! I must sit for so long through all the pretty voices and the mechanical scales for this one small reward.

'But you will practise?'

'*Sì,*' she said, doubtful again.

'Good girl.'

That night I sat at my window, lonely as one can be only in a city where so much is going on, so many voices and drifts of laughter are heard. I wanted to walk but was afraid that if I did

I would bump into Angelo again and he would think I had gone in search of him. He would be with his wife and family, bringing them home from church, or on their family walk, and he would see me and know I had gone looking for him. But that would be all right, if he was with them. No, I didn't want to see him with his wife and family. I must not see him again.

I had bread and fruit in my apartment. That was all I would eat. For three nights I had eaten with Angelo at the café. What did they think of this at his home? His wife would be a loud woman, railing at him in the kitchen, charred smoke stinking in her hair. She would be silent. She would sit playing her piano softly and would not look up when he came in, but glance at the door as he closed it behind him on his way to the bedroom. For a moment her hands would rest on the keys and then she would begin to play again. She played beautifully. She would meet him as he came in. She would weep, and he would stroke her hair and lift her chin to kiss her. She was ugly perhaps. He could not bear to look at her. She was beautiful, with many lovers. At night they talked about her lovers and his mistresses as they lay between cream embroidered sheets. He told her everything about me, and she laughed. She was jealous. He told her nothing about me. They loved. They slept apart.

There was nothing to tell her.

After three days I heard from him again. I found a note through my door inviting me to see *Tosca* at La Fenice. I arrived, breathless, at the bridge near the opera house where he had offered to meet me. I was early as it happened, and so was he. I had rehearsed what I must say to him. When I saw him I stopped running like a child and made myself walk casually, taking my deep breaths to slow my gasps. He greeted me noisily. I couldn't stop smiling at him.

'Cecilia! How are the pupils?'

'Oh, it's going really well, Angelo. I have one or two good ones, you know. And more to begin next week.'

'And now you're happy to spend your day off with me?'

'I would love to see *Tosca* with you,' I said, shy suddenly. 'It's my favourite opera.'

'You are a romantic lady, after all.'

'Maybe,' I shrugged, still smiling. Then I made myself say it. 'Would you not like to see it with your wife?'

He hardly responded, after all. 'My wife does not like music,' he said. 'She likes church.'

I laughed a little. It would be easy to leave it there. 'But *Tosca* is like church,' I reminded him, but only out of embarrassment and my old insane perverseness. I talked too fast, too lightly. 'It makes me think of the best things about church, the only things I miss. I love the *Te Deum* procession, don't you, best of all the opera processions? There will be choirboys and candles and incense. She will be very much at home with *Tosca*, your wife.'

He looked down at me, silencing my rush of sound. 'Do you really want my wife to come?'

'Yes. I do.'

'In that case.' He took the tickets out of his pockets and held them over the edge of the bridge. I tried to snatch them as he let go. We both laughed.

'Why is it so long since you went home?' He was still watching the white papers as they danced in the ripples made by the water traffic.

'Don't ask me about that.'

He turned, leaning his back against the wall. I turned too. He had his arm stretched out along the wall, supporting him. If I leaned back it would be supporting me.

'Did you quarrel?'

'No.'

'Then?'

'If you must know.' My voice was steady enough. 'They deceived me. Everyone deceived me about everything. Only one person told me the truth, in all my childhood. And she died.'

We began to walk. I could imagine the singers lounging in their dressing rooms, damping down the sweat that was already bubbling through the make-up. They would help each other with their dresses. I could feel the nervy hum as the orchestra began to tune up. I could see the maestro, tense and unsmiling backstage as the women from the chorus fluttered past him. I could smell the warm dust.

'I'm glad we're not going,' I told him. 'I'm not ready.'

'Of course not.'

'I would like to go back now,' I said. 'I'd like to be alone.'

The fruits of lemon and orange trees glowed like vivid lamps. My throat was dry.

'What will you do?' I asked him.

'I will meet my wife from church.'

'Good.'

I would not watch him walk away. I went in to my rooms and closed up all the shutters. I lit the lamp with its many small bulbs like candles and carried it to my dressing table. Its points of light pricked the corners of the room. Then I sat down in front of the mirror and unpinned the muslin scarf that I wore as a ribbon band so my shoulders and neck would be cool. And like a girl of sixteen this woman in her mid thirties tipped back the fading glory of her hair and smiled and smiled. Not too late. Please God let it not be too late. This time. This time.

For I had known all this before, and yet had never known it. Not this. Not this deep and swelling gathering of juices, not this peach-ripeness; not this tender yes.

Chapter Twenty-nine

Next day I went to see Tosca on my own. It was my opera, I felt. I came out, elated, my throat aching with Tosca's singing as though I had taken all the prima donna's notes myself. I decided then that I would stay in Venice. When I could afford it, I would teach only Rosa, and I would go to the maestro of La Fenice and ask for an audition. I would be in his chorus, and I would be happy. My life would be simple and sweet; it would be reduced to daily rituals.

The buying of bread was my favourite ritual. It meant leaving my apartment early and following housewives and the children, the old women in their peasant black, along the narrow passages. I could smell the bread before I arrived. When I had bought it in the dingy *panetteria* I would buy fruit from a child in the street. I would walk home in the sound of bells with my bread warm under my arm and would break off crisp chunks of it and eat it there.

When I set out early in my second week to buy my bread, the girl Rosa was sitting by my door. She scrambled to her feet, rubbing her eyes, as soon as she saw me.

'Have you come for your lesson, Rosa?' I asked her in my new careful Italian. 'Already!'

I showed her by my watch that I would be back with her in twenty minutes and she sank back to lean against the wall with her legs folded sideways, neat as a cat. So that day I hurried back with my bread untouched, fearful in case she took fright and slipped away. I brought her in and gave her coffee and bread, which she took with lowered eyes, silent. I watched without seeming to every gesture that she made, trying to know her. She broke her bread over her bowl and dipped it into her coffee, sucking it to dip again. She lifted the bowl to her mouth and lapped up with her tongue the little tessellated pieces of crust as they floated on the surface. She finished without speaking or looking up at me once, and then went to the piano and stood by it, waiting for me.

'So,' I laughed. 'Did you enjoy that? Then we're ready.' I left my own coffee unfinished.

I played the first chords for her to sing her arpeggios, and moved up and up the keyboard of the piano. Her voice soared with that cold power of thrill. I wanted her to go on and on. I wanted to stop playing for her and just lean back and listen to that soar of her voice, but when I lifted my hands she always stopped, nervous, and stood with her eyes cast down waiting for the next exercise to begin.

'Soon we will learn a song,' I told her. 'Would you like that?'

She looked anxious. She must go, she said, she had stayed too long.

'No, not yet,' I coaxed her. I was speaking half in English. 'Really, I have no pupils till this afternoon. Let's just choose the song you want to learn. I know one that you'll love. I loved it.'

I was excited. I jumped from my piano stool and bent down to open it up to search out the songs I wanted. I heard a quick flurry behind me and knew that she had gone.

With a sigh I closed the stool and fastened down the lid of the piano. The joy in the day had left for me. I went to the table and brushed the crumbs into the palm of my hand and flung them out of the window.

When Gianetta came I asked her if she had seen Rosa that day. She shrugged in her familiar laconic way and said simply that Rosa lived a long way from her, with the 'Filipinos'. Of course. I had not expected the other girl to live among the courtyards of marbled *palazzi*.

'Well,' I said. 'Never mind.'

'My mother asked me to tell you,' said Gianetta, as I opened up the piano for her, 'that she is having a party at the end of the month, for *il Carnevale*. She would like me to sing at it, and she wants you to teach me a special song.'

'What a lovely idea.' I had the song I would have given to Rosa.

'Can you come to the party too, she said.'

'That's very kind of her.'

'She would like you to play.'

So. I looked down at my hands, noticing how the sun had made the freckles spread. There would be a maid serving chilled wines, and there would be a maid serving pastries, no doubt, and there would be me, at the piano. I wondered whether I would be paid for this performance.

'She said I was to tell you that she is specially inviting people who have daughters who might like to learn to sing.'

I smiled at her. 'Your English is excellent, Gianetta.'

I had bought a new blue dress. Later I would show it to her and ask her whether it would be right for her mother's party.

A note was pushed underneath my door during the lesson. I knew it was from Angelo, and kept it there, a white patch on my mind, till the lesson was finished. As I showed Gianetta out she picked it up for me. He was asking me to meet him at the café for 'a little wine and some Venetian'. I would not go.

I set out in early evening and caught a glimpse of Rosa just outside the courtyard of my apartment. She must have been waiting for me again, but ran away along the river passage as soon as she saw me locking my door. I called out her name but my voice echoed dismally.

'Sometimes I think she doesn't exist at all,' I told Angelo. 'She's a ghost.'

'Whose ghost?' he asked me, smiling. 'The ghost who loves bread and coffee?'

But next day she came in during Gianetta's lesson. I nodded to her to sit down, hardly able to contain my pleasure. She had been running. When Gianetta left I made Rosa stand up and do her breathing exercises. 'Now, Rosa,' I said. 'I have another pupil soon. Why have you come at this time?'

She looked at me, wide-eyed, aware that she was being told off. '*Mi dispiace.*'

'It doesn't matter. We have a few minutes. But tomorrow could you come at eleven o'clock, say?' She shrugged. I showed her by the clock.

'*Non so, signora.*'

'You really don't know?'

She shook her head. Her breath came out in deep sighs.

'Now don't do that, or we'll have to do our breathing again.'

She frowned at me, understanding nothing but the tone of my voice.

'Do you like singing?' I asked her, trying my new Venetian dialect with care. Usually we exchanged our brief phrases in halting Italian.

She nodded. I almost caught a smile on her face.

'Well, Rosa. You must come when you are able to. It doesn't matter.'

I had the song ready on the piano. I had already begun to teach it to Gianetta. I would teach her another song, I decided. This one was for Rosa.

'Try this now,' I said. 'Just a little, Rosa.'

I daren't sing it to her. I played it with full accompaniment but just hummed the melody, glancing up from time to time to see whether she liked it.

'Well?' I asked her.

'*E troppo difficile*,' she said. It's too hard for me. I could have hugged her.

'But you'll try it.'

My next pupil had arrived with her noisy mother and her muzzled dog. As soon as they came in with all their fuss of greetings, Rosa ran out. Next time, I thought, I'll lock the door on her.

But I never did. I grew used to her brief appearances. Sometimes she came two or three times in a day, and sometimes not for days. Once she spent a whole afternoon with me, sitting wide-eyed on the floor while I played my piano for her. She sang me a song of her country, her small body responding to the power of the words that I did not understand and in gratitude and pleasure I came to embrace her in my way for it. She snuggled into my arms like a young child that day. Two minutes later, while my back was turned and while I was still speaking to her, she left. She reminded me of the birds that landed fleetingly on the narrow sill of my window, just touching down and lifting off again. I was impatient and abstracted with my other pupils till I had seen Rosa. I taught her the song a few bars at a time, note by note. She had no idea how to read music, or even, it seemed, the words. So. I would teach her to read. I would teach her to play. It was so simple. I measured my days by the minutes of her visits.

And in the evenings I walked with Angelo.

I told myself many times that Angelo was, after all, just a boy from my childhood. He was a beautiful Satan, I believe. He stepped into my life when my life was full and rich enough and made me reach out for more; when I was a child again he took my hand and led me through his city of painted air and islands, and I think he had the power of touching forbidden dreams.

'Why did you want to be a singer?' he asked me one day. His Italian-Irish accent always made me smile. 'Seenguhr', he said. 'Of all things! Whatever put such an idea into your head?'

'Because of my name,' I said simply, and he laughed.

'My name gives me no inclination to be an angel, I promise you. But you know what happened to St. Cecilia, don't you?'

I shook my head.

'Her throat was slit,' he said darkly. 'Fancy not knowing that. It would seem the most important thing to know about her.'

'Not at all.'

'Her throat was slit, and thirteen hundred years after she died they opened up her coffin and there she was, as if it had only just happened, fresh dead, you might say, in her green and gold robes that were stained with blood. And her head lolling to one side.'

'I feel as if it is myself you're describing, having her name,' I shuddered. 'I had an aunt who loved the gory details of the martyrs. I'm glad she spared me this.' I bit my lip, remembering briefly my Aunt Bridget, the way she would drop her top teeth to frighten us, the endless hoard of stories she had for us.

'People came for miles to look at her body. It was a miracle, of course, that she had such integrity.'

'That it was intact,' I corrected him. 'Incorrupt.'

'And within a short time it started to crumble, till it was just dust, just dust, nothing.' He held his arm up and opened out his fingers, as if he was trickling sand through them. He looked sideways at me and laughed aloud. 'But what an extraordinary thing that would be, Cecilia, to see that happening.'

We had stopped on a humped bridge and leaned over to look down at ourselves and at the bridges and houses and the lines of still washing in double image below us, the black gondolas with their red plastic seats and single roses, the hatted gondoliers, standing and watchful at their task, all cast in calm duplicity. A slow barge heaped up with the entire possessions of a household passed underneath. A stained mattress was flung across the top. Angelo's hand brushed against mine. It was just enough to send a rush of heat through me. As we moved away two women in black walked between us, scolding each other, and children shrieked past us to play barefoot on the bridge steps. Angelo crouched down on the top step to watch them.

'They say you can see a person's soul leave their body when they die. Or so I've heard,' I said.

He patted the top step and I crouched down next to him. The children began to show off, self-conscious at having an adult audience. 'I have seen it myself,' he said. 'I have watched over a dying person who seemed already to be lifeless and then in a second I saw the life that was in them just rise like a breath and vanish, like a candle flame being extinguished and leaving only wax.'

'I wonder why it is,' I said, 'that it's so important to Catholics that the bodies of the saints remain intact?'

'Because we all want to remain intact. So our souls and our bodies will be reunited.'

'That's pretty tough for the victims of bombs and fires.'

'Oh yes. Tough for them. Tough for all of us, if we don't like our bodies anyway. We're going to be stuck with them for all eternity.' He laughed round at me. 'You are so serious! I would like to make you laugh for joy. How can I do that?'

I had no answer for him. I was full of joy. He sat beside me, his fingers so near to mine that the air between them burned.

'I am a simple person,' he told me. 'If you want to understand me, that is all you need to know. I am what you see, and nothing is hidden.'

'What tiny imaginations people must have had,' I said, my voice a little dry in my throat. 'To think of the pleasures of heaven in physical terms. And to think the fires of hell meant the burning of the flesh.'

'There's no other way to think of them,' he said. 'If you're going to believe in them, they must be part of your living experience.'

'So this physical incorruption is victory over death.'

'And we have Eve to thank for death, remember that.'

'Oh, poor Eve,' I said. 'Poor women, always reviled.'

'Till Mary came,' he reminded me. 'The unstained woman and the virgin womb. What more could you want? Now will you be quiet!'

But his words were wings rushing me down the years to those shadowed corridors and whisper pistol-cracks.

'Do you believe all that?' I must have been shouting because the children had stopped their play and were looking up at me, half-grinning, but their faces were distorted and tilted at angles like the bridge and the buildings round me, and the blues of sky and water dissolved to the white of stone; and I must have been shivering because I had crossed my arms as if to hold myself and fold myself in against the cold that was inside me, and Angelo had reached round and put his arms around me till all my trembling stopped. It is now, I thought. Now is the time.

'I believe one thing,' he said. 'I believe it is good that you and I have come together.'

'Do you believe in God?' I asked him.

'Yes. Of course. Like I believe the earth is round, I believe in God.' He held me at arms length, puzzling at me. 'I must go Cecilia. Can I take you back to your apartment?'

'No. I want to sit here.'

'You are not well, I think.'

'Yes, I'm well,' I told him.

'Are you sure?'

'Sure. Sure. Quite sure.'

I tried to smile up at him, and he bent down to give me the Italian kiss. I turned my face away, wanting more.

'*Ciao.*'

I felt as if he was lumbering away from me in the sun's thickness; I felt he was a swimmer in a deep sea. As soon as he'd gone I wanted to run after him, and it was then that the thought came to me, and it was so powerful that it was not possible to resist it, and fearful as I was I knew I must do it. I must follow him to his home. I stood up unsteadily while the children stood with their stomachs rounded out and their fists tucked in to the small of their arched backs, watching me.

I ran until I saw him again and then stopped, following him little by little, dodging into shadows. He walked quickly, and I had to run without being seen. When he went over bridges and doubled back I had to stop and turn and bow my head, my heart pumping gloriously. Already it was growing dark. And soon I realised that we were nearing the Grand Canal and the quarter of Andrea's *palazzo*, and dreaded her seeing me and embracing me noisily, drawing me in to her safe ark for coffee and gossip. Angelo turned off and I nearly lost him. I caught sound of a door closing and guessed it was his and ran as close as I dared. I made myself walk up to it, listening out for house sounds, for laughter or quarrelling, anything.

The house was not so large as Andrea's, not so ancient or dingy. At any moment a child would come screeching down the steps and he would run after it to scoop it up. If he saw me I would try to look surprised. Now would he ask me in to meet his family? But I would have to say no. I was in a hurry. I was on my way to Andrea's, of course. Wasn't I already out of breath?

A woman came to the window and leaned out. She was staring right down at me. I could only stare back up to her, held in her gaze, unable to move or close my eyes or turn away, and it was as if there was no motion round me, nothing stirred for that long second, and my face was opened out in fear. And then briefly she smiled at me and leaned out further to pull in the shutters. I heard a man's voice behind her and knew it as his. She turned her face towards him, still with the shutters half-closed, and he came to stand behind her, and that was when I broke from the spell of stone and started foolishly to run, skittering down darkening passages and bumping into people, knowing by the sound of echoes when I was near a canal. I was lost in a maze of water, into which the city and all its lights were tipped. The bridges were round mouths gaping out of blackness. I could have stepped into air and tumbled into the mirror of myself.

I clung to a damp wall and edged myself along until I came out of blackness and echoes and into a square lit by strings of coloured lights. I sat outside a café and ordered a coffee that I did not want. I realised as I waited for it that I couldn't stop smiling. I wanted to laugh out loud. I caught the eye of a man sitting alone at a near table and he raised his glass of wine to me. I looked away quickly, trying to steady my breathing, unable to control my mouth. It starts again, I thought, and felt spurts of laughter rising up in me. I have only to turn back to look at this man and smile to him and he will move over to my table and want to talk to me and show me his country and teach me his language. He will stroke me with his friendship. I have no need of Angelo.

Berlie Doherty

Chapter Thirty

The next morning, early, my sleep was broken by the sound of a woman's voice railing. It was not uncommon, Venetians spill out their house sounds on to the streets, and the waters take them up in echo. But as I struggled to sink back into my drowsiness I was aware that the voice was coming from just outside my apartment. The woman began to beat on my door with her fists. I sat up in alarm.

'Who's there?' I shouted, fear in my throat.

The woman rattled the door, calling out again and again a word that I did not understand.

'What do you want?' I began to dress quickly. The woman persisted. Nothing that she said was intelligible to me. I crouched over my dressing-table to brush out my hair; again and again I brushed it trying to collect my thoughts while she thudded and shouted. At last I was ready to face her.

I spoke through the door to her. *'Chi è?'* Her voice was joined by another's, a younger woman's. I opened the door and they pushed themselves in, arguing loudly with each other, shouting at me, both of them. The younger one was my maid. I had never heard her speak before. The other woman was indignant and tearful; she spoke loudly, her hands gesticulating and wringing together.

'Stop it!' I shouted.

My maid gave a sigh of indignation and went through to the kitchen. I could hear her getting out the brushes and sweeping the floor vigorously, banging doors and cupboards.

I indicated the cane chair. 'Please sit down,' I said to the stranger. There was something familiar about her. She had hard, swarthy skin and wore tight black clothes. Her hair was oily and lank. As soon as she sat down she began to weep, in the loud, open-mouthed way that looks more like laughter. I sat down and watched her. My maid swept through into the room, scraping back furniture as she worked, making it screech. The woman began to gabble again and I recognised the name 'Rosa'.

'Che cosa è? What's the matter with Rosa?' I asked.

Again the confused babble of abuse and sobs, the hopeless gestures. My skin went cold. My own maid stood leaning with her arms crossed over the top of her brush and shouted out interjections. I couldn't make out a word of it. I telephoned Andrea. It was the first time I had used the phone since it had been installed in my apartment.

'Andrea,' I said. 'I think your maid is here.'

'Oh, God,' she said.

'What's happened to Rosa?'

'Is she in a state?'

'Of course she's in a state. I can't understand a word she's saying. What's happened to Rosa?'

'I'll come. Tell her.'

'I can't get a word in.'

'I'll be right over.'

I couldn't bear to stay in the same room as the woman, yet I wanted to hold her and say be calm, it's all right, nothing's wrong. I wanted her to hold me and say that. I went out to buy my bread, comforted by the ritual of it and by the coolness of the air. It had rained in the night; the streets shone. My head was throbbing with fright and bewilderment. When I arrived back at my apartment Andrea was just stepping out of a water-taxi.

'What's going on?' I asked her. 'She came at me like a mad woman. And she keeps saying something about Rosa.'

'She's Rosa's mother. I'm sorry. Perhaps I should have told you. It didn't seem relevant.'

I followed her into my apartment, where she went straight to her maid and sat by her, holding her hands. A long untidy story came out. I understood a little of it. I understood it to be about Rosa's lessons.

'Tell me,' I begged Andrea.

Andrea still held her maid's hands as she talked to me. From time to time she smoothed them down with her own, turning her head to smile at the woman, who was calmer now, snuffling a little.

'This is Sofia,' she said. 'Sometimes she brings Rosa to my house with her. When I have parties Rosa comes to help. And when she's not working with her mother she used to play with my Gianetta. They are of an age. And one day I heard the two girls singing together. I am a proud mother, Cecilia, you know that. But I'm not a fool. What I heard was my daughter's pretty voice, and I also heard Rosa's gift. I nearly cried when I heard that girl's voice, I tell you.'

'I know,' I said. 'I know.'

'And simply, I wanted a real singer to hear her too. She wouldn't have had a chance with this family.' She stroked Sofia's hand again. 'She will be singer,' she said in Italian, and again in the dialect of the Venetians.

Rosa's mother threw up her hands and wept again. Rosa was not a singer, she was a Filipino, she was a maid like her mother. She was needed at home. And now, since she had met me, she was never at home. She came and went at all hours. She stole money so she could come backwards and forwards on the water bus. She left the babies on their own, with the eight-year-old boy in charge. And when she sang she was like a clock. She sang in the house but not as she used to sing. She wouldn't sing the folk-songs that the family sang together. She sang like a clock, she insisted, like a clock. Sofia stood up with her hands pushing up her breasts and did an imitation of a voice exercise, getting it wrong, pulling her face into ugly shapes. '*Mo may mi ma mo ma mi mo. Come automate. Canta come un pappagallo,*' she shouted at me. She sank back into her chair, covering her face in her hands, babbling away again in Venetian to Andrea. Rosa sings like a parrot.

'No more lessons, she says,' Andrea told me. 'I'm so sorry, Cecilia. I'm so sorry.'

I felt numb with it, miserable. I could only stare out of the window. It was raining again. Grey shrouds hung around the buildings. 'She has great talent, tell her.'

'She knows that...'

'If only you had asked her mother first.'

'She would have said no. Simply no. I'm sorry.'

Andrea and Sofia left together as my first pupil for the day arrived. The maid was still tearful and indignant.

'Don't let it upset you,' Andrea told me. 'There will be more Rosas.'

'Of course,' I said.

I got through the lesson somehow, but my thoughts were miles away. I could see a child in a crack of a green hillside, standing barelegged with the wind around her, singing into the echo of boulders. I could hear that young voice singing. Take away the curse.

At the end of the week Venice was in carnival. The rain swept down, and still the flags went up, the musicians came into the streets, the waters glowed with the decorated boats. I went out in the evening to see it. Lanterns hung from windows and bridges, from the prows of the gondolas. Whole families were parading round together, talking and singing loudly, embracing each other. They wore masks such as I had seen hanging in the shops; black and white masks, and pale painted faces; the sad mouths of pierrots; gold laughing masks, wigs and feathers, baggy clown stripes, jewels; exotic costumes.

I did not belong to all this masquerade. I pushed my way through the people as they danced and flirted, too depressed to stay indoors. I knew that somewhere dancing in the *piazzas* would be Angelo and his family; I saw him with the stone mask of a cherub, and his dark eyes glinting through. I saw him at every corner. He would be there somewhere, watching me. In my entire life of aloneness I had never felt so lonely. I went back to my room and listened in the darkness to the clamour of it all.

'Cecilia! Open up!' I could hear Andrea's voice outside my door. She was full of laughter and excitement. 'Come on out!' she called. 'It's *il Carnevale*!'

'I know,' I called back. 'I'm tired.'

'No you're not. Open up.'

As I opened the door she and her husband and a younger couple swept in. They were all in carnival costume, wigs and shining gowns and pierrot suits, white faces and masks. They swirled round in their cloaks.

'Now then!' Andrea laughed.

I clapped. 'You look wonderful!'

'We've brought you a costume too.'

'No, really.'

'Yes, really.' She took my arm and steered me back into my bedroom, closing the door behind us. 'Cecilia, if you hide away from *il Carnevale* you will never belong to Venice. Never, never, never. I know how you feel but it's such fun! Now look.'

She tipped out the contents of her bag onto my bed. There was a long white dress with lace like feathers. She held it out to me. 'Put it on!' she begged.

When I had dressed in it she powdered my face white and painted my lips. She stroked perfume into my neck and my throat. 'Just breathe in,' she said. 'It is so beautiful you will float away.'

I gazed at myself in the mirror. The front of the dress was low cut. Deftly she painted a beauty spot where my breasts rose.

'What do you think?' she asked.

'It's tight,' I said. I couldn't stop smiling at my reflection.

'Nonsense. I wore it last year and I'm yards fatter than you. Now, your hair...'

'My dreadful hair.'

'You'll be recognised a mile away with that hair of yours. You must have my wig. It's all right, I'll wear my hood up.'

She took off the white powdered wig she was wearing and carefully tucked in my hair. Then she put a gold mask over my eyes. It covered half my face, making me look long-nosed and noble. It was edged with sequins. Wherever I turned my head they caught light and sparkled. My eyes gleamed through the slits. She gave me a fan made of white feathers, and made me twirl and twirl again for the others.

'How do I look,' I asked, thrilled.

'*Bella. Bella.*'

I flashed another look at myself in the mirror. I was on stage again. I was all eyes, yet my eyes were hidden.

We hurried out, my dress swishing as I walked. A sudden hullabaloo of music and laughter drowned our talking.

'*Il Carnevale*,' Andrea said into my ear. 'Tomorrow after my Shrove Tuesday party the fasting starts, remember. *Carne Vale*. Farewell flesh. Enjoy yourself!'

And I remember going into the *piazza* and holding out my hand to be kissed, sweeping low in a curtsey, dazzling behind my fan, tilting back my head to laugh, hearing my own laughter, my smile wide and bright, turning and turning to catch eyes and smile, to hide behind my fan and smile again; there was Angelo, and there, and there; they were all Angelos. I danced with all the Angelos. I felt their arms tender around me, I swooned in my perfume and in the smell of their skin, and always the music soared and skimmed and around me lights pattered like stars and I smiled, warm in my flesh, full and sweet and soft and giving in my flowing sap.

The next day was to be Andrea's party. She rang me several times during the morning, full of last-minute ideas and tricks.

'What do you think?' she asked me. 'Should it be quail or squid?'

'I don't know,' I said. 'Either.'

'I would do the squid in their ink sacs,' she said, 'and make *risotto nero*.'

'Perhaps the quail,' I suggested.

'It would be delicious,' she agreed. 'Stuffed with juniper berries. Of course, it looks like a chicken on toast the way we serve it here, but wait till you taste it!'

'Would you like me to help?'

'Clara won't even let me in the kitchen! I think she might just about let me stir the polenta, and that's the nearest I'll get to it!'

Gianetta came round for a last practice. 'Are you nervous?' I asked her. No. Nothing ruffled this girl. Of course, she had the temperament that would make a great singer. If only she had the voice for it.

I arrived in my gondola with my gift for Andrea, a trinket box I had found. She greeted me like a sister. She was wearing kingfisher colours with heavy jewellery that flashed as she moved. Her hair was piled up on her head. Already the house was full of guests. The room we were to dine in was one that I had never been in before. It was decorated with oil paintings and with tapestries and carvings done in green and gold. I could see that several tables had been put together and covered with a large gold damask cloth. The chairs were covered in the same gold damask, but as the guests were arriving Sofia struggled in with cane chairs from other rooms.

I had never seen so many people round a table in a house before. The clatter of their voices was overwhelming. I found I couldn't concentrate on their language any more. They made a fuss of me and I smiled; I replied to their questions in faltering Italian. I had no idea how I was going to keep it up through the long meal. There were still some guests to come, Andrea announced. More chairs were brought in; we were moved and squashed together. The old contessa had had enough. She bowed and went to bed, leaning on Gianetta's arm.

Candles and table-lamps were lit. The old dark walls gleamed with them. Behind their doors of latticed glass leather books with gold lettering glittered.

The late guests arrived and came in behind me, shouting their greetings, kissing and embracing the guests around the table. There was a large ornate mirror over the fireplace, and I watched their reflections in it before I, too, turned to be introduced. I had known it. They were the Caravellis. They were introduced to me formally, as strangers. Angelo's eyes blazed merriment. He loved the joke of it. I think he must have known about it for some time. I thought then of the nights and weeks we had spent together walking by canals and drinking wine in late cafés. In all that time, had no one seen us?

His wife's name was Livia. She was tall and very dark, heavily made up and bejewelled, as were all the women. She wore a black satin suit heavily shot with metallic blues and greens, her shoulders built up and her waist tiny. I was a peasant girl in a blue cotton dress with shoulder straps, my white comfortable shoes, my hair in its pale muslin band. I did not even feel grown up.

'I have heard a great deal about you,' she said to me in careful English, her accent thick and breathy. 'You are alone here? Well, you must not be alone. You must come and eat with us after Lent. Angelo my husband he speaks English perfect.'

'Actually I speak Irish,' he smiled.

'I am Irish,' I said, foolish, as if I'd never seen him in my life before. 'You're very kind. I'd like to come.'

And of course there it was, the thing was done, so simple. I had a licence. Yet he could have told her that he had known me as a child. Or I could.

The meal was beginning. Andrea hurried into the kitchen and brought out Rosa and Sofia with their antipasti trays of fennel and radicchio salad. They both ignored me. Rosa's eyes gleamed as she bent to serve me. Her hair needed combing. I ate slowly and carefully, avoiding Angelo's glances. As the course was finished and the guests took out cigarettes and cigars, and Andrea went back to the kitchen to prepare the sauce for the polenta, my neighbours asked me about the opera company.

'It feels as if it was in another world,' I said.

They looked puzzled. I must have got the words wrong.

I did not catch Angelo's eyes once; I ate in a dream while courses were brought in and out on their pewter dishes. I drank wine and avoided his eyes. I laughed and smiled. His glances burned my skin. The women moved round me in their serving and the voices rose and fell like tides of sound. I watched Sofia and Rosa. How alike they were, mother and daughter, cast in the mould of their race. How their daughters and granddaughters would echo them. How strange it must be to have possession of another person, to see your features and your nature in them, to know them as you know yourself, to have power over that person who was so like yourself, to sculpt them and weave them, and yet to lose that power.

My wine glass was being filled with sweet spumante for the dessert. I clapped when the crystal goblets were brought in. They were filled with iced grapes and quinces and cream. I smiled round at everybody except Angelo.

'This is why I came to Venice!' I told them all. 'Your food is as exquisite as your city!' I raised my glass to thank Clara in the kitchen for the wonderful meal. Clara has gone home, I was told. She will be eating bean soup with her family. I bowed my head. I had grown melancholy.

'*Signorina.*' Gianetta was standing beside me. 'I am ready.' Andrea was nodding to me.

Of course Gianetta sang well. She had taken her lessons well. She stood like a singer, and she was calm. The guests applauded loudly, cigarettes in their mouths. There would be more pupils for me. Rosa and Sofia were leaning against the wall with trays in their hands. I leaned over to Rosa.

'Sing,' I said.

'*No, signorina.*' She followed her mother into the kitchen.

'Will the *signorina* sing for us?' That was Angelo's voice. The call was taken up and I sank down on to the piano stool. Yes, I would sing. I wanted him to hear me. I wanted him to know at last what was within me. I could choose and not choose to give out my voice, and for many years people who had heard me sing had not heard my voice at all. It was my flame of rapture, my ecstasy. I held it back in my solitude or I gave it out once, twice, three times in my life. I sang the great aria from *Tosca. Vissi d'Arte.* I have known art. But never until I had known this love. I felt as if I had never sung it until I had met Angelo. It was an Act of Love. I sang for him.

Chapter Thirty-one

I should have known that Andrea was a woman of many surprises, and that the generosity of her imagination knew no bounds. After my singing she introduced me to one of her guests. He was the maestro of the opera house La Fenice. He kissed my hand, flustering me a little.

'Would you care to make a guest appearance at La Fenice?' he asked me. 'It would be a great joy to Venetians to know that we have a singer like you in our country.'

'I would like it greatly,' I told him, bold with success. I felt Angelo's eyes warm as suns on me from across the room, and tried to be calm.

'We plan to repeat *Tosca* for a short season next month, but there is one night when our Tosca wishes to be away from Venice. Normally it could not be done; I would not have it. She is a great prima donna. But maybe now there is a way?'

My heart had stopped with the word '*Tosca*'.

'I could sing it tomorrow,' I told him. 'I know the music like I know my name.'

'Am I dreaming this?' I asked Angelo the next day, as he walked with me to rehearse at the opera house.

'If you're dreaming this then you're dreaming Venice,' he said. 'And you'll wake up and it will all have drifted away, and you'll be standing in a wet field in Ireland. Cecilia, I wish you'd tell me what happened to make you cut yourself from your family.'

'I couldn't begin,' I told him. 'You mustn't make me. You mustn't make me think about it.'

'Families are important,' he said.

I turned away from him, upset still. 'If families are so important then why do you spend so much time with me?' I wanted to hurt him.

'I was a child when I married,' he said. 'I thought I was in love.'

Say you are now, I wanted to ask him, but daren't. How little I knew him, yet I was a cup held out for him to pour himself into, drop by drop.

I went into the hot darkness of the opera house, to the familiar sound of instruments tuning and the trickle of arpeggios from the rehearsal room, and I was as nervous as a mouse and trembling sick inside.

I sang through my parts of the opera for the maestro and a small rehearsal orchestra. The two men playing my lover Mario and my would-be seducer Scarpia joined me in the afternoon. I had heard them sing many times before. I was in awe of them: their names were known throughout the world. I would be worthy of them, I promised myself. They were courteous and kind to me, and I knew the part so well they had no reason to doubt my right to be with them. They joined me for a walk-through rehearsal that went without problems.

The great singer playing Mario flashed smiles at me as we left the theatre. 'You will be splendid,' he promised me, coming very close, his plump hands fluttering out towards me.

I spent day and night thinking about my part of Tosca the opera singer, about her passion and her virtue, about her love for Mario. I felt that if I never sang again I would have fulfilled myself in this role. And I knew now that I could do it. My voice grew in those days of rehearsing. I couldn't wait for the night of the performance now. In my mind Mario was Angelo, and I sang for him. I knew how Tosca would sacrifice everything for his love. How well I understood that. One day I would tell him that.

After a late rehearsal the maestro came round to my dressing-room to speak to me. The dressers stood, shy and smiling in his presence. He held out his hand to me and bowed.

'You have an angel in you!' he told me. 'They will love this Tosca. Venice will love you.'

'Thank you, Maestro. I've waited all my life for this,' I told him. 'When I was a child I was told I couldn't sing.'

He threw back his hands, clouting the imaginary faces of my abusers, and I laughed with him. 'They don't deserve to live!' he suggested. 'There will be many great roles for you now. You will create them, with the passion you have in you.'

He stepped away from me and bowed a little formally, his kind face creased with pleasure.

When he left me to finish dressing I found myself dithering with the thrill of it, too agitated to do up my buttons or to fasten back my hair.

'Here, I'll help,' one of the dressers said. She smiled at me in the mirror. 'Such great happiness!' As if she couldn't help the movement she stroked my hair, then pinned it briskly. 'Will your family be here for you?'

'Oh, no.' I looked away, seeing things to tidy on my dressing table. 'They don't even know, as it happens. They live a long way away.'

'What a pity. It should be shared.'

'But I have a friend,' I confided. 'He will come.' I held him in my mind, waiting outside for me, sitting at one of those café tables, his head a little to one side as I came to him.

When I went outside in the early evening he was there, watching the huge barges that had been moored round the back of the theatre ready to unload scenery flats. Men shouted, their voices echoing across the water.

'Look,' he said, taking my hand and leading me round to the front of the theatre where the posters were displayed. 'The name of the guest prima donna!'

'Nobody has heard of her!' I laughed, proud. We looked a long time at it, the letters of my name seeming unfamiliar, not mine at all. 'I've waited so long for this!'

'Now you're not to get too famous,' he told me. 'How far would I have to follow you?'

His fondness made me bold. 'The world's a tiny place, after all.' With great daring I rounded my first finger and my thumb to an O and held it to my lips and then towards his. 'Look how tiny.' And he hooked his finger into that O and drew down my hand and held onto it.

'I'll tell you something,' I said, my voice not steady as he circled his arm round me. 'When I am waiting in the wings for my first entrance, when I have to sing Mario! Mario! - it's you I'm thinking of. When I'm in his arms, I'm in yours.'

'Of course,' he said.

We walked slowly back to my apartment. Fog came with the night cold, and drifted in white swathes across the canals. My flesh burned with his closeness. Somewhere deep inside me there was something un-named, something that rose and spread and fell again, and rose again. Angelo's hand touched mine.

'I want to come inside with you,' he said, when we reached my door. He put his hand across the key as I was turning it in the lock. 'I want to spend this night with you,' and unbidden, the longing that was in me turned as cold as death.

'Please go,' I said.

He laughed, thinking that I was teasing him at first, and his laughter turned to puzzlement as I shook my head again. I couldn't look at him now.

'What's wrong?' he asked me.

And I could only answer, 'Nothing. Nothing is wrong,' though I was heavy with a deep and knowing grief.

He took both my hands and kissed them.

'Please go, Angelo.'

I remembered the face of the child, hauled from his desk by the teacher, how he had turned his head to me, shocked.

'Go away! Please!'

He let my hands drop.

'Then I will wait,' he told me, 'until you are ready for me.'

I watched him walk away, and closed the door. I did not switch on my light. Lassitude drained through my limbs, and the muscles in my head and throat were tight with grief, for it was a kind of grieving. I let my clothes drop onto the floor and went over to my windows. I opened them out onto the canal. The fog rolled and shifted. I leaned against the sill and let my voice howl out, thin and high and wailing, as if it would never stop, wave upon wave of grieving, an animal voice, not mine, a beast in agony.

At last I slumped towards my bed. My body was an empty inert thing, it was made of heavy clay.

I let myself loll back. My head was swimming and my limbs felt watery and heavy, as though they could dislocate themselves and float away from me. I lay like a woman bereft, as indeed I was. Far away I could hear the last tired revellings of late home-goers. I heard the bells of San Marco and it was like hearing the bells of my own requiem. But it was not Angelo that I mourned for. It was for me, it was for the shadows of all the women in this dance of death: for Eve, and Mary, and Martha, for Rose, and Agnes. For my mother. For every moment of my blighted history. I would have lain myself out with my arms stretched at my sides and taken the knife point of pain and let flow my blood for him, and with him I would have risen up out of the darkness.

Did I not know there was a skin beneath this skin, and another, and yet another?

When the bells ceased I closed my eyes and let my sigh come deep. Oh, that restful silence. The embrace of it. I felt the dribble from my mouth soak warm into the pillow that had been embroidered for me by nuns. I was washed in a green sea, where people lurked like a family, shaking their heads, and the light that slanted through the water was like a flicker of fire. I was in search of my mother, and when she swam away from me I was in search of something that I wanted to call God.

Oh that the air would turn to sea and I to a fish to swim and enter the cave of her green womb again, and to lie there a long time in the beating blood-dark; that long, long sigh.

Chapter Thirty-two

Dawn came with a burst of angry red. I poured sweet oils into my bath and lay in it for a time, quite calm. I packed my belongings and had them sent on to the station. I was half in a state of dream.

Then I went on to the rehearsal room and sang till my tight throat found its ease and there was nothing left in me but this music that is in me still. Nobody spoke to me and I spoke to nobody. From early evening I stayed in my dressing-room till the time came for the opening of the opera. My huge triumph. They dressed me in rich red and gold; they piled up my hair and fastened a flashing tiara there and I sat, mute.

I knew that Andrea would be there to see me, and that bright-eyed beside her would be Gianetta and Rosa. I knew just how Rosa would be feeling. Her mother too, would be there, drawn in by Andrea's generosity and love, and she would be proud and nervous to be in one of the rows and rows of mirrored boxes that circled the auditorium. She would be anxious for her daughter, too, and yet would be full of tears when the music moved her.

And when I stood in the wings I knew that Mario would be out there in that murmuring audience, with his wife who would love the *Te Deum* because it would be like church for her. I felt I could see him, his head a little to one side, smiling and eager for my appearance on stage.

I waited to breathe my first 'Mario! Mario!'

But that was yesterday's, that tiny passion. I was tensed now for the moment way beyond that in the second act, when Baron Scarpia would try to seduce me, would ask me for that great sacrifice, my most precious thing, my integrity, my curse-gift, my worthiness. That, in exchange for Mario's life!

When the moment came, I sank to my knees to sing my great aria. He wanted Mario's life or my love, and in despair I promised myself to his desire. But then I saw the only solution. I must destroy the thing that would destroy me. I knew every shade of Tosca's thinking as I gazed and gazed at the knife on Scarpia's table, knowing her solution and the terrible justice of it. I circled round it, my eyes drawn to it again and again.

And when he came to me with his lust I swung round with all the fury of virtue and plunged the knife into him many times and set the candles of death around his body, and stared then at him locked in terror, and I did not know at that moment that I was on a stage.

The roar of applause frightened and roused me a little. 'Bravo!' The audience shouted. 'Bravo!' I didn't look up or smile when Scarpia and Mario Cavaradossi pulled me in front of the curtains for the second act ovations. I stayed in my trance of terror, knowing now for sure that Mario's death would follow on, and then Tosca's own.

And when all the long last ovations were over and I had received the flowers that were sent up for me from Mario and from Andrea I slipped away to my dressing-room. I couldn't speak to anyone, bound as I was in the spell that had been cast. The maestro followed me. His face was beaded with sweat. Like a proud father he embraced me. He found his handkerchief and wiped his face with it many times.

'Smile!' he told me. 'It's over! It's all over.'

I sat down, confused. People were knocking at my door and he shouted to them to go away.

'Your next role will be *La Traviata*,' he told me. 'I will see to that. Your great passion will soar!'

He spread out his arms, laughing down at me.

'No,' I said. 'I must go away.'

'Go, if you must!' He nodded. 'But come back to Venice and sing *Violetta* for me.'

He took one of the flowers from the bouquet that Angelo had sent for me and kissed it. Then he handed it to me, and I took it from him, laughing out loud. And when I went outside Angelo was waiting for me. I went to him and let him hold me.

'Now are you ready?' he asked me.

'Yes,' I said.

And I believe neither of us spoke after that through all our slow journey back along the canal and into the *rios* that led to my apartment, or through the night, until I was roused from my reverie. But I did not go into this night blindly or like a child, with no sense of guilt or danger, of future or past, wanting nothing but the moment. I had released myself.

When we reached my rooms we sat at either side of the window that overlooked the *rio*. We were watching each other and the golden light of the rippled reflections that the water cast up onto our faces. We were watching each other's eyes from that great distance, and I was warm with it, and grew soft inside myself. The sky bloomed green, and still we watched each other till our features faded into a vibrant darkness. A long barge with a lantern slung on it rippled past, casting a yellow light across his face, and still he was watching me. Then the deep dark came, and I felt he was imagined.

I heard a soft crinkling sound, and with a start I knew that he was undressing. I did the same, my fingers steady this time, steady and slow, and all that could be heard in the room was the stealthy swish of fabric and the slap of the water below. He stood up and came over to me and just faintly then I could see the gleam of his flesh, and I don't know what it was I was beginning to feel, fear and thrill maybe, but when he stood just by me and I felt his breathing I had new senses, I was not a physical being. Where he softly touched me my flesh ached with burning. Now is the time. And when I felt the flower of his manhood grow and thrust against me it was as if I were turned into liquid air. This time. He lifted me up and carried me to the bed… *Yes*… and a darkness came over me then as he came down on me, for I was awash with agony and rapture.

And he drew his face away from mine… *Oh, this time, this time*… and there were patterns of liquid light shimmering round me and I was going down in it, down in it, pinned to a knife-point of pain, and there was his voice somewhere booming somewhere, and high in the air there was a screaming that was as shrill as light; and then, oh then, came a flowing of seas that rose to drown the shrill cry and to drown it again and to drown it for ever.

I surfaced at last and lay for a long time in his arms, watching the darkness, as calm as sleep.

He said to me then, 'You were a virgin, weren't you?'

'I was.' I felt the sweet tears rising in me. I was weak now in my strength.

At last I must have slipped into sleep, and woke again to find the room speckled with the lights from the chandelier lamp. Angelo was dressing. When he saw me watching him he came over to my bed and knelt down by it, stroking my damp cheek.

'I didn't know,' he said. 'Did I hurt you?'

'No,' I said. 'You took the hurt away.'

He smiled, not understanding.

'I must go home now,' he said.

I nodded. 'You must go back to your wife.'

After all, he was a married man.

'I'll come to you again,' he said.

'No. I'm going away,' I told him.

'You can't go now!' he laughed. He stroked my cheek again.

'I'm ready to go,' I said. 'I have a pilgrimage to make.'

'You will come back though?'

'Yes. Venice is my home.'

'But you won't be coming back to me?'

I took his hand and kissed his open palm.

'No,' I said. 'Not to you.'

Berlie Doherty

Chapter Thirty-three

Europe ticks away from me: the solid light, the churches of water, the vivid colours, the mountains, the flat green fields, the golden heliotropes.

It had been raining for hours. As I arrive the sun is just coming through, watery with it, making the fields rich and the pavements gleam. I can smell the sea. Joy surges up in me. I ask at the station if I can leave my luggage there. It's a kind of insurance, though I know I won't be staying long. I have brought little with me; Venice will call me, the world is opening up its arms to me. I pull up the collar of my coat. The air is soft and cool, just beginning to blow my hair free. I want to run now, a child again. I want to run singing up the hill.

Halfway up the hill I stop to lean against the wall. I can see the train snaking away from the valley. I can see the church. I can see the tide seeping out over wet sand. Gulls scream round the fishing-boats. Soon the cockle-gangs will be going out with their pails across the mud.

And there now I can see the house. You'd think it was a small bird on dark waters, that white house on the hill. You'd never hear the pitch of its heart from here. I look away from it again. Long ago I had left it, for ever, I thought. I had spoken out the thoughts that were in me and had opened up a locked door with my words. I had lifted the skirts of the tabernacle.

The house looks much smaller. I can smell the rich, kippery smoke of its turf fire. A pitchfork has been propped up in the porch, ready for work to start again. There's a rusty bike lying by the wall. I bend to pick it up, noticing how the lining of the basket is stained and torn.

And I can hear voices inside the house, and the sound of dishes being clattered together, chairs pulled away.

Let her be alive still.

Let her remember me.

I take deep breaths and try the door.

It is open. I knew it would be.

Berlie Doherty

has written over 60 books, as well as plays for radio, theatre and television, short stories and poetry. She has won major awards and prizes in all fields, including the Carnegie Medal (twice), the Writers' Guild award (twice), Film and Television Award and Royal Philharmonic Society award (for a libretto), and was shortlisted for the International Astrid Lingren award.

Berlie has been published in 21 different languages, and has travelled the world extensively, speaking at International literature festivals and conferences.

She began over 30 years ago by writing short stories for BBC Radio 4 Morning Story, and has published one short story collection, 'Running on Ice'. Much of her writing is for young adults, though she also writes picture book texts, children's books and has two adult novels, 'Requiem' and 'The Vinegar Jar', due to be republished in 2014 by Cybermouse MultiMedia Ltd.

Berlie is best known for 'Dear Nobody', which won many awards both as a young adult novel and as a play for theatre and for radio. It has also been made into a television drama.

Her book for children, 'Street Child', (also a play script) is read and performed extensively in schools throughout the country, and she is currently completing a long-awaited sequel.

You can follow Berlie at www.berliedoherty.com or on Twitter, where she reveals the life of a writer.

Her most recent novel is 'The Company of Ghosts'.

'Dear Nobody' is available in paperback at all good bookshops and on Kindle.

Other Books available from Cybermouse
(& all good bookshops)

'Mine'
An absorbing 'Coming of Age' novel from the pen of
Caroline Pitcher

'…on my 'I wish I'd written this' list.'
Berlie Doherty

'11 o'clock Chocolate Cake' also by **Caroline Pitcher**

*'…a delicious slice of teenage life. Readers will be engaged at once…
Great stuff…'*
Adèle Geras, Times Educational Supplement'

'The Jeweller's Skin'   **Ruth Valentine**

*'This beautifully-crafted novel is the first effort from a well-established
poet. The prose is gorgeous, and the narrative, which shifts through
different periods in the heroine's life, is gripping and moving. Highly
recommended…'*
Tamar Yoseloff

'The Fox & The Fish'   **Bill Allerton**

*'…casually very clever, and full of 'words'. It's so puzzling and allusive
and fast that it makes the world more interesting when you stop…
This book is sexy, and kind, and playful.'*
Rony Robinson: Author, Playwright and Sony/Radio
Academy Award winning presenter of BBC Radio Sheffield's
Morning Show

**Our books are available from all good bookshops, from Amazon and
Amazon for Kindle, or direct from ourselves at;**

www.cybermouse-multimedia.com.

Lightning Source UK Ltd.
Milton Keynes UK
UKOW06f0206300915

259535UK00007B/107/P